ties that tether

ties that tether

JANE IGHARO

JOVE
New York

A JOVE BOOK
Published by Berkley
An imprint of Penguin Random House LLC
penguinrandomhouse.com

Library of Congress Cataloging-in-Publication Data

Names: Igharo, Jane, author.
Title: Ties that tether / Jane Igharo.
Description: First edition. | New York: Jove, 2020.
Identifiers: LCCN 2020016125 (print) | LCCN 2020016126 (ebook) |
ISBN 9780593101940 (trade paperback) | ISBN 9780593101957 (ebook)
Subjects: GSAFD: Love stories.
Classification: LCC PR9199.4.I37 T54 2020 (print) |
LCC PR9199.4.I37 (ebook) | DDC 813/.6—dc23
LC record available at https://lccn.loc.gov/2020016125
LC ebook record available at https://lccn.loc.gov/2020016126

Printed in the United States of America
1   3   5   7   9   10   8   6   4   2

First Edition: September 2020

Cover art by Fatima Baig
Cover design by Emily Osborne
Book design by Ashley Tucker

To God, for every narrow, crooked road
you straightened to bring me here.
Thank you.

chapter
1

Culture is important. Preserving it, even more important. It's the reason I've always abided by one simple dating rule.

Tonight, I've broken that rule.

It all started when he kissed me, when his silken lips and skilled tongue moved against mine with a perfect and sensational mixture of tenderness and force. It was the kind of kiss that rid me of all my wits and made me act spontaneous and reckless for the first time in my life.

That kiss brought me here—to his hotel room.

We stagger through the door. Our bodies, entangled, navigate blindly, attempting to reach the bed. He slides a hand into my blouse and, in one swift movement, unhooks my bra.

This wasn't where I envisioned my night going. A few hours ago, I was having dinner at Louix Louis, located on the thirty-first floor of the St. Regis Hotel in downtown Toronto. My date was not the man currently undressing me, but Richard Amowie, the engineer my mother referred to as *"husband material."* Like me, he was Nigerian—of Edo descent. He was also a Christian and, from the series of questions he had been asking, the kind of man who believed a woman's single purpose was to breed babies and cater to her husband. Was I surprised by his archaic mentality? Not at all. My mother's matches usually have this trait in common. As well as being Edo—the most important trait of all.

"What do you do for fun?" he asked, slicing through a well-done steak. "Do you like to cook? Are you a good cook? Do you know how to make Edo food?"

Despite the glamorous restaurant with a glistening coppery interior, I was not on a date. I was being interviewed for the position of dutiful Edo wife by a man who couldn't chew with his mouth closed. The sight of his jagged teeth breaking apart the wine-glazed beef made nausea tickle my throat. My appetite morphed into disgust, and I had no desire to finish the walnut-crusted salmon on my plate. I looked through the large window, at the stunning view of downtown Toronto—clusters of high-rises invading the sky with height, the sight of Lake Ontario spread out in a vast expanse of shimmer and blue, and the CN Tower posing majestically as the city's greatest beacon.

"Well?" Richard asked, one eyebrow raised. "Do you? Do you cook?"

"Yeah. I do."

"Edo food?" This specification was important to him.

"Yes. I learned when I was a kid—back in Nigeria."

His brow dropped, defusing the tension on his massive forehead. "Good. Very good." His lips stretched and widened, hitting his cheekbones and exposing his teeth.

It was official. I had advanced to the next round.

"Want to know my favorite?" he asked. "Black soup with fresh catfish. I love it."

"Yeah. So did my father."

"He died, right? When you were back in Nigeria."

"Yeah," I said. "Before my family and I moved to Canada. I was twelve at the time."

"Oh." He chewed his dinner with the temperament of a ravenous goat, not taking a moment to offer a gesture of condolence. "But you're twenty-five now. So, it was a long time ago." He made the statement with a casual ease as if referring to a childhood pet rather than my father, a man who died too young and agonized on a hospital bed before he did. "So. About your job," he continued. "What is it you do again?"

"I'm a creative director at an advertising agency." At that moment, curious about his follow-up question, I pulled a lock of my box braid behind my ear and leaned into the table.

"Impressive. But you would quit once you had a family to take care of, right?"

I chuckled, amused and stunned by his idiocy. "No. I absolutely would not quit."

"Really?"

"Yeah. Really."

His gaze was stern and steady on me, an intimidation tactic I fought by conveying the same look, but with a hint of disdain to go with it. It occurred to me then that if looks could seal fates, he would have ignited to cinders.

"Well." He blinked rapidly, his glare quivering under the strain of mine. "You're stubborn." He knifed the steak again. "Your mother didn't mention that. Personally, I prefer my women to be a lot more . . ." He pondered, eyes narrowed and darting as if considering some vast complexity, and then his stare stilled on me, and he said: "Submissive."

At the utterance of that word, rage seethed inside me. "And I prefer that my men weren't chauvinistic pricks with the brain and table manners of a caveman!"

It was a statement loud enough to capture the attention of

the diners at the nearby tables. Inquisitive eyes shifted between me and Richard, inspecting, speculating, and then concluding.

The date or interview was officially over. I stood and grabbed my trench coat. "It's obvious we aren't a good match."

"Yes," he said. "Very obvious." Because of the attention he had gained, he was trying to portray a composed facade, but his straight lips kept reverting to a tight frown. His fingers rolled into fists that trembled, the guise of the perfect husband shedding to reveal his true nature.

"Goodbye, Richard." I left him alone at the table with strangers eyeballing him and offering silent and likely accurate judgment.

It was past eight at the time, and I ended up in the hotel lobby, heading for the lounge instead of the exit. A drink made by a professional seemed more enticing than anything I could mix at home.

The lounge had a more relaxed vibe than the restaurant; the beige-and-gray palette, cushioned seats, and electric fireplace created a modern and cozy ambiance. I ordered a whiskey sour and sipped with relief. The alcohol unwound the tension that had accumulated throughout the night. My back slacked, and I leaned into the comfortable chair, but the thought of my mother made my spine spike up straight again. She would blame me for how the date ended. At the realization, I emptied the sweet cocktail in my mouth. The flood of alcohol warmed my insides and made my eyes close.

I racked my mind for a solution—a way to either survive or avoid my mother's wrath. I considered multiple possibilities, including hopping on a train to Montreal. While still contemplating, a deep voice broke through my thoughts. I opened my eyes, turned to the seat next to me, and saw the man who had spoken. He was looking at me, waiting for my response, but I had no clue what he had asked.

"Excuse me?" I said. "Did you say something?"

"Yeah. I was just wondering if you were okay." He smiled, and a deep blush snuck up his cheeks, staining his white skin. "You downed that drink pretty fast. And for a minute, it looked like you were sleeping . . . at a bar."

"What makes you think I wasn't meditating?"

"At a bar?"

I shrugged.

"Well, if that was the case, I apologize for interrupting your meditation."

"Apology accepted." I turned to my empty glass, and he turned to what looked like scotch. I watched him from the corner of my eye, sipping his drink and working his thumb against his phone. "I wasn't meditating," I confessed, no longer able to ignore the guilt of lying.

"Oh." He switched his attention to me. "Then you lied. And accepted my apology."

"Yeah." I smiled, a playfulness suddenly bubbling inside me. "I could give it back if you want."

"No." His blue eyes dashed across my face, a quick examination. "Keep it. On behalf of whoever upset you tonight, I apologize."

"And how are you so sure someone upset me?"

"I just am." He lifted the tumbler to his lips and drank. "Am I wrong?"

I shook my head.

"Who upset you?"

"Um . . ." The question was intrusive. I didn't owe the stranger an answer, but somehow, he put me at ease. "My date."

"And what did he do?"

Another intrusive question I could have dismissed, and yet, my loose lips offered the answer without restraint. "He was a sexist ass."

"Those still exist?"

"Yep. And my mother knows exactly where to find them."

"Your mom set you up?" Amusement curved his flushed lips, which stood out against his pale complexion.

"Yeah. It's kinda her thing. This one didn't work, so she'll probably arrange another for next week and another after that if necessary."

"Sounds like torture. I think that warrants a second drink." He waved the bartender over, and I ordered another whiskey sour. He insisted on paying, and I objected a few times before giving in.

He was a gentleman, and as I recall, a well-dressed one, sporting a navy-blue blazer over a white button-down and black dress pants. His hair had a perfect side part that separated the dark, wavy strands into precise proportions. The strong angles that structured his square-shaped face were made soft by the calm blue of his eyes and the gentle fullness of his lips. He had an elegance about him that was neither intimidating nor arrogant.

"I'm Rafael," he said, extending a hand.

"Nice to meet you, Rafael." I gripped his hand, and he gripped mine. It was a standard gesture—simple, nothing intimate or remotely profound—and yet, it stirred a reaction from both of us. His jaw tightened as if he were fighting some frustration, and my heart raced, triggered by an indefinable thrill. "I'm Azere." The motion to separate our hands was reluctant.

"Azere," he said, uncertain, my name a foreign flavor he had yet to acquire a taste for.

"It's A-ze-re," I repeated, enunciating and emphasizing the distinct Nigerian rhythm paired with the name.

He gave it another attempt, and although the pronunciation improved, his Western intonation remained inflexible. "It's a beautiful name."

"Thank you," I said. "So. You know my deal. What's yours? What are you doing here, drinking at a bar alone? Did you have a crappy date too?"

"Actually, I'm staying in the hotel. I came in from New York for an interview."

"And how did it go?" I watched his lips for the answer.

"Well, I hope it went well. If it did, then I'll be moving back to Toronto. My family lives here. I used to too before I moved to New York."

"And you're moving back because you miss your family or because—"

"Because New York has too many memories," he said, his stare far off.

"Memories of what?"

He opened his mouth to answer but then sealed it. *Or memories of who?* I wanted to ask, hoping he was as liberal with information as I had been, but he changed the subject. The conversation quickly transitioned to less personal topics. We moved to a settee adjacent to the fireplace. The mood felt light and the conversation effortless. I was utterly fixated on him, paying no attention to the thinning crowd or midnight's quick approach, only aware that I had been touching him as we spoke, my hand falling on his arm and his shoulder and his leg. Each touch sent a zing through me that rattled my core. It was a warning, telling me I had encountered something dangerous and had to proceed with caution. And so, I did.

Moving forward, I forced my hands to stay at my sides, to twirl a lock of my braid, to tug on the hem of my short skirt. Although that was a mistake as it drew attention to the faux leather that clung to the curve of my hips and revealed my chestnut-brown skin. Rafael's gaze instantly dropped to my thighs. When he looked up again, his stare was deep and prolonged. My heart raced.

"We're closing up." The bartender's voice boomed through the lounge, capturing the attention of the only remaining people— Rafael and me.

We stood in sync. He held my coat as I slid an arm through each sleeve. When I faced him, our eyes connected. For seconds, verging on a minute, I stared at him, inspecting his eyes. They weren't simply blue, but an ever-evolving tide of blues—sapphire, azure, violet, and periwinkle—all intricately woven together, circling dilated pupils.

It was during this moment, while I was studying his eyes, that it happened. He kissed me. It was unexpected. Yet, somehow, I had been waiting for it since he offered an apology for the mistakes of someone else.

Sweet and forbidden—that's how I remember it tasting. It was everything I wanted and couldn't have. There was a rule I had to obey, and it was simple: never get romantically involved with a man who isn't Edo.

The rule rang in my head. Though, as his lips worked against mine, I felt the rise of defiance. For the first time in my life, my heart was putting up a fight against my mind. Intense sentiments contended with forced reason, and I knew I wanted him. There was no denying it, so I clung to him and kissed him fiercely.

Again, the bartender urged us to leave. We ignored him and pressed our bodies tightly together, the need to feel skin intensifying with each stroke of our tongues and exchange of our breaths.

"Seriously, guys!" He stood in front of us. "It's past midnight. We're closed."

Rafael initiated our separation; I didn't have the willpower to.

"Sorry about that," he said to the bartender, whose face had turned red with irritation. "We'll go." But he didn't make a move. His focus was strictly on me. His lingering stare implied he wanted more—so much more than the feel of my lips.

"Yeah. Whatever. Why don't you guys take this to one of the many rooms in this place?"

The suggestion was the push we both needed to take things further. Rafael grasped my hand and squeezed it, a silent request I responded to by bobbing my head. He led the way, and I followed, each step rushed until we finally reached seclusion.

Now, in his hotel room, rumpled sheets snake through our limbs and conjoin our naked bodies. His breath is warm and feathery against my skin, like a wisp of summer air. Sex with a stranger. It's a new occurrence for me, something I never thought I could do. Somehow, it isn't what I expected. He isn't indirectly asking me to leave with excuses of having to get up early in the morning. He's holding me—my back to his chest—and pressing kisses along the curve of my neck.

"You're beautiful, Azere."

Azere. He hasn't mastered the Nigerian rhythm paired with my name. Though, the way his Western intonation caresses each syllable creates a new rhythm that's just as lovely.

"It's late, Rafael. Maybe I should go."

"Stay," he says. "I want you to stay."

"Okay." I twist to look at him and trace his handsome features with my fingertip. "Sure. I'll stay." *Because I want to more than anything else.*

"Good." He smiles, wide and genuine. "You know, I turn thirty today."

"Really?"

"Yeah."

"Well, happy birthday, Rafael."

"Thank you." He brings his lips to mine and takes his time exploring my mouth. "I swear, Azere, I could kiss you forever."

"Well, maybe not forever. Just for tonight."

Because tonight, for one night only, I am not the obedient daughter of a conservative woman who is adamant on preserving her Nigerian heritage. Nor am I the daughter of a patriotic man who feared his family's departure to a foreign country more than the cancer that was killing him.

Tonight, I belong to no one but myself, driven by my desires and impulses despite any consequences that might follow.

One night. It's all I can have and all I can give to Rafael, a man who seems worthy of so much more.

chapter
2

One of the perks of working at Xander, North America's top advertising agency, is the downtown workspace. It has that new age corporate design thing going on—open-concept layout, industrial ceilings, glass walls, light fixtures that resemble descending UFOs, and splashes of vibrant colors that imply playfulness. Through the floor-to-ceiling windows, there is a spectacular view of brownstone structures and slick glass skyscrapers towering over ever-bustling civilians. Another perk of working at Xander are the snacks available at every staff meeting. At the moment, I'm enjoying a raspberry-chocolate-chip muffin.

The warm, fluffy loaf breaks apart in my mouth, and I stifle a moan. Dev, the chief operating officer, is saying something that must be of importance, but I'm savoring the sweetness of the chocolate chips and the tartness of the berries and paying very little attention to anything else. Every bite relieves the cramp in my empty stomach until I'm no longer hungry. I have to stop skipping breakfast.

When Dev's orotund voice suddenly captures my attention, I

realize I've missed something important. A few minutes ago, he mentioned a new hire. Unfortunately, I tuned out before receiving all the details.

"And here he is!" Dev says, elated. He stands and arranges his plaid blazer over his protruding stomach. "Everything settled with HR?"

"Yes. It is."

Still chewing, I turn to the door and offer a glance at the person who just spoke. The glance is too brief, and within a second of looking away, I'm doing a double take and carefully examining familiar features—a strong but relaxed jaw, flawless ivory skin gleaming with sun flavor, pink lips with a gentle fullness, and compelling eyes with an infinite supply of blues.

Holy crap.

I gasp, and a chunk of muffin hitches in my throat, obstructing the flow of air. As I cough and wheeze in the most inelegant manner, I try to rationalize the current situation. I align all my memories, retrieve forgotten pieces of the past, reexamine minor details that once seemed irrelevant, and stitch them all together to form a clear understanding of the present.

It's him. It's been a little over a month, but I remember that face.

It's the face of a man I thought I'd never see again. And yet, here he is.

"Azere," Dev says just as my throat clears. "Are you okay?"

"Mm-hmm. Yeah." Air courses through my throat like water through an unclogged pipe, and I exhale. "I'm fine." *Far from it.*

"Right. Anyway, as I mentioned before, we have a new hire." He gestures to the person standing beside him. "Everyone, meet our new marketing director. Rafael Castellano."

In a moment so brief it almost doesn't exist, I hear the devil laughing at me, mocking a predicament triggered into motion by my lust and stupidity. *Lust and stupidity.* No, those weren't the only factors that created this dilemma. Fate had a hand in this too. And fate is a cruel force, toying with us all, manipulating our lives, making lessons out of them and riddles and jokes—the type of jokes that are bittersweet. This joke, however, is straight up bitter. I can't handle it. My heartbeat is manic. My nerves aren't fluttery butterflies but nails, stabbing my stomach. *This can't be happening.*

"Nice to meet you all." Rafael is addressing the room, but he is fixated on me. "I look forward to getting to know each one of you."

I've already gotten a chance to know Azere. Actually, I know her very well. I expect him to say this, but he doesn't.

We watch each other, neither of us blinking. The moment is so intense, goose bumps sprout to the surface of my dark skin, causing the thin hairs on my arms to spike up. In my chair, I shiver. I squirm. The subtle movement breaks his concentration. He blinks sharply and tears his eyes from mine. The meeting continues, but I don't take note of anything that's discussed. The room is spinning, and my sanity is slowly receding because it's too fragile to handle the madness that is currently my life.

How is this possible? How the hell is this possible?

Lost in my thoughts, I zone out. When I regain focus, the room is emptying. People are rising and leaving, but Rafael and I remain seated. We have things to discuss.

Once we are alone, I stand. Though light-headed by the recent discovery, I manage to balance my weight on my stilettos and walk to the window, away from the open door and prying ears. Rafael follows.

"Hi," he says.

"Hi." A simple greeting that doesn't quite suit our predicament. "So. Your interview. It was here—at Xander."

He nods.

"Why didn't you tell me?"

"It never came up, and I had no idea you worked here. Small world, right?"

Too damn small.

"It's good to see you, Azere. Really good." He flashes his teeth in a grin that makes my heart move in leaps and bounds. "By the way," he says, gesturing at my face, "you've got a little something right there."

"Oh." I touch the corner of my lips and dust away crumbs. "I had a muffin."

"Oh yeah? What kind of muffin?"

"Raspberry chocolate chip," I say. "It was so freakin' good. I kinda devoured it. Hence the crumbs." At the sound of my own laughter, I shake my head and instantly regain my wits. *What the hell is wrong with me?* I'm supposed to be figuring this situation out and, of course, setting some ground rules that will allow us to coexist on platonic terms. Instead, I'm giggling like an infatuated idiot. Time to get back on track. "So . . . um . . . you work here now."

"I do." He watches me, stare fixed and consuming, and takes a step forward. The space between us is small—too small for employees who should, for the sake of their careers, appear like they've never engaged in a sexual relationship. I should take a step back, but his scent fills the sliver of space between us, and I stand static, close my eyes, and breathe him in.

He smells so good—like air. The kind that's sweet, fresh, untainted. I inhale deeper. Hints of musk and cedarwood accompany the scent of clean air, creating the perfect blend. Days after our hookup, this scent remained on my skin as if my pores had opened and swallowed it, every part of my body desperate to hold on to some piece of him.

"Why did you leave without saying goodbye, Azere?"

"What?" I look at him.

"You left without saying goodbye. I woke up in the morning and you were gone." A deep frown makes his eyes shrink to thin lines of blues. "Why?"

"Umm . . . well." I tug on a lock of my braid and expel a heavy, shuddery breath. "Look. Rafael, can we just act like that night never happened? We both work here now. I don't want it to get weird, and I certainly don't want anyone to know. No one can ever know, Rafael. No one. Please."

"Azere, you don't even have to ask. I won't mention it to anyone. You have my word."

With his assurance, I breathe easy. "Thank you."

"I know this situation is completely insane and unexpected. Believe me. I'm just as shocked as you are, but I think we should talk about it. Maybe over lunch or dinner."

"I'm sorry, but I don't think that's a good idea. I think it's best we just stay away from each other—keep our distance."

He scowls and opens his mouth as if to object, but before he can speak, I escape in a manner more fitting for sneakers than the heels I'm wearing.

In the open-concept workspace, prying eyes dart from computer screens to me. As I sprint to the kitchen, the sound of my heels contends with the low murmurs of my colleagues. Today, I'm wearing my jewel-toned satin stilettos, an imitation of the iconic Manolo Blahniks Mr. Big proposed to Carrie with in *Sex and the City*. They're stunning but the wrong choice for a day when I want to go unnoticed.

Christina, my best friend, is the only person in the kitchen. She's yawning while stirring a spoonful of honey into a cup.

"Chris, where in the world have you been? You missed the staff meeting."

"Yeah. It's been a crazy morning." She brings the cup to her pursed lips and takes a sip of what smells like peppermint chai. "Saw you chatting with the new guy. What was that about?"

"Nothing. Just answering some of his questions about the office." I'm proud of the lie. It's quick, simple, and definitely believable.

"Mm-hmm." She drinks the tea leisurely, her hazel eyes watching me from above the rim of the cup. "He's hot. Don't you think?"

"No. Not really. I don't . . . I don't think he's hot at all." Another lie. Though, this one lacks all the elements of believability.

"Oh. Okay. Well, rumor has it that the instant he walked into the conference room, you forgot how to chew and choked on a muffin." She chuckles, and her nose scrunches up, its length shrinking. "Then you proceeded to gawk at him like a damn fool for the rest of the meeting. Did I hear wrong?" She arches a perfectly groomed eyebrow, daring my denial.

"Look." I sigh, and the sharp release of air makes my lips tremble. "I wasn't staring at him because he's hot or anything." *Damn the stupid rumors.*

"Then why were you staring?" She waits for an answer I'm not ready to provide. "Azere, I'm not judging. Hell, I probably would have been staring too. He's one gorgeous excuse for a man." Her hand flaps, fanning her flushed face. "Oh, the things I would love to do to him. Whips, handcuffs, and hot wax would definitely be needed."

At her admission, my eyes widen. *Hot wax?* I have questions but lack the audacity to ask and the resolve to stomach the answers. "Yeah. I gotta get back to work."

"Hold up." Christina stands in front of me, preventing my exit. "What's with you?" Tilting her head, she observes me. "I'm getting a vibe."

"A vibe?" I laugh. "Should I credit that to your supposed psychic abilities?"

"Or just good ol' instincts." She's still inspecting my face. "Azere, what's wrong?"

There's so much I could tell her, so many issues currently bothering me. One is sitting a few feet away, confined by glass walls in an office directly across mine. The other issue is a suspicion I've had for days, a suspicion I'm not ready to confirm or tell my best friend about. Fortunately, the third issue doesn't require secrecy because it's something Christina has heard many times before.

"It's my mom. I'm having dinner with my family tonight, and she's setting me up. Again."

"Azere, just tell her you don't want to meet another potential husband. In fact, tell her you don't need a man."

"That's definitely not happening." I glare at my friend. "Immediately when I say that, she's gonna call the pastor over for a prayer and deliverance session. Her exact words will be"—I clear my throat and conjure a Nigerian accent—"Azere, at your ripe age, if you don't need a man, a husband, you must be possessed. You must be very possessed, but Jesus will deliver you."

Christina giggles. "Okay. Fine," she says, settling down. "But, Azere, if you really want a man, you gotta stop letting your mom set you up. She's a terrible matchmaker. Maybe it's time you pass the baton to me." She grins widely, exposing the gap between her two front teeth. "I'll set you up. With my cousin. Leo."

"Hmm. Leo." I consider the name. "From your father's side of the family?"

When she nods, I shake my head.

"Chris, I only date Nigerians. You know that."

"Yeah. And how's that been working for you?"

I say nothing, and she eyes me.

"Mm-hmm. Exactly. Now, let me set you up with Leo. He's a great guy, and he's super cute. He looks like a young John Travolta with a hint of an older Robert Downey Jr."

"I'm having a hard time envisioning that combination."

"No need to. You can meet him in person. You two could work out. And if you're wondering, a Nigerian woman and an Italian man can make a pretty cute kid. Check it out." She waves her hands over her body like she's a displayed prize on *The Price Is Right*. "I'm proof."

I smile and nod in agreement. Christina is a beautiful woman. The mixture of black and white in her DNA adds an undertone of russet to her beige skin and a delicate kink to the brunette locks that puff out and coil past the length of her neck. We interned at Xander together—right out of university. The first time I saw her, attempting to balance a stack of files on her arms, I noticed her eyes. They were wide and frantic, a stunning hazel hue that complemented the ginger-colored freckles on her cheeks. I took half the load off her arms, and the next day, she thanked me with a latte. We became inseparable soon after, having lunch together every day, ranting about our boss, and bonding over our shared Edo heritage.

Christina, unlike me, was born in Canada. I became a citizen at twelve, shortly after immigrating.

Canadian. It's a title that is both empowering and demanding as it requires me to give up portions of my Nigerian culture so I can fit into my Western setting. And I've been doing that for years—compromising, losing bits and pieces of my original identity in an attempt to reinvent myself. However, the one thing I can't compromise on is the ethnicity of my future husband.

"So," Christina says, "should I give Leo a call and tell him someone special wants to meet him?"

"Absolutely not."

"What?" Her thin lips shrink then turn downward. "Why not?"

"Chris, you've known me for years. You know what I want."

"Yeah. You want to marry an Edo man and have his babies. Sounds good. But what makes you think life is gonna turn out just as you expect?" She scoffs. "It hardly ever does, Azere. Maybe it's time you become a little flexible, open up to new possibilities— let go of the life you've planned and accept the life that's waiting for you. I'm just saying." She shrugs and struts out of the kitchen, her heels clicking and clacking against the ceramic floor.

Let go of the life you've planned and accept the life that's waiting for you.

For a moment, I wonder what that would be like. If I hypothetically let go of the life I have always envisioned, the life I have meticulously planned, what else would there be? What else would be waiting for me?

chapter
3

Rafael Castellano

Sweat gathers at the root of my hair and drips down my forehead. According to the watch on my wrist, I ran six miles—six miles that did nothing to relieve the stress of being newly employed at a company where my one-night stand coincidentally works. The shock and disbelief of seeing Azere quickly turned to elation and relief. Though, she didn't share the sentiments.

The private elevator slides open, revealing my spacious, two-story penthouse. I step out, walk to the kitchen, and grab a bottle of water from the refrigerator. I guzzle down the chilled drink, knowing I'll soon be interrupted by the quick pitter-patter of small feet. Right on cue, the interruption arrives. The toy fox terrier hastens toward me, his tongue hanging out of his open mouth and his tail wagging at an incredible speed. He stops at my feet and barks, demanding my attention.

"Hey, Milo," I say, crouching down to pet him. "Did you miss me?"

He licks my hand, his way of answering.

"Missed you too, buddy. Did you enjoy your walk with Jenny? Were you a good boy?" He usually is. As I rub a spot under his chin, I recall getting him two years ago. He was exactly what I needed, someone other than myself to take care of. Unfortunately, we haven't spent much time together lately. I've been occupied with moving back to Toronto. Now, with my new role at Xander, I'll be occupied with trying to prove myself and impress higher-ranking colleagues who already expect so much from me. The pressure to succeed is higher than ever. To make matters worse, I haven't been able to focus entirely on my new tasks. I've been thinking about her a lot.

Azere.

Today, while sending emails and taking phone calls, I found myself periodically looking straight ahead at where she sat in the office directly across mine, holding her gaze in the brief moments our eyes connected. The image of her in my arms—naked and spent—came to mind throughout the day.

It comes to mind now.

I still recall the details of that night—not just the pleasure derived from touching her and being touched by her, but the hint of emotion that sprouted out of my guarded heart like a plant through the ground. Being with her—laughing, talking, touching—was the first time in three years I felt something other than utter bleakness. It's still a mystery how she managed to do that—reacquaint me with my old self, a man who was unburdened and easygoing. Azere did all that in one night, and then she was gone. The only evidence of our encounter was in my mind, and sometimes, I found myself questioning if I had imagined it all. And then today, I saw her—flesh and blood, muffin crumbs dusted on the corner of her lips, and eyes wide with surprise. It was as if our meeting again was the contrivance of some unseen immensity—God, angels, something. Now, she wants me to stay away from her. Fulfilling that request will require mustering a colossal amount of willpower.

"Come on, Milo." I stand and walk through the open-concept space, stopping at a shelf in the living room. "How about some music?" I sort through the collection of records, choose one, and place it on a vintage record player. Seconds after dropping the tonearm, traditional Spanish folk music projects through the copper horn.

The music reminds me of the many summers my family spent with my grandmother in Spain. If I listen closely enough— beyond the combination of the guitar, the bandurria, and the castanets—I can hear my feisty grandmother singing along, her voice rising and falling with the same theatrical flair as the singer on the record. I can hear my siblings chuckling as we link hands and attempt to perform the sardana. My parents' voices are also audible—my father passionately negotiating with business associates and my mother talking and laughing with her sisters. The effervescent music and the familiar chaos fills the empty, quiet spaces in the penthouse; with it, the constant ache of loneliness lessens.

On the balcony, I lounge on a chair and Milo hops on my lap. Lake Ontario expands beyond the terrace, city lights and the auburn and indigo hues of dusk reflecting over its swaying, glistening form. The view is serene; it's the reason I bought the lakefront property. This close to the water, the air is cooler, which I prefer. I enjoy the breeze, the music, and the company of Milo, who is receiving some much-deserved love and attention. When I close my eyes, my mind wanders off to her again.

Azere.

I think about her—how she walks purposefully, gracefully in stilettos. I think about how her long lashes brush against the thin crease of skin beneath her brown eyes. I think of all her small gestures that seem as seamless and fluid as a dance. Like the way her fingers twirl a lock of her patterned hair—around and around, pulling and smoothening.

Each memory makes my heart race.

My eyes flash open, and as I look over the vast, tranquil lake, I can't help but wonder if the memory of our night together is etched in her mind as it is in mine.

chapter
4

My suspicion has been confirmed.

Denial is pointless now, and yet, it's the one thing capable of getting me through this night.

I pull into my mom's driveway and park the black Toyota. Tears burn my eyes, and I fan them away. I cried in my apartment immediately after learning the truth, a truth that will surely upend my world. It's best I keep this information to myself. My family can't know—no one can.

Just pretend like everything is okay. You can do this, Azere.

I twist a lock of braid between two fingers. Feeling the intertwining pattern of the neat plait relaxes me. I continue the motion for seconds before stepping out of the car.

I've got this.

The pavement is wet from rain that only just stopped. Along with the petrichor drifting in the warm May air, there is a trace of my mother's cooking. The aroma of the signature ingredients—ground crayfish and red palm oil—reminds me of life in the Nigerian village I was born and grew up in.

It was nothing like this charming suburban neighborhood. As I admire the trimmed lawns, some with For Sale signs wedged in them, I remember that houses in my village weren't sold and bought. Generations of my family lived, thrived, multiplied, and died in one house, our single history just as important as every building block keeping the structure standing year after year. I remember how we all shared a lifestyle and an identity that was crafted by those who came before us. My father, like his father, was a farmer. My mother sold foodstuff in the market. When she was young, she would balance a tray of smoked fish on her head and hawk on the streets. At nine, I did the same. With one hand supporting the tray on my head and the other braced on my hip, I strolled down the streets laden with red sand and dust, the same streets my mother had walked and her mother before her.

I remember at home, in our immense compound, I plucked guavas and cashews from the trees my grandfather had planted as a child. In the mornings, I walked two miles through narrow, crooked roads to attend the school my great-grandfather had helped construct. In the evenings, as the scorching heat of day waned and termites fluttered toward lit kerosene lanterns, my father told my sister and me greatly exaggerated tales of our ancestors—the fighters and the cowards, the dreamers and the unbelievers, the vengeful and the justified.

In Nigeria, my entire life was an extension of my lineage. There—in a close-knit community, tucked away from the rest of the world—nothing existed but the paths my ancestors had paved, the buildings they had molded with sand and concrete and sweat, the lands they had cultivated and bled to defend, the traditions they had created and nurtured, the myths they had fabricated and adopted as truths.

In that village, life was simpler, more familiar. I miss it.

The faint sound of a dribbling ball redirects my attention to the suburban neighborhood, to Jason Carter who is approaching me and bouncing a basketball against the pavement with weary disinterest.

"Hey, Azere." He tucks the ball in his armpit, and an impish grin appears on his boyish face. "What's up, babe?"

"Babe?" I frown and cock my head. "Seriously?"

I babysat Jason when he was a kid. When he was a sweet kid. Now, he's eighteen. He has a rugged beard patched along his weak jawline, an ego with its own zip code, and an agenda to add my name to his developing little black book.

"Or do you prefer sweetheart?"

"Funny," I say. "That's what I used to call you right after tucking you in bed."

"Well, if you wanna relive the past, I'm up for it. But just so you know, I sleep naked now."

"Yeah." I give him a once-over, shifting my eyes from his head to his feet. "I'm sure there's been no progress."

"Seeing is believing, babe. Once I get you alone, I'm sure I can make you a believer. But you gotta promise. If I show you mine, you gotta show me yours."

"Gosh." I cringe. "When did you become such a perv?"

"I'm just a man who knows what he wants." His fingers move through his hair, tousling the confusion of thick brown curls and blond tangled frizz.

"Well, man." I lick my thumb and bring it to his face. "Looks like you've been playing in the sandbox."

My wet thumb smears a patch of dirt on his cheek. When I pull back, he gawks at me—his skin flushed and his mouth wide open. Above our heads, moths flutter around the glow of the streetlight.

"You might want to close that big mouth of yours." I pat his cheek and turn away. The stone walkway leads me to the front door of the quaint bungalow.

"Well, look who it is," my sister, Efe, says when I step into the air-conditioned house. She's standing by the entry table, sipping red wine with perfect ease. "Mom has a surprise for you, and it's in the living room." She struts toward me, her yellow sundress flapping against her knees.

She looks like me, with the same glistening chestnut skin and full lips. Our slight differences are aspects that make her prettier. Like the slanted cheekbones that shape her oval face and her honey-brown eyes that have a sharp lift at their corners, creating a cat eye.

"So," I say. "What does this one look like?"

"Rich. He looks rich." She strokes a lock of her chemically straightened hair behind her multi-pierced ear. "He smells rich too."

"Rich has a smell?"

"If you have the nose for it. He kinda looks familiar too, but . . ." She squints and taps her pursed lips, thinking.

"Yeah? But what?" I urge.

"I don't know. Can't make the connection. But maybe you know him."

"Right." Groaning, I kick off my shoes. "*Oya*, let's get this over with. Where's everyone?"

"Uncle is entertaining your guest. Mom's getting dinner ready. We've all been stalling, anticipating your arrival." She tilts her head and observes me from an angle. "Azere, you don't look so good. You look . . . terrified. What's wrong?"

"It's nothing. I'm fine. Mom's waiting."

I rush down the corridor, and pictures of my family, framed on the beige wall, blur at the corner of my eye. Nerves and dread rattle in the pit of my stomach. I inhale and exhale at a steady, controlled pace.

"Mom?" I say, entering the kitchen. My voice is a whisper muffled by the swishing of the kitchen ventilation.

"Mommy," I speak louder this time, "good evening."

She focuses on her task, separating browned plantains from sizzling oil and tossing them into a bowl lined with paper towels.

"Sorry I'm late."

Seconds after my apology, she spins around, and her floor-length lilac dress sways against her petite physique. "A-ze-re." When the syllables in my name are emphasized, it means I'm in trouble. "I expected you an hour ago." She scowls and pins her dark lips in a rigid line. "Ah-ahn! What took you so long?"

Despite thirteen years in Canada, her Nigerian accent is still thick. Sometimes, it's like her accent is calling out to mine, saying: "Hey, authentic Nigerian Azere, come out and play." And that's when the accent, the one I tried hard to hide after my move to Canada, forces its way out. This happens whenever I'm at home with my family, when I don't feel the complete pressure of being wedged between two worlds, when I'm not a Nigerian Canadian. When I'm just Nigerian. Then I speak freely, mixing pidgin English with Edo or simply speaking fluent English but with a Nigerian intonation, altering the rhythm of each word.

"Mommy," I say, "*lahọ*. Don't be angry. I'm here now. Sorry for being late."

"Don't tell me sorry *o*. Sorry for yourself."

I hate it when she does that, when she turns my apology into an insult. *Sorry for yourself*. Try to apologize to a Nigerian mother and that's usually the phrase you get in return.

"Anyway." She leaves her position by the stove and circles me. She's inspecting my outfit, ensuring I appear appealing to my latest suitor. As she moves, the fluorescent light gleams on her smooth, dark skin that's oiled with shea butter. "Azere, why are you dressed like this? Eh?" She yanks on the loose-fitting blouse I'm wearing. "What is the meaning of this nonsense? Your figure is not even showing at all. What kind of *wahala* is this? It looks like your breasts are playing hide and seek."

"Mostly hide," my sister chimes in.

"Lord, have mercy." My mother rubs the creases that line her tense forehead. "In fact, why aren't you wearing Nigerian clothes? Eh? I know you have many. Or did you throw them away to make room in your closet for jeans and T-shirts?"

"No, Mommy. I still have them."

"Then why aren't you wearing one? You're meeting your future husband for the first time. And let me also add that this boy is a doctor. A medical doctor. You should have dressed like a bride. Instead, you look like a farmer going to harvest cassava. To make matters worse, you are too thin. Look." She pokes my collarbone. "They're all sticking out."

"*Osanobua*," I say, grumbling. "Mommy, they've always been like that."

"No. Not when you were living in this house, eating Nigerian food on a regular basis. Now you are on your own, eating those *yeye* Canadian food every single day. Quinoa salad, avocado toast, smoothie bowl." She rolls her eyes. "If you were eating Nigerian food, you would be more robust and have enough flesh to cover your bones."

"Right." I have no words. None.

"Anyway, what can we do now? You are here, he is here. Let us go."

"Okay," I say. "Sure. But I just need a minute."

"A minute to do what? To do what, Azere?"

To mentally prepare myself for another tragic setup.

"You have kept that man waiting long enough." My mother grimaces, and her round face distorts awkwardly. "He did not come here to gist with your uncle." Because she's irritated, her Nigerian accent deepens. She speaks slowly, stressing the syllables in each word. "You are not wast-ing an-oth-er min-ute—not ev-en a sec-ond." She grips my arm and hauls me toward the living room. "*Oya*. Let us go. And don't forget to smile and flirt with your eyes."

Flirt with my eyes. How the hell does that work?

To my right, Efe shuffles beside me. She gives me two thumbs up, and I stick out my tongue at her.

"Look who has finally arrived," my mom announces when we enter the living room. "Ah-ahn." She scans the space, then turns to my uncle, who is sitting in a brown armchair, effortlessly projecting confidence and authority as patriarch of the family. "Where is Azere's future husband? Where did he go?"

"He stepped out to take a work call," my uncle answers. "He should be back shortly."

"Thank God." My mother exhales. "I thought Azere found a way to chase this one off without even meeting him."

I roll my eyes and turn my attention elsewhere. "Good evening, Uncle," I say.

"*Omwinwen*." He calls me his child in Edo, our language. He's been calling me that since I was twelve—since my father, his younger brother, died.

After the funeral, my uncle—who immigrated to Canada in his early twenties and had a successful career as an engineer—brought my family over to live with him. He shouldered the responsibilities his brother left behind. *Omwinwen*. At first, it was strange to hear him call me that. I wasn't his child. I had never even met the man until my father's death. And though he had my father's full face, deep-set eyes, sienna pigment, and dimpled smile, the distinction was clear. He was not my father.

He was a widower. He lost his wife to cancer and was the father of a boy, Jacob. My uncle understood loss and honored the ties of family. My mother, my sister, and I lived with him for four years after coming to Canada. Selflessly, he took care of us. He provided necessities and more and even financed my mother's nursing school education. He never resented our presence, nor did he deviate from his unassigned duty. In time, reservations and technicalities were put aside. I loved and respected him. He became my father, and his son, my brother.

"Azere," my uncle says, looking over my shoulder. "Your visitor is here. Turn around. Greet him."

Reluctantly—because I must, because defying elders in my culture is highly frowned upon and basically a one-way ticket to hell—I obey. And when I see the man my uncle has dubbed my visitor and my mother has dubbed my future husband, I gasp.

Shit.

He walks forward and extends a hand to me. I look at that hand and then at him, clenching my jaw and fisting my hands, restraining myself from reacting.

He has a lot of nerve, showing up here.

The last time I saw him was the night he took my virginity. It was the last night of church camp. We were counselors, and after everyone had fallen asleep, we snuck out of our cabins. He was waiting for me at the rim of the woods, hiding behind a hefty tree. When he revealed himself, I jolted, and his lips came over mine before I could yelp.

"Shh," he spoke into my mouth as he kissed me.

With a flashlight guiding our way, he led us farther into the woods. We stopped at a dome tent he had set up. Inside, he peeled off my clothes. His hands and lips touched every inch of my body.

"You okay?" he asked as he eased into me. When I nodded, we made love. He walked me back to my cabin after, and that was the last time I saw him.

I was nineteen at the time—naive, overly optimistic, and foolishly in love—and he broke my heart in the worst possible way. Because of him, I acquired insecurities I never had, and my memories of my first love, my first sexual encounter, were tainted. Elijah Osunde did all that. Now, six years later, he's standing in front of me, holding out his hand for a handshake. A handshake.

"Azere," he says. "How are you?"

"To be honest, I've had a pretty horrible day, and seeing you here confirms that there is a force in the universe who has dedicated this day to my personal torment."

Efe releases a loud snort but settles when our mother fixates on her.

"Azere." With just my name, my uncle discreetly warns me to behave. "Why don't we give them a moment to get better acquainted?" He stands and makes an exit. Once in the dining room, he calls for my mother.

"Zere, you better behave." Her warning is indiscreet. She hisses, grabs Efe's arm, and marches off.

After my family leaves, I focus on the man in front of me. "What the hell are you doing here?" My voice is hushed, but the anger in it is knife-sharp.

"Azere. You look"—keen eyes move over my body—"amazing."

"Answer the question, Elijah."

"Your mom invited me. Our mothers are apparently friends. They thought we could—"

"They thought wrong." *They thought so wrong.* "You need to leave, Elijah."

"Your mom invited me to dinner," he says. "Leaving is rude."

"No, rude is taking my virginity and then going MIA. Remember that, Romeo?"

"But, Azere, I thought you understood why I had to leave."

"The fact that you left isn't the problem. The problem is how you left. How you left me."

"Azere, I was twenty-three and very stupid."

"And I was nineteen and very intolerant of stupidity. Six years later, nothing has changed. So please." I press my eyes closed, forcing back tears on the verge of falling. "Leave, Elijah." I look at him. "Just go."

"Zere, I made a huge mistake. Okay? I didn't handle the situation well. I wish I had."

I wish he had too because up until that point, when he left and broke my heart, I envisioned a future with him. I envisioned eventually becoming his wife and the mother of his children, and he told me, on so many occasions, he envisioned the same. We were in love—a love that, in our youth, was consuming, obsessive, invigorating, ardent. And then he was gone along with the promise of our future.

"Azere, I want another chance."

"Another chance?" I'm stunned. A mixture of chuckles and puffs surges from my mouth. "Another chance to do what?"

"To be us again—to be everything we were supposed to be." He takes my hand in his, and I flinch before settling into the sweet familiar. "Zere, after all these years, there hasn't been another girl who has come close to being everything you were to me. Everything you still are to me."

It's unfortunate that I can say the same. It's unfortunate that I haven't loved another man as fiercely as I loved him or met one worthy of envisioning a shared future with. It's so very, very unfortunate.

"Azere, give me another chance. Please."

"Elijah." I pull my hand from his grip. "I can't."

"Just let me prove myself to you. I'm not the same person. I swear. Just look at me."

Yeah, I'm looking and admiring just a little. With his swarthy complexion, he looks like a young Morris Chestnut. His shaved head is lined neat and sharp like the goatee framing his lips.

He's wearing a black suit with no tie. The first two buttons on the white oxford shirt are undone, revealing a hint of his firm chest. He's more handsome than he was six years ago. If I didn't have such a strong grip on my resentment, I would be tempted to accept his apology.

"Elijah." I shake my head, rejecting any lustful thoughts that might compromise my good sense. "I need you to leave. Right now."

"Come on, Azere."

"Right now, Elijah. If you don't, I'll . . . I'll . . . tell my mom."

"Tell her what exactly?" He laughs, mocking my juvenile statement. "Your mom loves me. She already calls me her in-law."

"Well, once she finds out you took my virginity at church camp, I'm sure her opinion of you will change. She'll probably chase you out with a broom, or maybe she'll grab the hot oil off the stove and aim for your head. And so you know, my mom's aim is on point."

"Zere, are you serious?"

I cross my arms over my chest, indicating I am indeed very freakin' serious.

"Okay. Fine. You win." He throws his hands up in surrender. "I'll go. Just let me say goodbye."

"There's no need for that." I usher him to the front door and anticipate his exit. "What are you waiting for?"

He holds the knob as if he doesn't know how to work the damn thing. "Azere, I'm sorry. Really. I am." There's a hint of remorse in his eyes. "I hope one day you'll forgive me. Good night." Finally, he leaves.

When I slam the door, my mother steps out of the dining room. Efe follows her like a loyal dog.

"Where is Elijah? Did he just leave?" She frowns. "A-ze-re, what did you say to that boy?"

"Nothing. She said nothing." Efe, sweet Efe, comes to my defense. "He's a doctor. He probably had a work emergency—had to deal with a patient or something. Right, Azere?"

"Yeah. Exactly. Efe's right. He's off saving lives. Being a hero. Doing his thing."

My mother, who can sniff out my bullshit like a shark can sniff out blood, is glowering at me suspiciously. She knows I chased Elijah off. Soon, a lecture—long and dreary—will commence. I refuse to be present for it.

"Efe." I grab my sister's hand and drag her down the corridor. "Let's catch up."

We leave our mother alone, muttering and brooding.

chapter
5

The first non-Nigerian man I ever lusted after was Antonio Banderas. At sixteen, I saw *The Mask of Zorro*—a story of action,
romance, and a fearless outlaw with a sultry accent. Over the
span of a month, I watched the movie repeatedly. I focused on
the way Antonio's hair swayed in accordance to his movements
and the way his lips moved while kissing the woman he loved.
My mother, determined to keep my sister and me rooted in our
culture, didn't appreciate my Latin obsession. She tore down the
poster of Antonio in my room and replaced it with a poster of Jim
Iyke, a Nigerian actor. That's what my mother has been doing
since we moved to Canada—shoving my culture down my throat,
so I don't forget where I come from.

In my old bedroom, I flop on the queen-size mattress. The
poster of Jim Iyke is still on the lavender-colored wall, right
above the bedframe.

"Didn't go well with your potential lover boy?" Efe says.

"Nope."

"Wanna elaborate?"

"Nope." I look at her. "How come Jacob's not here?"

"The detective is working late tonight," Efe says, lying beside me. "He's obsessing over some murder case. Anyway, you probably want this back." She shoves a credit card in my face. "Thanks again for paying."

"Sure." I take the card and slip it into my pocket. "Did you get all your textbooks?"

"Yep. Officially ready for law school in the fall. Now, I can spend the rest of the summer being reckless."

"How about you spend your summer in the library instead, prepping for classes?"

"Nah," she says. "I'm twenty-three, and I plan to milk this young-and-free thing until Mom starts nagging me about getting hitched."

"You know that's coming at some point, right?"

"Not anytime soon. Not when I have Mike, a best friend who also doubles as a mock boyfriend. The fact that he's Edo and Mom loves him is the cherry on top." A satisfied grin extends across her face.

I can't help but be jealous for not having the same option. If only Christina were a Christopher.

"Anyway." Efe lets out a sharp breath and turns to me. "You know Mom's gonna come in here at any moment. And you know what she's gonna do, right?"

Lecture me, criticize me, and bring up the promise.

"We should get outta here, get some ice cream, catch a late movie, and most important, avoid Mom. There's a new romance movie out."

"Efe, you're feeding my obsession."

"Puh-lease." She scoffs and rolls her eyes. "Your unhealthy obsession with romantic movies has nothing to do with me."

This is true. "Fine. Let's go watch two lovestruck fools jump over hurdles in pursuit of their ever after." In my opinion, these are the only stories worth knowing.

In sync, Efe and I spring to a sitting position, and just as we're about to stand, our mother appears in the doorway.

"I need to talk to Azere," she says, her tone stern. "Alone."

"Yeah. Of course you do." Efe squeezes my shoulder, offering encouragement before leaving the room.

"Azere." My mother sits beside me and releases a lengthy sigh.

"So . . . um . . . How's work, Mom?" I ask, hoping to divert her from the conversation she's aiming to have. "Anything interesting happening at the hospital—any *Grey's Anatomy*–type drama?"

She watches me blankly, not a glint in her unblinking eyes nor a hint of humor on her straight lips. "Azere, I am not here to gist about work."

Well, of course she isn't.

"Azere, I am here to talk about the path you are currently on."

"Path? What path?"

"You are single." She says it like it's a terminal disease. "I don't know what is wrong with you. I have introduced you to several eligible men, and yet, here you are. Maybe you are being influenced by these modern women—no husband, no children. All they want is their career. You want to be a feminist."

She has obviously been misinformed. I should enlighten her on what the term means, but I don't have the energy to debate with a woman who doesn't like being corrected.

"Azere, listen. If you want to be a feminist, fine. But please be a married feminist with at least three children. In our country, a woman's honor is her husband and her children. A career means nothing. I married your father when I was twenty. You are twenty-five now." She touches my cheek and looks at me dolefully as if I'm truly being afflicted by the deadly disease: singleness. "Enough time has passed. I have allowed you and your sister to reap all the benefits of this country. It's time to honor your own country. Zere, it's time to honor your culture. Or have you forgotten the promise you made to your father?"

And here we go.

"No, Mommy. I haven't forgotten."

And even if I did, she would refresh my memory. She was present when I made the promise. We were both sitting on the edge of the bed, watching my father take his last breaths. He'd lost a lot of weight at that point. He was so feeble, he could barely lift a finger. We were at a hospital in Benin City. We had been there for weeks, watching my father undergo several treatments. In truth, there was no cure. The cancer had spread too quickly. One day, the doctor told us my father most likely wouldn't make it through the night. Even then, I was determined to prolong his life. I spoke to him, reciting the stories he once told my sister and me. I even narrated a future where he was alive and well. Hours passed, and he remained inert. When my mouth started to dry and my eyes began to droop, he stirred.

"Your uncle is taking you to Canada," he said, his voice a faint quiver. "Do you know where that is?"

I shook my head.

"It's right beside America."

I knew about America, so I nodded.

"Everything is different there. It is nothing like Nigeria, like our village. Some people travel abroad and get carried away. They forget where they come from. They forget about their culture. They forget who they are. *Omwinwen*, don't be one of those people. No matter where you go, honor your culture."

"Baba, I will."

"Do you remember what happened to Mama Efosa?" He was referring to a woman in our village who had complained her daughter, in America, had forgotten her culture after marrying a white man. "Do you remember what she said about her daughter?"

I nodded.

"Azere, promise me you won't do that. Promise me you will never get involved with a white man or any man who is not Edo. Azere, when you are of age, marry a good Edo man and give him children. Just like your mother did and your grandmother and so many others before them. Promise me."

"Baba. I promise."

It was an agreement made with sincerity, an agreement that gave my father peace as he died, an agreement I reflect on every day of my life, an agreement that haunts me and demands so much from me.

Efe was asleep when I made the promise. I am so grateful she didn't have to do the same. She's twenty-three and free in every sense—detached from the promise my mother considers sacred. I, however, am bound to that promise—sentenced to live cautiously and love selectively.

"Azere, Elijah is a good boy," my mother says. "He is Edo and a medical doctor. Your father would have loved him. He would have been proud."

"Mom, I—"

"I don't know if you remember too well, but Elijah used to go to our church when he was younger. In fact, he was even a youth leader." She smiles, proud. "He is a very good Christian boy. I even suspect he's a virgin like you, saving himself for marriage."

Oh, Lord. If only she knew.

"Azere, believe me. Elijah will make a good husband."

"Mommy, I can't be with him. Or anyone else. Not right now."

"And why is that?" Her face hardens with irritation.

"Because I . . . well . . ." I'm losing a grip on the denial I've been holding on to all night. *I can't pretend anymore. Everything is not okay.* "Mommy, I have to tell you something. I'm . . . um . . ."

"You're what, Azere? Speak!"

I can't. The words are stuck. They clog my throat, and I can't breathe. I stand and sprint out of the room.

Outside the house, I clench my chest and gasp frantically for air. During my intense struggle to breathe, a brisk breeze dashes over my face. It has the effect of a firm slap, snapping me back to my senses. Instantly, my erratic heartbeat slows and air passes through my throat. The panic attack is over.

Now, as I breathe with ease, the truth becomes a force impossible to contain, and I confess what I couldn't to my mother.

"I'm pregnant."

chapter 6

In most romantic comedies, the lead character usually has a sidekick—someone bold, witty, and capable of providing comedic relief and harsh truths the lead isn't willing to face. In the movie 27 *Dresses*, Casey is Jane's best friend and the blunt voice of reason who goes as far as slapping Jane for pining over a man who only sees her as his errand girl.

If I were the lead in a romantic comedy, my sidekick would be Christina. Though, at the moment, I'm not confident about the status of our friendship.

Last night, after returning from my mom's, Christina called me. The conversation didn't go so well.

"Girl, are you caught up on *Insecure*?" she said when I answered the phone.

"No, I just—"

"Spoiler alert, Issa got a new man. And he is gorgeous."

She proceeded to rave about the latest episode, detailing each scene and even reenacting a three-person dialogue. And that was when I lost it. My whole world was falling apart, and she was babbling about a show that surely couldn't be more dramatic than the crap I was going through.

"Shut up, Christina!" I snapped. "For once, I wish you would get your dumb head out of your dumb ass." The insult was juvenile, but I knew the impact it would have on her. She hated when people called her dumb, when they insulted her intelligence. It was the one thing capable of eating at her self-esteem. Yet, I spat out the slur because I wanted to take my frustration out on someone.

"Azere." She spoke after a few seconds of silence. "I don't know what your problem is. Maybe you had a bad day. Hell, maybe you had a bad week. Whatever it is, you didn't have to come at me like that." She sniffed. "You just didn't." And hung up.

I was wrong, and now, the day after our little quarrel, I'm hoping the cheeseburger in my hand will make my apology more acceptable.

"Wanna share a burger?" I say, hovering over Christina. She's sitting at an empty table in the office lunchroom, picking at a kale salad. "Well?" I shake the brown bag, and she rolls her eyes. "Did I mention it's a double bacon cheeseburger on a pretzel bun?"

"Sit."

I do as she's instructed and try to contain my relief. "About last night." I dig into the paper bag, pull out the box of fries, and place it in front of her. "I'm so sorry, Chris."

"I might be willing to forgive and forget, but what was with the bitch attack? You said some mean shit."

"I'm sorry, Chris. Really. It wasn't about you. The thing is . . ." Before offering an explanation, I survey the lunchroom, searching for prying ears. My colleagues are either engaged with conversation or technology. "Okay." I take in a deep breath. "A little over a month ago—say about five or six weeks—I went on a date my mom set up. It was at the St. Regis with some guy called Richard. The date didn't go so well. After it ended, I went to Astor, the lounge in the hotel."

"Oh, I love that place," Christina says, grinning. "Super swanky. Remind me to write a Yelp review." When she notes my straight face, she shakes her head, coming to her senses. "Sorry. So not the point."

"The point is, I was drinking and sulking, and there was this guy . . . this white guy. He was from out of town. And we hung out a little. And one thing led to another. And . . . well, I . . ."

"You what, Azere?" She shuffles to the edge of her seat. "Go on. Spit it out."

"I had sex with him. In his hotel room."

"What?" Christina's expression bounces between confusion, curiosity, and utter disbelief. "What the hell, Zere? Why are you just telling me this now, and what happened to only dating Nigerian guys?"

"It wasn't a date, Christina. We just hooked up. I wanted to have some fun and then put it behind me but . . ."

"But what?"

"But I can't exactly do that because my one-night stand . . . um . . . well, he works here. He recently started working here. Recent as in yesterday."

Those are the only clues I give, and instantly, her eyes still on me and fill with understanding.

"You slept with Rafael?" she whispers.

"I had no idea he was gonna start working at Xander. Then yesterday, he just showed up."

"Azere, are you messing with me?"

I shake my head.

"Well, damn. Talk about an insane twist of fate." She puffs and ruffles her springy curls. "Your one-night stand turns out to be your new coworker. If this shit ain't serendipitous, I don't know what is."

Serendipitous. The word reminds me of the movie *Serendipity*. After a spontaneous and somewhat magical encounter, Jonathan and Sara part ways without exchanging contact information, leaving it to fate to reunite them. Despite the years that pass and the miles between them, Jonathan and Sara—through a series of hilarious and heartwarming coincidences—meet again. In the movie, destiny has a sweet sense of humor. In my case, destiny has a wicked sense of humor.

"Christina, there's more." *More complications throwing my life out of balance.*

"Well, tell me." She abandons her salad and tosses fries into her mouth like they're popcorn and my story is an Oscar-nominated drama. "Just spit it out."

"I'm pregnant."

"I'm sorry." Her eyebrows shoot up, almost touching the sleek baby hairs that line her forehead. "You're what?"

"Pregnant. I'm pregnant, Christina."

"Seriously?"

"Yeah." I nod. "Seriously."

"Shit. I did not see that coming." For a few seconds, she says nothing. She gawks at me, her wide eyes unblinking. "What the hell, Azere?" she finally says. "What were you thinking? Didn't you use a condom?"

"Of course I did. We were safe, but I guess it wasn't foolproof." I groan and push my fingers through my braids. "This is bad. This is so bad."

"Zere, honey, you don't look so good. You're sweating."

She doesn't have to make the announcement. Moisture seeps through my pores, drenching my face and my neck and my armpits, making my skin icky.

"I'm pregnant, Chris." That word, *pregnant*, bears a distinct hint of bitterness that tickles my gag reflex. "And trust me. When my mom finds out, she's gonna kill me. And I know people say that all the time, but this is no joke." I tap my chest, trying to calm my rapidly beating heart. "Getting pregnant out of wedlock is one thing. Getting pregnant by a one-night stand is another. Getting pregnant by a man who isn't even Nigerian, is taking things to a whole other level. My mom won't forgive that." I can't contain my emotions any longer. Tears finally fall, and I feel like throwing caution to the wind and jumping off a cliff. I search the room for an open window.

"Azere, look at me." Christina snaps her fingers and promptly gains my attention. "Listen to me. We'll figure this out. Do you understand?"

I hesitate, and she squeezes my hand.

"Azere, you're gonna be fine. Do you understand me?"

"Yeah."

"Good. Now, what did your gynecologist say about—"

"Um . . . I never met with my gynecologist. I just took a home pregnancy test. I picked one up at Dollarama yesterday and took the test before going to my mom's."

"Wait. I'm sorry. I'm confused," Christina says, shaking her head. "You said Dollarama. Did you buy a home pregnancy test at the dollar store?"

"Mm-hmm." With the back of my hand, I rub tears and sweat from my cheeks. "Yeah."

"Honey, does that sound rational to you?"

"It was cheap," I say, sniffing.

"My point exactly. You're betting your life on a test you bought for a dollar?"

"Plus tax."

"Azere, you need to get a real test from a doctor."

"I already made an appointment with my gyno. It's this afternoon."

"Good. When we get a real confirmation, we'll take it from there. Now, what about Rafael? I'm guessing you haven't filled him in."

I shake my head.

"Good. Don't tell him anything—not yet. Wait until you're totally sure. Got it?"

"Yeah." I nod. "Got it."

"Good. Now, eat your lunch."

Just as I unwrap the silver coating on the burger, Arianna, the office receptionist, comes prancing toward me.

I'm sure an invisible fan follows the girl wherever she goes. Long, blond hair flutters in the air, moving to the beat of her steps. A short, beige skirt clings to her toned thighs like skin. The cleavage exposed by her red blouse is small but eye-catching. She's one tall, hot blonde, and she knows it.

"Hey, pretties." She glances from Christina to me. "Dev wants to see you."

"Me?" I ask. "Why me?"

"I'm not sure, but it sounds important. He's waiting in his office with Rafael."

"Wait. What? Rafael?"

"Yeah. The new guy." She smiles, a small gesture that proves her interest in Rafael exceeds professional boundaries. "Anyway, bye." She waves and struts away with all the flair of a runway model.

"Oh my gosh." My heart jerks, a new frenetic beat derived from the utter shock of the news. "Christina, do you think he told Dev? I mean, why else would he want to see us both?" My fingernails dig into my sweaty palm. "He must have told him. Shit. The whole HR crew is probably in there too. I'm so screwed."

"Azere, relax." She draws circles along my spine. "It's probably nothing."

"You think?"

"Mm-hmm. Yeah. Totally." She isn't the best liar, but she's trying, trying hard to convince me my world isn't imploding. I love her for the attempt.

At Dev's door, I dally while contemplating whether to enter or take off. It's just him and Rafael, seated across each other, exchanging words that aren't audible. There are no HR reps present, but maybe they'll make an appearance at any moment. *Any moment.*

Suddenly, taking off seems like the most rational action.

"Azere," Dev calls out. "Come in. Sit."

I obey. What choice do I have?

"Hi, Dev." I acknowledge Rafael only by glaring at him from the corner of my eye. *What the hell has he done? And how do I fix it?* I'm on the edge of my seat, too anxious to relax into the cushioned chair.

"Azere, Dev called us in for a work-related matter," Rafael says to me, straight-faced. "A new campaign." He must sense my discomfort.

"Yes." Dev folds his arms and reclines into the leather chair, giving us his undivided attention. "FeverRun energy drink. The product is on the verge of launching in North America and will require a huge campaign. I'm assembling a very small team to put together a pitch. In case it isn't obvious, the very small team is you and Rafael."

"I'm sorry, what? Just the two of us? Working? Together?" I clench my teeth, maintaining the stoic expression that's concealing the rampage in my head—the crying, shouting, sulking. *No, no, no. Why am I working with him? Why is this happening?*

"Check your emails. I sent you both the product profile. Look through it, do your research, and get to work. You'll be pitching tomorrow."

"What? Tomorrow?" My mind is reeling. Everything is happening so fast. "You expect us to put together a presentation in less than a day. Why the rush?"

"The company was with another agency but experienced some issues." He pauses and touches the thin strands of hair strategically arranged over his bald spot. "Anyway, they're considering us as well as two other agencies, and I want to give them a solid pitch—an overview of our campaign to assure them we're the right choice. I'm sure you and Rafael can handle that."

"Dev, correct me if I'm wrong, but FeverRun is a Nigerian brand. Right?"

"It is. And?"

"Well, I'm Nigerian, so I can probably add a favorable perspective to the campaign. You know who else is Nigerian? Christina. She's also a very talented copywriter. So maybe we should work together on this instead. I mean, that makes more sense to me."

"Azere, I'm not assigning Christina to this campaign because of her ethnicity. It's certainly not why I assigned you to it." He puffs and rubs his temples. "Your work on the Fruit Infusion campaign was impressive. Frankly, it was brilliant, and I thought you and Rafael would make a great team. He's only just started working here, but make no mistake, he's got years of experience in the industry. We're very lucky to have him."

"Thanks, Dev," Rafael says, standing. "We'll get started and have everything ready for tomorrow." He leaves the room, and I'm forced to follow even though I'm not satisfied with the conversation.

"Hey. Rafael." I stride after him and almost trip over my rushing feet. "Wait up."

He keeps moving and doesn't stop until he's in his office.

"Thanks for finally stopping, Road Runner."

"You tried to get me off the campaign." Anger makes his tone brisk and rough. "Seriously, Azere? This is my career."

"Rafael." I close the door, giving us as much privacy as we can get with transparent walls. "We're supposed to be staying away from each other, not working together. That's what we agreed to."

"No, that's what you decided. What you selfishly decided."

"Excuse me?" I'm taken aback. "Selfishly? How am I being selfish? I'm just trying to make the best of this situation."

"You've been acting like this situation only affects you. Maybe if you stopped avoiding me and stopped trying to kick me off campaigns, you would see that I'm in this with you, Azere."

He says nothing else, and neither do I. Looking at the digital clock on his desk, I calculate a minute of silence between us. A full minute spent not looking at him. A full minute spent observing the view through the window and the office's minimalist decor. A full minute realizing the truth in his words and the fault in my actions.

"You're right," I say. "We're in this together."

It was easier to keep him at a distance. It helped me ignore the memory of us—our naked bodies sprawled over wrinkled sheets, our lips pursed and locked, and our hands keenly exploring. That memory, as sweet and forbidden as our first kiss, is so hard to dismiss, especially when I'm looking at him and fighting the urge to touch him. But that's my fault, not his. He shouldn't be punished for my inability to disregard a one-night stand.

"I'm sorry, Rafael."

This time, when we fall silent, my eyes don't wander. I focus on him. The view through the window is a blur. The decor in the room dissolves to white space. Everything is suddenly void of shape and color, except for him. I become acutely aware of only him, of only us. He breathes and I breathe and that's all there is, the gentle rhythm of our inhales and exhales creating a harmony of their own.

"You thought I told Dev about us. Didn't you?" he asks, his voice low and mild.

"Yeah." I drop my head, ashamed of the truth.

"I gave you my word, Azere."

"No offense, Rafael, but I don't know you well enough to hold you to your word."

"Okay." He frowns but nods. "Fair enough."

"But maybe it's time we start to coexist." It's the only reasonable approach. "Maybe it's time we get to know each other. As coworkers, of course."

"As coworkers." He hesitates but nods again. "Okay. Yeah. I would like that." He smiles, and in an instant, the atmosphere becomes lighter. "So, about the campaign. How about we do our individual research and meet in an hour or two to go over ideas."

"I'm actually leaving in two hours. I have an appointment today—a very, very important appointment." *That will confirm if I'm indeed carrying your child.* "So, how about I meet you in your office when I get back around five?"

"Sure." He clears his throat and looks me over. "So . . . can I get your number?"

"Um . . . why?"

"In case I need to reach you while you're at your appointment."

"Oh. Okay. Sure." I extend my hand, and he places his cell in my palm. "Use this responsibly," I say, inserting my number. "No prank calls."

"I'll make sure my thirteen-year-old self gets the memo."

"You do that." I hand him the phone, make a move to leave, and then halt when he calls me.

"Dev had a lot of wonderful things to say about your work."

He watches me intently, a glint in his blue eyes. "I really look forward to working with you, Azere."

"Thank you, Rafael. I look forward to working with you too."

As I walk out of his office and maneuver between the rows of desks in the open-plan workspace, I turn around. Through the glass walls, our eyes connect, and he smiles. I hate myself when my heart skips, when my skin turns hot, when I smile back at him.

chapter
7

I'm sitting in my gynecologist's office, praying for a miracle—
confirmation the dollar-store pregnancy test was indeed bull.

A dollar is pretty cheap for a reliable test. *What the hell was
I thinking? What if the test is wrong? What if I've been stressing
for nothing? What if I'm not pregnant?* This could be a possibility,
but I refuse to be optimistic or pessimistic.

"Azere." Farah, my gynecologist and close friend, enters the
room with a clipboard in hand. She smiles, and her extended lips
lift her round cheeks. "What are you doing here? Didn't I see
you like three months ago?"

"This is a different kind of visit."

"You sound serious." She walks to the table and occupies the
chair across from me. "What's up?"

"I think I'm pregnant." I blurt it out. There's no alternative.

"Hmm." Farah smooths the black hijab veiling her hair. "The
last time we spoke, you told me you weren't sexually active."

"Well, I was. For one night. Hence my current dilemma."

"Wait." She stands and strides toward me. Her dark eyes have
grown broad with interest. "You had a one-night stand?"

"Yeah. At the time it felt right. But now . . ." I curse under my breath. "Farah, I'm in serious trouble. I'm freaking out. You, more than anyone, should understand what I'm going through."

"Me? Why me?"

"Well, what would your traditional Pakistani parents say if they found out you were pregnant and unwed? They would basically disown you, right?"

"Well . . ." She taps a finger on her chin and contemplates the scenario. "Yeah. They probably would."

"Okay. Now, throw this into the mix. The guy who knocked you up isn't the Pakistani man they envisioned you starting a family with. He's white."

"Hmm. Interesting." She contemplates again. "In that case, I'd simply have to leave the planet. See if there's a vacancy on Mars."

Exactly.

"Wait." Farah shakes her head. "Your one-night stand is a white dude?"

"Yeah."

"Oh." She sighs, then walks to the far end of the room where there's a cart. "Well, let's do this." She rolls it to me, looks through it, and pulls out a needle and a vacutainer. After connecting the two objects, she goes through the cart again and pulls out a plastic band. "Make a fist."

"I took a home pregnancy test. It was positive. Think it might be wrong?"

"Those things aren't always accurate. A few of my patients have put themselves through the wringer because of those tests."

"So I might not be pregnant?" My heavy heart lightens. So much for not being optimistic.

"Azere, how about we wait for the results? No speculations until we get the results." She ties the plastic band around my bare forearm and wipes a spot with a damp cotton ball. When the needle pricks my skin, I wince. Blood fills the vacutainer, and she slides the needle out.

"When will I get the results?" I ask. "Today?"

"Definitely not. But since you're a VIP, tomorrow."

"Thanks, Farah."

"No problem. So." She clears her throat. "What if you are pregnant? What will you do? Will you keep it?"

I've been considering that question since last night, and I still don't have an answer.

"Just so you know, whatever you decide, there's no judgment. Do what's best for you, Azere."

What if what's best for me puts me at risk of losing another parent?

chapter
8

Walking through a deserted office is equally unnerving as walking through a graveyard. It's past six in the evening, and the natural light that usually radiates through the large windows has dimmed significantly.

My heels click and clack, the sound echoing against the uncanny silence. If I were a character in a Gothic romance such as the stunning and terrifying *Crimson Peak*, I would be the overly curious girl, walking through dark corridors with a candelabra in one hand and the length of a nightgown bunched in the other, opening doors she shouldn't dare to only to find the most intriguing creature waiting for her.

"Rafael?" I enter his office, and he looks up from the computer. "Hi. Sorry I'm late. There was traffic. Really bad traffic." I pull off my jacket and settle into a chair.

"It's fine, Azere." He sits up straight. "Don't worry about it."

"There's a storm coming," I say. Through the floor-to-ceiling window behind his desk, the view of the city is clear. Dark clouds extend over the beautifully lit metropolis, indicating an impending storm. The few people on the street are pushing forward, contending with the strong wind that's hauling them back. I watch them struggle to reach the subway entrance and then turn to Rafael. "It's really bad out there."

"Yeah. Everyone took off in a hurry, trying to avoid getting caught in it."

"So, it's just the two of us?"

When he nods, I pull my laptop out of my handbag and try to remain calm.

Maybe this is a bad idea. A brewing storm, an empty office, a hot one-night stand turned colleague, and a single black female with little self-control and a lot to lose. These are the exact ingredients for a memorable night and a regret-filled morning. I instantly consider kicking off my heels and running for the exit. I consider it, but the thing is, I really love my shoes. They're nude Mary Jane pumps. They pair well with anything, especially the red knee-length dress I'm wearing. I should come up with an escape plan that doesn't involve leaving them behind.

"Azere."

I shake off my reverie and look at Rafael.

"Everything okay?"

"Um . . . yeah," I say. "Everything's fine." I trash the escape plan, open the laptop, and then a file. "I've got a few ideas for the campaign. Would you like to hear them?"

"Yeah. Sure. Go ahead."

"Okay. Since the product is being introduced in a new country, I think it should get revamped. Let's start with the slogan." I glance at my notes. "The energy drink is called FeverRun. The slogan is: 'Live long, prosper, and stay energized.' First, that's a horrible slogan. Second, I don't appreciate the *Star Wars* reference."

"*Star Trek*," Rafael says. A smirk twitches at the corners of his lips. "It's a *Star Trek* reference."

"Yeah. Of course. I knew that." Frankly, I don't know the difference between the two sci-fi series—not really my genre. I wonder if it's his. "Anyway, the slogan should be short and sweet."

"What do you propose?"

"Catch the fever. It also works with the name of the product."

"Yeah. It does." He squints and mulls over the phrase. "I like it. A lot."

"Great. Now, for my next idea." I glance at my notes again. "In Nigeria, the spokesperson for this product is Genevieve Nnaji. She's this gorgeous, talented actress. She's a huge deal. I think we should get a beautiful, talented Western actress. Then we should mirror both actresses, from two different cultures, in the commercial and print ad."

"How would we mirror them?" he asks, leaning forward.

"We show the audience how similar they are despite their differences. We show how they both depend on FeverRun for an energy boost. We can show them in everyday settings—going to the grocery store, going to the gym, spending time with their families. By doing this, we—"

"Find commonalities between two different cultures."

"Exactly. Also, this method will help the product transition well into its new environment while remaining true to its origin. So? What do you think?"

His focused, steady stare is indecipherable.

Maybe he hates it. My confidence instantly plummets. "Rafael, if . . . if you don't like it, we could—"

"It's brilliant."

"Really?"

He nods, and I grin. Confidence boost in three . . . two . . . one.

"Awesome. Because that's all I've got."

"Well, I had nothing, so—"

"I kinda saved your ass?" I bite my tongue. *Shoot.* Confidence overload. "I'm sorry."

He grins, clearly not upset. "I'm starving." He stands and loosens the black tie around his neck. "I'm going to run out and pick up something to eat. Can I get you anything?"

"Well, I am pretty hungry." I rub my rumbling belly as if the circular movement can ease its ache for food. "But I'm not sure what I want. Why don't you surprise me?"

"Surprise you?"

"Yep. And just so you know, I don't like mushrooms or onions."

"I'll keep that in mind." He grabs his wallet off the desk and strides to the door. "I'll see you in a bit."

"Okay. I'll start building the presentation." I place my fingers over the keyboard but pause before hitting the keys. "Rafael!"

He stops and turns around—a single figure in the isolated space. "Everything okay?"

"Yeah. It's just that it doesn't look too good out there. The storm and all. So be careful. Okay?"

He glances at the window, and when our eyes meet again, he nods, a silent assurance before walking away.

TWENTY MINUTES AFTER HE LEAVES, HE RETURNS WITH A brown paper bag. I smell the ingredients in the Chinese food he's bought—ginger, basil, chili pepper, sweet soy sauce. When he places a takeout box in front of me, I open the cardboard container and spoon a portion of chicken fried rice into my mouth.

"Mmm, this is delicious," I say while chewing. "Thanks, Rafael."

"You're welcome." He digs chopsticks into his box of chow mein. "Glad you like it."

For an hour, we alternate between eating and working. He

listens to each idea I propose and builds on them. He's smart and insightful, and our collaboration is effortless. When I return from the kitchen with two cups of tea, he's hunched over the computer, typing. His tie and blazer are off, and the first two buttons on his white shirt are undone. His wavy hair is messy, flopping over his forehead—no perfect side part to separate the dark strands into precise proportions. When he looks at me, I notice something oddly familiar in his eyes—a hollowness. I recognize it because I saw the same in my father's eyes as he died.

The man who raised me was vivacious. His dark eyes were layered with secrets, stories, riddles, and mysteries. Though, as sickness consumed him, his eyes grew vacant as if his soul had been scooped out and all that was left was the vessel—the shell of a man. An intolerable amount of pain did that to him—left him empty. And I sense the same happened to Rafael somehow. Pain, too great to sustain, hollowed him out, took something from him. I'm certain of it because in his striking blue eyes, there is a deep, eerie void.

What happened? Was it loss or betrayal or heartbreak? What emptied you out?

"Azere."

His voice pulls me out of my deep thoughts. "Yeah?"

"Are you okay?"

"Yes. I'm fine." I settle in the chair and extend a cup to him. "Here's your tea."

"Thank you." He sips the hot beverage slowly. "We're almost done. I'm only adding some finishing touches."

"Oh. Great." The digital clock on his desk reads 9:15 p.m. "I'm so ready to get outta here."

"It's not safe outside," he says, setting down his cup. "Not yet. You should wait until the storm ends."

"Oh, it's nothing. I live twenty minutes away—in one of those apartment buildings along King Street. I'll be home in no time. Plus, I think the storm is letting up."

As if on cue, thunder erupts suddenly, roaring and causing me to yelp and flinch. Lightning flashes; its silvery blaze rips through the black sky and emits an unearthly glow through the window. My heart is racing, but I keep a calm disposition. Casually, I flip my braids over my shoulder and arrange the pleats on my dress, faking coolness while sipping my tea.

Rafael miserably attempts to suppress a laugh by rolling his lips into his mouth. "Are you okay?"

"Yeah. I'm fine."

"Right." His lips are straight now, but there's a glint of humor in his eyes. "You know what? You still haven't answered my question."

"What question?"

"Yesterday, I asked why you left my hotel room without saying goodbye. You never gave me an answer." He searches my eyes. "Why did you leave without saying goodbye, Azere?"

"Rafael." I place the cup of tea on the table and huff. "I really don't want to talk about that night."

"Why not?"

"Because . . . because it's hard enough that I think about kissing you every time I see you. It's hard enough that I want to touch you. I'm just trying to deal with this crazy situation, but talking about that night makes it harder."

The confession seemed to have surged out my mouth like water through a faucet. Now, he's looking at me like I've lost my mind. Maybe I have.

"I'm sorry. That was really inappropriate." I stand and hesitantly grab my things, avoiding eye contact as I do. "I'm gonna go."

"Azere, wait." He's at the door before I can walk through it, obstructing the exit with his large stature. "I wanted to kiss you yesterday—the instant I laid my eyes on you." He moves forward until there's no space between us, until his chest is pressed to mine, until his breath warms my skin and his scent fills my nostrils. "I want to kiss you now. So fucking bad." He tilts his head, brings his lips a mere inch from mine, and takes my breath away—breathes it in, claims it as his own, a part of me now in him.

"Rafael." The urge to touch him and be touched by him seems impossible to resist. Yet, somehow, I manage to step back, to stand separate from him, to keep my hands static at my sides, to suppress all the desires that threaten my logic. "We can't."

"Azere." A low grumble sounds in his throat. "Why not? Is it because we work together?"

It's a lot more complicated than that, but his response is simple and reason enough for us to stay apart.

"Azere, it's not like we report to each other. You're not my superior and I'm not yours."

"I know, Rafael, but I think it's best we have a professional and totally platonic relationship. I just want to do my job without any complications. Can you respect that?"

He tousles his hair and exhales, deflating his enlarged chest. "Yeah. Of course. Our relationship can be strictly . . . um . . . professional." It seemed to have taken him a lot of effort to get those words out. "And I won't bring up that night anymore."

"Thanks, Rafael."

"Now, will you stay? At least until the storm lets up. I don't want you driving in this weather, Azere. Come on. Sit." He carefully ushers me back into the chair as though afraid I might run if he's inattentive.

I retake my seat and resume sipping my tea. Together we look over the work we've done and finalize the presentation. By 9:55 p.m., the rain stops beating against the window, and the wind stops whooshing and stirring objects into the air. The storm appears to be over, but Rafael is cautious, checking several news websites, confirming the storm has indeed ended and the route to my home is safe.

He escorts me to the underground parking lot. I'm grateful for his company because the space is isolated and unsettling at night.

In my car, as I fasten my seat belt, he leans down, and his face appears in the window. I roll down the glass and inspect his fatigued eyes. I ask when he plans on going home. He doesn't give a direct answer. He grabs my seat belt—the part that doesn't touch the chair or my chest, the part that just sort of hangs in limbo—and tugs it as if testing its sturdiness. The action seems overly cautious, but I don't question it. In fact, a part of me appreciates his care, his attentiveness.

"Keep your eyes on the road," he says, his hand falling away. "Watch out for slick spots. Okay?"

I nod. "Sure."

"And about the presentation tomorrow. You should make it."

"Me?" I point to myself, confirming his statement.

"Yes, you. You came up with the ideas. You'll be the best person to explain them."

"Okay. Sure. I can do that." I search his eyes—blue, beautiful, and hollow. "Well. Good night, Rafael."

"Yeah. Good night, Azere. Drive safely."

I do. I get home in one piece. I take a shower. I brush my teeth. I wrap a scarf over my braids, securing them for a routine night of tossing and turning.

In bed, I nestle under a thick duvet and inhale deeply, relishing the scent of lavender embedded in the plush fabric. A little after midnight, I say a prayer for myself and the ones I love. And then, just before I fall asleep, I say another prayer.

For him.

chapter 9

Rafael

Alone in the office, I send my dog sitter a text message, asking how Milo is doing. She replies with a picture of him curled on her lap.

With confirmation that he's fine, I take on a new task. My fingers move against the keyboard, matching the speed at which my brain is working.

Focus, work, focus, work.

Like always, the basic mantra serves its purpose by centering my mind. Currently, the words I'm typing and reading are my sole focus—my only thought. But then my eyes land on the empty chair across from me. In an instant, another thought, a sharp thought, penetrates my mind.

Azere.

Earlier, she was sitting in that chair. I smile at the recollection.

Damn it. Focus, Rafael. Focus, work, focus, work.

The mantra has always been the driving force in my career. For years, it kept me proactive. Tonight, it loses that effect. I can't stop thinking about her. I prioritize her over the tedious combination of words and numbers on the computer screen.

Where is she now? Did she get home safe? Is she okay?

I snatch my cell off the table. Maybe I should call to confirm she's home, safe. When the phone chimes, however, my focus veers. It's a video call from someone who never takes no for an answer. Declining will only provoke her to call repeatedly. To avoid that outcome, I click the green button, and my sister's face appears on the large screen.

"Hey, big brother," Selena says, grinning.

She's wearing a band of flowers over her dark hair; the scarlet carnations match the color coating her lips. Her face holds my attention until my eyes move to the picturesque backdrop—the breathtaking sight of Valencia. Buildings with ancient and Gothic architecture align the seaside. Dawn dyes the sky with variations of purples, yellows, oranges, and reds. The warm hues are reflected on the rippling sea. It's times like these, seeing the scenery, that I envy my family for spending yet another summer in Valencia with our grandmother.

"Earth to Rafael." Selena waves her hand, signaling for my attention. "Thought you might appreciate the view. Just didn't think you would abandon me for it."

"Sorry." I smile; it's the same smile I've worn for years, the one meant to convince my family that I'm okay and not utterly broken. "So. How are you? Missing home yet?"

"Not really. I love it here. But how about you, Rafa? What's it like, living in Toronto again? Is it a little weird?"

"Actually, it feels good—familiar, like home."

"Cool." She yawns. "Sorry. I'm exhausted. I went dancing last night. Then to a club. And then to some random house party.

Pretty crazy night. I just got in. Thought we could chat before I head to bed."

"Well, you didn't have to call. It's five thirty a.m. in Valencia. You should be sleeping."

"And it's eleven thirty p.m. in Toronto. You should be at home with your adorable dog. Instead, you're at the office. Working. Right?" She arches an eyebrow, awaiting my response. "Rafael, why aren't you at home?"

"Because I have work to do."

"Right." One finger falls on the cameo choker she prematurely inherited from our grandmother. Selena is never without the antique jewelry. She wears it with everything and rubs the pendant when deep in thought. Much like she's doing right now. "Rafael—"

"Don't, Selena. Don't say what I think you're going to say. If you do, I'll end this call." My finger hangs over the End button.

"Go ahead. Do it. And I'll catch the next flight to Toronto just so I can punch you in the gut. And after you've recovered from my almost deadly blow, we'll have the conversation."

She's twenty-six, four years younger than me, and capable of delivering threats that make me reconsider my actions. I drop my finger and tuck it under the table.

"Thought so," she retorts. "Now. As I was about to say, I'm worried." Her big dark eyes well up with emotions. "About you, Rafa. Mom's worried too."

"Mom worries, Selena. It's what she does. And you—"

"What about me?"

"Where's Máximo?" I ask.

"My twin is somewhere in Ibiza likely squandering his trust fund on alcohol, drugs, and prostitutes." She rolls her eyes. "*Maldito idiota.*"

"Now, there's someone you should worry about."

"I'm going to mass on Sunday. I'll say a prayer for him, then. That's all I can do for that one—bid his case to God and hope for a miracle." She shrugs. "Anyway, I really wish you were here, Rafael. With us. *Abuela* misses you. We all do."

"And I miss you guys too. But I have a job, Selena."

"Your job is your entire life, Rafael. You never take vacations or days off. It's not healthy. Especially because you've been using work as a coping mechanism."

"That isn't true. My career has always been important to me. You know that."

"Yeah. But it became your obsession, the center of your world after—"

"Don't! Don't say another word! I don't want to talk or think about it."

But it's too late now.

Dark memories seep into my mind like ink. I try to push them away, but one image appears and then another. There's blood. So much blood. It's everywhere, coating my shuddering hands, drenching her white summer dress, trickling into the chair's thin creases. It's everywhere.

"Rafael." Selena's firm voice halts the memories prone to play in a torturous, incisive loop. "It's been three years. You're entitled to a fresh start. That's why you moved back to Toronto, but it looks like you're falling into the same pattern—isolating yourself, consuming yourself with work." She sighs. "How long are you going to live like this? How long are you going to punish yourself for what happened?" Tears settle at the rims of her round eyes. "It wasn't your fault, Rafael. It wasn't."

Yes, it was. And I've been shouldering that guilt for three years.

"I just want you to be happy." She rubs her teary eyes. "That's all I want. Is there currently anything in your life, aside from your job, that makes you happy? Is there anything or anyone that gives you the slightest hint of joy?"

My eyes shift to the chair across from me, to the space Azere once occupied. I watch the spot as if she's still there, twirling her long hair around one finger, mistaking *Star Wars* for *Star Trek*.

"Rafa."

I look at my sister.

"Well?" she says, hope flickering in her eyes, waiting to ignite. "Anything? Anyone?"

When I say nothing, the twinkle of hope vanishes.

"I guess I'll bid your case to God as well."

"Yeah." I nod. "Maybe you should."

She forces a smile that extends to half the length of her regular smile. "I should go to bed."

"Yeah. Of course. Give *Abuela* a kiss for me. And tell Mom and Dad and Max I said hi."

"We'll be home in the fall. We'll see you then. I love you, Rafael. You know that, right?"

"Of course, I do." How could I ever doubt it? She's always been there for me. I shut her out, and she kicks down the door. I push her away, and she fights her way back in. I've never told her, but she's my best friend. She's the only person who completely understands me. One day, I'll tell her what she means to me. Tonight, I'll keep it simple. "I love you too, Selena."

She waves goodbye, and her face disappears and so does the spectacular view of Valencia.

Alone again, I spin on my chair and look through the window. There are no stars tonight, no silver dots gleaming and decorating the vast mass of nothingness. Everything is bleak. I should feel hopeless like I have many nights before. Instead, I feel the slightest hint of something else. Joy. It's so small. It probably measures to a speck of sand, but I feel it anyway. And I know the source of it.

Azere.

chapter
10

I step out of the conference room, my head bopping to Beyoncé's "Diva." The song is on replay, an earworm that's the perfect soundtrack for this moment when I've just slayed the FeverRun presentation. As Rafael and I walk our new clients—Mr. Ojo and Mr. Oliha—to the elevator, I restrain myself from dancing.

"Azere," Mr. Ojo says, turning to me. "Excellent pitch. We look forward to working with you and Rafael."

"Likewise," I add.

"Why don't you both join us for dinner tonight—to celebrate."

"You know, that sounds great." Dinner will be the perfect distraction while I wait for the test results. "Where do you have in mind?"

"Heritage, an amazing West African restaurant. I go there whenever I'm in Toronto. Are you familiar with the place?"

"Of course. I love that restaurant."

"Wonderful. Then we'll see you both at seven." The elevator doors open, and our clients step through them.

"Azere," Rafael says once the steel doors slide closed. "You did an amazing job on the presentation."

"You both did an amazing job," Dev raves, stepping out of the conference room where we left him. "Brilliant presentation." He grins widely, and his mustache extends along with his lips, his features exaggerating until he looks like a caricature of his former self. "Well, I have to go. I've got a conference call in . . ." He glances at the two-tone watch on his wrist. "One minute. I'll catch up with you two later." He marches off in an ungraceful haste.

"So," Rafael says, "I guess I'll pick you up at six thirty."

"Pick me up? For what?"

"Dinner. You know the location, I don't. We'll go together."

"You know, there's this magical device called a GPS."

He scowls, and I shrug.

"What? There is. Just throwing it out there."

"Azere, we're a team. Let's go together." He says it as if expecting no further objections, and I don't offer any.

"Why don't we discuss next steps for the campaign in my office?" I ask.

He follows my lead, and when we're behind the glass door, in a space that has my signature style, he looks around—from the cactus plants on the windowsill to the blushing pink swivel chair behind the glass desk.

"Nice office."

"Thank you," I say, following his stare. "It's much nicer than yours."

His eyes land on me, a brow raised and a playful smile on his lips. "Is it?"

"Mm-hmm. I mean, look at that view." I gesture at the large window. "It's pretty damn impressive."

"Eh." He shrugs. "It's okay. I've seen better."

"Um . . . Rafael." Suddenly somber, I squint, lean into him, and examine a spot on his neck. "What's going on there?"

"Where?" Noting my serious, assessing gaze, he frowns and runs his fingers along his neck. "What is it?"

"It's your skin. Looks like it's turning a little . . . green." I cross my arms and smirk. "With envy."

His hand falls away from his neck, the worry on his face fading as he watches me, his lips gradually stretching until he bursts out laughing. "All right. You got me."

"You should have seen your face."

For a little while, we just laugh. And it feels so good to only have humor between us—nothing else, nothing complex.

When we sit, he lays out his plan with details of the team he wants to put together, then he asks for my input. I like working with him. He's intelligent and easygoing. Now, if the test results would prove I'm not pregnant, things can remain like this—professional and uncomplicated and my life can unfold as I've always envisioned.

The landline on my desk rings, and I pick it up reluctantly. "Hello?"

"Hey, Azere," Arianna says. "You have a visitor. And just so you know"—her bubbly voice reduces to a whisper—"he's hot. Really hot." She ends the call without giving me the visitor's name.

"I'm sorry, Rafael," I say, dropping the phone. "But can we pick this up later?"

"Um . . . yeah. Sure." He's polite, but I note disappointment in his low tone and hesitancy in his movement as we leave my office.

"So." I drum my fingers on the receptionist table that wraps around Arianna, enclosing her in a sphere. "Where's this so-called hottie?"

Arianna's eyes float above my head, and her glossy lips stretch into a wide, goofy grin.

"I guess that would be me."

I recognize that voice—deep, smooth, with a generous dose of confidence, or as some may describe it, cockiness. Though disinclined, I turn around and brace myself for no other than . . . "Elijah."

"Hey, Azere."

Here he goes again, looking like Morris Chestnut circa 1999. In the movie *The Best Man*, there's a scene where Morris Chestnut's character ogles his fiancée as she descends a flight of stairs. Right now, Elijah is giving me that exact look. His lips form a confident side-slung grin, and his suggestive gaze moves along my frame. I wish he would stop. I wish he would leave. More than anything, I wish he wasn't here.

"Elijah, what in the world are you doing at my job?"

"I wanted to see you. Thought I could take you out to lunch."

Lunch? Does he believe he can waltz into my life after six years and hit Play on our relationship? Obviously, he needs a reality check. And I do love giving reality checks.

"Arianna," I say, "can you give us a minute?"

"Huh?" She wrenches her eyes from Elijah. "What?" When I repeat my request, she pouts. "Fine. I was due for a break anyway. Bye, handsome." She waves at Elijah and sashays off with a lot more flair than usual, as if begging for an audience.

"Eli, you can't just—"

"Azere, you look beautiful. Amazing actually."

"Oh . . . um . . . okay." *Shit.* I can't give a good reality check when he's throwing compliments at me all willy-nilly. "You . . . you can't just show up here, Elijah." Already, I've lost the edge in my voice, and what's a good reality check without some bass and sass? "How'd you even know where I work?"

"Your mom," he says. "She kindly shared your phone number, your work address, and your home address."

"Of course." I'm not surprised. "Well, you need to leave."

"Azere, your mom is a very persistent woman. She wants us to—"

"What? Date? Get married? Have three kids?"

"Well, I was thinking two kids and maybe a dog." He grins to show he's joking, but my face is passive.

"Elijah, you're blowing my mind right now. Did you honestly think you could show up after all these years—smile a little, flirt a little, and reclaim me? What? Thought I would forgive you and fall back into your arms like some damsel with no damn sense?" I scoff. "You thought wrong."

"Azere, I understand you're still upset. But it's not like I left to hurt you. Everything happened so fast, and I didn't really have a choice. I was wait-listed for medical school at Stanford, but it was the end of summer, and I thought I wouldn't get in."

When Lenny from accounting appears, Elijah stops speaking. Lenny's loitering by the elevator, idly scratching the bald spot in the middle of his head. It's clear he's interested in the conversation Elijah and I are having. He keeps glancing in our direction. When the elevator finally arrives, he makes an unenthusiastic exit.

"Anyway," Elijah says, redirecting his attention to me, "that night, after I walked you back to your cabin, I checked my email. There was an acceptance letter from Stanford. Classes were scheduled to begin in a week, and I had made no preparations. My mom picked me up early the next morning and a day later, I was on a flight to California."

"You already explained this to me, Elijah. Remember? A month after you'd been gone, you finally called. A month later." And therein lies the problem. "Do you understand how it felt to wake up the next morning and find out you were gone? You didn't even return my texts or calls."

"Zere, I didn't know how to face you." He takes in a big gulp of air and releases it. "I made all those promises to you, and I meant them all. Zere, I wanted to be with you but . . . but . . ."

"But you were a coward," I say, my tone curt. The edge has returned. "You were a selfish coward. I was only nineteen." Something trembles in my chest—the early beginnings of a sob. I suppress it. "I trusted you. And you took my virginity and left without a word or an explanation." Six years later, this fact still makes me want to break down and cry. "How the hell did I ever love a man like you?"

"Azere, I wasn't a man then. I was a stupid boy who made a huge mistake."

His eyes are remorseful. I want to look away, but they're pulling me in, forcing me to acknowledge his sincerity, compelling me to offer my forgiveness.

"Azere, I never wanted to hurt you. Never. I'm so sorry. I know I screwed up everything between us, but I'm back in Toronto for good now. I'm doing my residency here, I want to build a life here, and I want another chance with you. Azere, I'll do anything for another chance."

"Go to hell, Elijah." I whirl around and start to march off, but he grabs my arm before I can get far.

"Zere." He stands in front of me and expels a sharp breath. "Listen to me. I still love you."

The first time he told me that, I was nineteen. It was the week before church camp—the week before I lost my virginity. He was driving me home from a summer fair. His ability to consistently toss a basketball through a moving hoop earned me one of those gigantic stuffed animals people rarely win. I was practical in choosing a name. I called the bear Brown Bear, honoring its chestnut fleece. As Eli drove, I huddled the prize against my body, preventing it from plummeting over the dashboard.

"That thing is bigger than you," Eli said, laughing.

"It's so fluffy," I squealed. "I love it."

"I love you."

It was an unexpected confession that made my hold on Brown Bear loosen. Assuming it was a slip of the tongue, I said nothing. The ride to my house was quiet, uneasy. When he pulled into the driveway, he parked his red Mustang and came to the passenger door. With both hands on Brown Bear's paws, he pulled the gigantic stuffed animal out of the car and waited for me to step out.

"Thanks," I said, averting my eyes from his. "I had fun today."

"Me too. Your mom home?"

"No. She has a shift at the hospital."

"You ever gonna tell her and your sister we're dating?"

"Maybe when it gets serious."

"When it gets serious?" There was a sharpness in his voice. Maybe it was irritation or hurt. I couldn't tell, and I couldn't look at his face to confirm. "Zere, I just said I love you."

"Oh." My eyes rose to meet his. "You meant that?"

"Of course I meant it. I love you, Azere." He took a step toward me, but the stuffed animal in his hands kept us apart. "This stupid thing is starting to get on my nerves."

"Hey!" I said playfully. "Don't diss Brown Bear! I love him. But . . ." My voice softened. "I love you more."

"Really?"

"Yeah. Really."

We stood there for a long while, grinning too broadly, regarding each other with lustful eyes, an oversize bear between us— the perfect depiction of fools in love.

Even now, after all these years, I still taste those words on my tongue. *I love you.* Though, now, they carry a bittersweet flavor. He did that—took the sweet simplicity of our love and ruined it.

"Elijah, I have to get back to work." I tilt my head toward the elevator, gesturing for his departure.

"Azere." He ignores the obvious hint. "I know it's asking a lot, but I need to know. Will you ever forgive me?" His pleading eyes almost trigger my compassion.

"No," I say. "I don't know," I correct. "Elijah, please leave."

This time, he has the good sense to obey. He turns around, shoulders slouched and hands stuffed in his pockets, and walks away. The elevator arrives, and he steps inside.

When I return to my office, Christina is in a chair, flipping through the *Cosmopolitan* I bought a month ago but never got an opportunity to read.

"Finally! There you are!" She tosses the magazine on the desk. "I've been waiting for you."

In the company of my best friend, I try to forget about Elijah and his recent attempt at redemption. "Well, here I am. What's up?"

"I want to know about the presentation. How did it go?"

"You know, for someone who claims to be psychic, you're kinda always clueless."

"Azere, I've told you several times. I'm a part-time psychic. Some days, I have it. Some days, I don't." She folds her arms across her chest. "Now, tell me about the presentation. How did it go? How did you do?"

"Great." I flip my braids over my shoulder and smirk. "Nailed it."

"Awesome. Proud of you." She clears her throat. "So . . ."

"So . . . what?" Something tells me she isn't genuinely interested in my recent success.

"How was last night? You know, working late with Rafael. As I recall, there was a thunderstorm. Did you two get cozy, rekindle that old flame, relive the past?" Her thin eyebrows dance suggestively.

"Christina, I'm having a great day. So do me a favor and keep your dirty thoughts to yourself." I drop into my chair and click on the computer. "I have lots of work to do, so skip away, little one."

"Fine. But before I go, how was your appointment with your gyno?"

"I should get the results today, but I doubt I'm pregnant."

"Um . . . okay." She frowns and eyes me. "What makes you so sure?"

"As you pointed out, I took a test from the dollar store. It was probably a knockoff or expired. I'm not pregnant."

"Okay." She doesn't look as hopeful as I sound.

"Right now, things are going well for me. This campaign could really help my career. Do you know how long I've wanted an opportunity like this? I can't be pregnant."

"Okay." She still doesn't look as hopeful as I sound. There's concern in her eyes. Concern for me.

I can't help but wonder if that concern is warranted.

chapter
11

At exactly six thirty in the evening, there's a knock on my apartment door. I'm fussing with the spaghetti straps on my maxi dress, ensuring they rest flat against my shoulders. It's my favorite dress—made of *ankara*, an African wax fabric designed with vibrant colors and bold prints. The colors on this material are ruby red, fuchsia pink, and sunflower yellow. The vivid shades swirl together, creating patterns of circles both big and small. My mother would be happy to see me in this dress. To her, I don't wear enough Nigerian clothes. There's some truth to that.

Once the straps are smooth on my shoulders, I admire myself in the full-length mirror. The matte red lipstick adds a hint of seduction to my smile, and the red strappy heels offer the elegant height nature denied me.

Another knock reminds me there's someone waiting outside my apartment. I open the door to find Rafael looking both understated and elegant in a simple combination of black dress pants and a white oxford shirt.

"Hi, Azere." He glances over my physique, eyes lingering before finally meeting mine. "That's a very beautiful dress."

"Thank you." I would appreciate another compliment, one relating to how I look in the beautiful dress. But considering we recently vowed to keep our relationship professional, maybe that would be inappropriate.

"Shall we?" he asks.

"Yeah. Sure."

The ride in the elevator is quiet and a little uncomfortable. I stand parallel to him, my head a few inches short of hitting his shoulder. Rafael's quite tall, and as he looms over me, so does his signature scent—clean air and cedarwood. I close my eyes and breathe him in.

"Damn, you smell good." My eyes fly open. *Oh Lord. Did those words just come out of my mouth?* I turn to Rafael, biting my lip.

He's staring straight ahead. There's a tiny crease between his bent eyebrows.

"I was actually talking about the . . . um . . . the elevator," I say. "Yeah. The elevator smells . . . really good." Surely, those words have never been uttered by any sane human being. But at this moment, I can't classify myself as a sane human. My attempt at damage control is worsening the situation, making me appear unhinged. "So . . . um . . . when I said, 'You smell good,' I was actually referring to the elevator 'cause sometimes, I like to personify objects. And the elevator is an object. Yeah . . . I didn't actually mean you, Rafael. I don't like . . . go around smelling people. That would be weird. So. Yeah."

Silence. I'm mortified. I gape at the steel doors waiting, praying for them to open.

"That was honestly the worst attempt at a cover-up I have ever heard," Rafael says. "For a second, I was scared you might hurt yourself." He's still staring straight ahead, but slowly, he begins to laugh, each chuckle gaining volume until I'm laughing along with him and caring very little about my previous embarrassment.

I'm more relaxed as we enter the parking lot. Making a fool of myself definitely helped to lighten the mood. When we approach a sonic silver Lexus, I halt.

"Is that an LC 500?" I ask, examining, admiring, and basically drooling over the elegant coupe.

"Yeah. It is."

This isn't the car he drives to the office. I've seen him pull up in a black Range Rover. Xander pays well, but not well enough to afford two luxury vehicles. Maybe he has a side hustle. A really good side hustle. I don't concern myself with his finances and instead focus on the car.

"It's beautiful." My fingers skim over the door panels that pull inward in perfect contrast to the front and rear fenders that flare out. "This is my cousin's dream car. He's kinda obsessed. He's gonna freak when he finds out I rode in one."

"And how would he react when he finds out you drove one?"

"Drove one?" I tear my eyes from the vehicle and look at Rafael. "Huh?"

Rather than clarifying, he walks to the driver side of the car and pulls the door wide open. "Would you like to drive, Azere?"

"What? Me? Drive? Seriously?"

When he nods, I scurry to the open door.

"Wait." I pause before sliding into the seat. "Are you sure about this? Are you sure you want to trust me with your car . . . your expensive car?"

"I'm sure. Go ahead," he urges. "Get in."

Objections? I have none. I gather my maxi dress in one hand and settle into the cockpit. Cool leather presses against my bare skin, and I grip the steering wheel. Like the rest of the luxurious interior, the wheel is black except for the hand-stitching that creates a neat and uniformed pattern of white thread around its circumference.

"Ready?" Rafael asks, settling in beside me.

"Umm . . ." I adjust the seat and the mirrors, secure my seat belt, and grip the wheel again. "So ready." After pushing the power button, the car comes to life.

On the highway, I accelerate past the speed limit and swiftly swerve in front of cars.

"Wow. Azere, I would actually like to make it to the restaurant in one piece."

"Sorry." I reduce pressure on the gas and glance at him. "I got a little excited."

"Seems like you're a bit of a daredevil. Like my sister."

"Oh yeah?"

"Yeah. She's a small thing who tends to overcompensate by doing outrageous things." He laughs, and his eyes crinkle at their ends just as his lips curve upward. "A few years back, I was in Toronto to visit my family, and she insisted on treating me to lunch at 360, the restaurant in the CN Tower. I went, expecting to enjoy a good meal."

"But what really happened?" I ask.

"She had another activity in mind—the EdgeWalk."

"No! She wanted you to walk around the CN Tower—one hundred and sixteen stories from the ground?"

"Yep," he says. "One hundred and sixteen stories from the ground."

"Well?" I'm curious. "Did you do it?"

"I attempted to—got suited up, took one step onto the ledge, looked down, and lost my nerve. Selena, only twenty at the time, was perfectly fine. I, at twenty-four—having seen my life flash before my eyes—was having a panic attack and crying. I couldn't do it."

I try to stifle a giggle but fail. "You cried. I'm envisioning it, and it's seriously funny."

"It was terrifying," he admits. "Damn right, I cried."

I laugh harder, and he joins in, and I turn just in time to take note of the dimple on his left cheek.

He tells me more about his spunky sister and her audacious and often hilarious antics, and I laugh so much, my throat becomes sore. I learn he's of Spanish descent. His parents are from Spain. They were childhood sweethearts who came to Canada as international students. They got married after graduating university and started their lives together in Toronto.

"My parents are the hardest-working people I know," Rafael says. "I think it's an immigrant thing—the pressure to succeed as the *other* in their new home coupled with the fear of disappointing their family back at home."

I know exactly what he means. It's the reason my mother, a woman who once sold foodstuff in a village market, was determined to get a master's degree in nursing. It's the reason I worked tirelessly in high school and in university—not only to graduate with honors but also to stand on the podium as valedictorian. It's the reason my sister aims to be a partner at a top law firm by the age of thirty.

Immigrants chase success differently because we have something to prove to the people we left behind and the people who note our differences—our accent, our appearance, our religion, our culture—every day. The fact that Rafael understands this makes me gain a new appreciation for him.

"After a few years in Canada," he continues, "my parents saved up some money and bought their first property. Then two years later, they bought another. And then many more followed. They've been in the corporate real estate business ever since."

"So they must be rich or something."

He shrugs. "They're well-off . . . I guess."

"Well-off parents. Is that how you're able to afford this very expensive car?" From the corner of my eye, I watch his reaction to the intrusive question.

Shaking his head and smiling, he doesn't appear offended at all. "I had a trust fund. With the help of my father, I invested in some real estate. My sister did the same."

"Your daredevil of a sister?"

"Yeah. Her. She can be responsible when she chooses." He laughs gently. "What about you? Do you have any siblings?"

"Yeah. I have a little sister. Efe."

He asks one question after another, and I answer them all, offering him the same entertainment he offered me. I tell him about Efe's rebellious younger years and how our mother, the overly superstitious Nigerian woman who believed every problem was caused by juju, prayed zealously for the deliverance of her child.

"Punishments never worked on Efe, so my mother concluded someone had cast a spell on her." I laugh. Though at the time, my mother took the matter seriously. "She prayed for Efe every day—morning and night."

"And did they work . . . the prayers?"

"Well, something worked because Efe eventually grew out of it. Today, she's a model daughter. Well, to some degree."

The lane I'm on extends into a main road, and I exit the highway.

"And what about you?" Rafael asks. "Were you as rebellious as your sister?"

"Me? Rebellious? Never. I was older. I had to set the example for Efe. I had to give my parents one less kid to worry about. I had to make them proud." That's what I've always strived to do. "They asked me to work on the farm, and I did. They asked me to go to the market, and I did that too. No questions asked."

"What was it like, living in Nigeria?"

"Whenever I tell people I grew up in a village in Africa, they imagine mud huts and a safari in my backyard. They imagine a society stricken with poverty and disease and incomprehensible people." I roll my eyes. "The truth is, my village was far from being a metropolis. Sure, it was quiet, rural, and simple. But our ancient customs and the simplicity of our lifestyle didn't make us uncivilized. We were a community of teachers and doctors and farmers and vivacious marketwomen whose sharp wits and quick tongues could easily rival many university graduates. My mother was one of those women."

Rafael's blue eyes seem to urge me to continue.

"And yes, we lacked a few things the Western world couldn't do without, but that still didn't make us uncivilized. We had streams and water wells instead of running faucets. We had power, but the power-holding company seized it regularly. If you had a generator, cool. But if you didn't, you had to light up those kerosene lanterns.

"My family, like many, didn't have a generator. But my fondest memories are of when the lights went out, and my sister and I would gather around a lantern and listen to our father tell stories." I make a sharp turn into a small street and into the restaurant's parking lot. "That was the best part of my childhood." I pull into an empty spot. "I loved it."

"How old were you when you came to Canada?"

"Twelve."

"Have you visited since?"

"No." I turn off the car and lean back, my head falling on the cushioned headrest. "But I will. Someday soon." I tilt my head, and our eyes connect.

We should step out of the car now. We should walk into that restaurant and spend the evening entertaining our clients. But it surprises me that I don't want to do those things. I want to stay in this car. With him. But when he opens the door, when he lets the outside world invade the light atmosphere we have somehow created, my heart sinks. He walks over to my side and pulls the door open as well. More of the outside world infiltrates what I consider to be our sacred space—a space where, perhaps, a friendship was formed.

I step out and unclench my fist, allowing the full length of my dress to fall free and move in the wind. Around us, cars speed by, chatting crowds bustle through the restaurant doors, Afrobeat booms from speakers on the patio. The world pulses with chaos, and everything that occurred in the car seems distant—like it never happened.

Maybe it's best this way.

"Well." My voice is soft and raspy, an effect of the laughter I enjoyed minutes ago. "I guess we should go inside." I spin around and hasten toward the restaurant, suddenly eager to put space between us.

"Azere," he calls from behind, but I don't stop pacing until he holds my arm. "This fell off." He loops a gold bracelet around my wrist. The jewelry is secure, but his hand doesn't retreat. Between two fingers, he holds a heart-shaped charm that dangles from the bracelet. He studies it with focus and curiosity.

"For my sister," I say. "Her name is engraved on it."

He holds another heart-shaped charm, and his thumb glides over the letters. "Who's Itohan?"

"My mother."

Again, he holds another heart ornament. "And Jacob?"

"My cousin."

He holds another. "Samuel?"

"My uncle."

Last, he holds a charm that differs from the rest—a silver star studded with white crystals. "Joromi?"

"My father."

"Why a star?" he asks, still studying the charm.

"Because he's in heaven—one of God's stars. I like to believe that's what happens when our loved ones pass. They become stars, always shining down on us."

"Yeah." He nods and drops his head. "I like to believe that too." He releases the charm and focuses on me.

I focus on him also. I search his eyes, look past the infinite shades of blues until I'm confronted once more by that eerie void. Again, I sense that pain—too great to sustain—that hollowed Rafael out, took something from him. I suddenly wish I had the means to give it back.

"Thank you, Rafael. For noticing that it dropped. I would've been devastated if I had lost it."

"Well, we can't have that." He smiles, and so do I.

Together, with little distance between us, we walk toward the restaurant, and as we step through the doors, a silly thought occurs to me.

If Rafael wore a bracelet with charms that represented his loved ones, how many charms would be silver studded stars?

chapter
12

The restaurant's decor is striking. In here, it's easy for your eyes to wander from one conspicuous object to another. More than anyone else at the table, Rafael is engrossed in the setting. A few minutes ago, he was examining the detailed pattern on the cushioned seats. Now, his focus is on the carved wooden mural that covers one wall. Amid smooth ebony wood, there are intricate designs of faces, animals, masks, and shapes that seamlessly link together like the knots that combine to form a knitted blanket.

There is so much more to observe and admire, like the magnificent sculpture of an African warrior that seems to be in the likeness of Shaka Zulu. Though, when the waitress approaches our table, Rafael's attention moves to her.

"This is yours," she says, placing a plate of tomato stew and fried yam in front of me. "And this is for you." She sets two plates in front of Rafael and notices his confused expression. "Your first time?"

"Yes," Mr. Ojo answers. "We convinced him to try what we are having."

"I'm sure you'll like it. Here are your finger bowls." She distributes three small bowls to the men.

"What are these for?" Rafael asks.

"To wash your hand," the waitress says. "You're eating with your hand." She grabs the handle on the serving cart and strolls away, snickering just a little. "Enjoy."

"Azere." Rafael turns to me. He's utterly muddled. "What exactly is this?"

"This is *eba*," I explain, pointing at the white mound with a doughlike consistency, "and it's made with cassava flour. And this is *egusi* soup which is made with spinach, a variety of seasonings, and ground melon seeds. You have to eat both together. With your hand."

"I will show you how," Mr. Ojo says. "First, you rinse your right hand in the bowl." He follows his own instruction. "And then you're ready to feast." He digs all five fingers into his mold of *eba*, gathers a small portion, and dips it into the bowl of soup. Once the *eba* is coated in the leafy, yellow broth, he throws it in his mouth and swallows. "Mmm. Delicious. Try it, Rafael."

He appears skeptical but doesn't hesitate. He mimics Mr. Ojo's actions, and when the portion of *eba* is in his mouth, his jaw moves.

"No," I say, holding up my hands. "Don't chew."

His mouth stops moving, and he stares at me with wide eyes.

"Rafael, you don't chew *eba*. You swallow."

He nods and does as I've instructed. "Did I do it right?"

I laugh. "Yeah. You did. Now, what do you think? Thumbs-up or thumbs-down?"

"It's different but good. The soup . . . it's amazing." He continues with the process he's been taught—dig, dip, swallow.

Halfway through dinner, as Rafael is licking his soup-coated thumb, my phone vibrates. I retrieve the buzzing device from my purse. It's Farah calling. *Shit.* I've been on a total high since the presentation. And then there was that car ride with Rafael that further lifted my spirits, and now, I'm enjoying a meal that almost tastes as good as my mother's recipe. So I'll admit: this whole pregnant situation skipped my mind. Until now. The phone is still vibrating. I inhale and exhale at a steady pace and soothe myself with positive thoughts. *I'm not pregnant. Everything is okay.*

"Sorry." I look at Rafael apologetically and turn to our clients. "I really have to take this." I grab my purse, and hurry through the restaurant doors, pushing past a hyper crowd until the cool evening breeze hits my skin. "Hello?" Apprehension strains my voice, making it faint.

"Azere," Farah says. "How are you?"

"Please no small talk. Just tell me, Farah. What's the result?"

It's silent for a few seconds. *Has she hung up?*

"Hello? Farah?"

"Azere. You're pregnant."

Rapidly, white noise pours into my ears, whooshing and swelling until I can no longer make out Farah's voice. In fact, I can't make out anything. Through the tears that blur my vision, only sharp smudges of streetlights and colors appear.

Why did I get my hopes up? Why was I optimistic? Why did I hope for the best? I'm so stupid. So, so stupid.

Disorder floods my mind while anxiety strains my palpitating heart. I'm losing my bearing, body swaying on the verge of hitting the ground, when arms curve around my waist and secure me in a tight, protective embrace. I sniff and take in the scent of clean air and cedarwood—sweet, fresh, earthy.

Rafael.

"Azere, what's going on? What's wrong?"

His inquiry provokes more tears.

"Hey. It's okay." His hold on me tightens, and I bury my face in his chest. "It's okay."

If he knew the truth, he would understand that everything is not okay. In fact, it's far from it.

"I . . . I . . . need . . ." Stutters and whimpers compromise my speech. "Home." That's all I can say. "Home."

"Okay. Of course. I'll take you home."

He leads me to the parking lot. The people loitering outside the restaurant are watching, but I don't stop crying, and his arm around my waist remains fastened. At the car, he opens the passenger door and waits for me to settle into the seat.

"I'll be right back, Azere." He closes the door and strides off.

My phone vibrates in my hand. It's Farah. She's probably calling to see how I'm handling the news. Rather than answering, I send a text message, telling her I'm not ready to talk. Then I turn off my phone, close my eyes, and count backward—"one hundred, ninety-nine, ninety-eight"—attempting to avert focus from the disarray in my head. "Ninety-seven, ninety-six, ninety-five . . ."

THE RIDE TO MY PLACE ISN'T LIKE THE RIDE TO THE RESTAU-rant. The lighthearted atmosphere is gone. He asks questions, but I don't answer.

"Azere, what's going on? Are you okay? Is there something I can do?"

I gaze through the window for the duration of the ride, unable to speak, unable to look at him.

Though, when he parks in front of my apartment building, my stare goes to his chest—to the spot where I buried my face and cried. Now, the saltwater has dried and marked the white button-down with yellow blotches. There's also a smear of rouge, a permanent blemish on what looks like an expensive shirt. Right now, the other emotions stirring in me take priority and won't make room for embarrassment. So rather than cowering away, I fill the silence with words. "What about the clients?"

"Don't worry. I took care of it."

"Oh. Okay." I'm too tired to probe for clarification.

"What's going on, Azere? You can talk to me . . . if you want."

I should tell him the truth. He deserves to know, but I can't bring myself to do it. At least not right now, when I'm still processing the information.

"I should go." I push the door open. "Thank you, Rafael." And I am grateful for his understanding and kindness, but I don't have the energy to express the depths of my gratitude. "Good night."

"Azere," he says before my feet touch the pavement, "please take care of yourself."

In my current state, I can't make any promises about my wellness, but I force a tight-lip smile, giving him slight assurance.

In the lobby, while waiting for the elevator, I rub my temples, coaxing the chaos in my head to settle. And as it does, as the tempest of regret and confusion and grief gradually simmer to silence, a single thought occurs to me.

I am so screwed.

chapter
13

When I was a little girl, I had a dream—fairy-tale themed. It was nothing original—a charming prince meets a spirited girl, they fall in love and live happily ever after. As I grew, life lessons poked holes into my fairy-tale-themed dream. At sixteen, after the divorce of a friend's parents, I decided ever after could be cut short if the prince turned out to be a cheating SOB. At nineteen, after my first heartbreak, I became cynical and eliminated the idea of eternal love. At twenty-two, after going on a few dates arranged by my mother, it became obvious that princes come under the guise of various animals—frogs, pigs, snakes, dogs, rats. And sometimes, no matter how much you kiss them, they don't change.

Now, looking at the list on the ottoman titled "*How to Fix My Messed-Up Life*," I realize how far I've diverted from my childhood dream. Sitting on the sofa with my legs huddled to my chest, I consider if that dream can be salvaged as it lays under the ruins of my chaotic life. When my phone chimes, notifying me of a text, my attention shifts. After reading the message, I rub my eyes—to ensure I'm seeing correctly—then look at the screen again.

Hey. It's Rafael. I'm downstairs. Can I come up? I brought dinner.

He's here—at my apartment building. This morning, I sent him an email, explaining I wouldn't be coming into the office. After last night, I needed time to recuperate and to think without being so close to him. Now, past seven in the evening, he's here. What do I do? I hear Christina's voice instructing me. *Tell him you're pregnant, Azere.* It's what she advised me to do yesterday when I called and told her the news. *Tell him you're pregnant.* The thought terrifies me. Can I do it? As I consider, my phone chimes again.

You must be busy. I don't want to intrude. Never mind. I'll go.

Before I can think rationally, my fingers move against the screen, and I send a message.

Come up.

The reality of what I've done hits the instant *Delivered* appears under the message I sent.
Shit.
He's coming up—to my apartment. I stand and quickly stuff tear-soaked tissues into the teal love seat and straighten the ivory throw pillows. In the sitting room, cream curtains drape tall windows, black-and-white pictures of old Hollywood actresses adorn the gray walls, and a charcoal ottoman rests on an ivory shag rug. Not a thing out of place. My apartment remains the perfect combination of cozy and chic.

I rush to the bedroom, pull off my pink pajamas, and throw on a white T-shirt dress. I check my hair in the mirror; thankfully, it doesn't need any work. With a white scarf holding my braids in a high ponytail, I look like Janet Jackson's character in *Poetic Justice*—in the last scene when she accepts Lucky's apology, kisses him, and gets all giddy. I love that scene. It's the best part of the whole movie.

A knock at the door interrupts my thoughts.

He's here.

Nervous but very determined to overcome that emotion, I march to the door. Even though my palm sweats against the brass knob, I turn it and pull it open.

"Hi, Azere."

"Hi." I still can't believe it. He's standing at my door with a brown paper bag in his hand, his signature scent ebbing in the air, presenting me with further evidence of his actuality. "What are you doing here, Rafael?"

"I wanted to check on you." He scratches the back of his neck as if nervous and unsure of himself. "After yesterday and today, when you called in sick, I wanted to make sure you were okay. How are you feeling?"

"I felt a little sick earlier, but I'm better now." It isn't a lie. I was hit with a wave of nausea this morning—an effect of my current status, I suppose. "You brought me dinner."

"Yeah." He drops his head and takes a sudden interest in his black loafers, watching them instead of me. "I thought you might be hungry."

He thought I might be hungry.

For a moment, I don't see my one-night stand turned colleague turned father of my unborn child. I see the man who shared stories with me yesterday and made me laugh, then held me while I cried and told me everything would be okay. I see a friend, and somehow, the sight of him at my door doesn't seem outrageous. In fact, it's rather comforting.

"Come in." I pull the door wide open, permitting him to enter.

"Are you sure? Are you sure I'm not intruding?" He awaits confirmation with his stare darting from my face to the floor. He looks so hesitant and incredibly adorable and terribly handsome, and my subconscious is begging me to keep him like he's a stray pup.

"Yes. I'm sure, Rafael. Come in."

Gingerly, he steps inside.

"You can put the food right there." I gesture to the tray on the tufted ottoman and lock the door. When I turn around, he's hunched over, looking at the notepad on the ottoman.

"*How to Fix My Messed-Up Life.*" He scowls after reading the large scribble. "Azere. Are you . . . are you okay?"

"I'm fine." I grab the notepad and shove it under a throw pillow.

"Really? Because it doesn't seem that way. Would you like to tell me what's going on?"

Maybe I should. Here we are, alone. It's the perfect opportunity to tell him the truth, but once I do, there will be no going back. My already chaotic world will blow up in shards. There will be nothing left—no version of normalcy to hold on to, no possibility of a happily ever after to hope for. There will be nothing left to salvage. And I don't think I'm ready for that.

"Azere, you can talk to me."

"Someone's a tad bit nosy."

"I'm concerned and maybe a little curious."

"Well, Mr. Curious, did you know curiosity killed the cat and its owner?"

He frowns. "Really? I thought it was just the cat."

"Nope." I shake my head. "Both. It killed them both."

He chuckles—teeth exposed, dimples deepening, and eyes radiating warmth. When he stops laughing, he doesn't push any further. I flop on the couch, and he sits beside me—a little too close. My subconscious taunts me with all the possible outcomes of this situation. Outcomes I refuse to entertain because they involve X-rated activities.

"Here." He opens a takeout box and hands it to me. "I got Chinese because I wasn't sure what else you might like."

"Chinese is perfect. Thank you."

"So, what are you watching?"

I open my mouth to answer, but then his knee sways to mine, and I tense. I'm not sure if the action was accidental or intentional. Truthfully, it doesn't matter because my temperature, fueled by temptation, rises. Now, instead of looking at the television, I look at him—his biceps and chest that fill his shirt, his smooth, flushed lips that are fuller at the bottom, the gap between his thighs that leads to his pelvis.

Oh Lord.

Desire heats my insides and sweat sprouts to the surface of my skin. My nipples, covered by a thin fabric, are in jeopardy of hardening and protruding. This is bad. Really bad. Mentally, I'm whacking a rolled-up newspaper over my head.

Bad girl, Zere. Bad girl. Behave. Get it together.

"Azere, are you okay?"

"Mm-hmm." I clench my hands, preventing them from doing what my subconscious desperately wants them to do. "It's called *Isoken*." I look at the television, my attention on the movie I muted and neglected minutes before receiving his text message. "It's my favorite movie." I take the remote and turn up the volume. "It's really good."

"*Isoken*. I've never heard of it," he says.

"It's a Nollywood movie—a Nigerian movie."

"Oh. What's it about?"

"A successful career woman who has everything but a husband. So her mom sets her up with this guy who's basically the perfect Nigerian man, but then she falls in love with a . . ." I bite my lip before the last words fall out. Suddenly, the premise I've recited many times to friends and family weighs heavy on my tongue as if it's gained a significance it didn't have before. I cock my head and watch Rafael who in turn, watches me.

"Falls in love with a what, Azere?"

"Um . . ." I loop a braid around my finger and tug. "A white guy."

"Oh." He lifts an eyebrow. "She falls for someone who isn't Nigerian."

"Yeah. She does."

"Well." He digs chopsticks into a box of chow mein and turns to the television. "This sounds very interesting."

We watch the movie while eating—me scooping portions of rice into my mouth and him enjoying stir-fry noodles. The sight has me a little dumbfounded—Rafael in my apartment, sitting beside me, watching a romantic movie. He laughs at the funny parts and watches the last scene, smiling.

"That was great," he says, turning to me. "They ended up together."

"Well, it is a requirement for every romantic movie—a happily ever after."

"And you're the expert on the genre?"

"Well, my sister does call my love for romantic movies an unhealthy obsession." I shrug. "I just call it an obsession."

"And why the obsession?"

"My father." A faint smile touches my lips. "In the evenings, when the lights would go out, he would tell my sister and me stories about our grandfather and great-grandfather and so on.

But sometimes, he would tell us love stories. Those were my favorites." My smile expands. "A cruel king who falls in love with a kind palace maid; a poor farmer who saves a princess's life and wins her heart; childhood sweethearts who are separated by war but later reunite." I nod. "Yeah. My dad was a great storyteller. He got me hooked on the whole happily-ever-after idea. Hence the obsession."

"Then you believe in happily ever afters—that things just somehow work out, that people who are meant to be together, end up together." He watches me deeply as if looking for more than an answer, as if looking for hope—assurance.

"I don't know, Rafael. They're just stories. And in stories, struggles are simplified to guarantee a solution and a happily ever after. Reality is more complicated. People are more complicated." And this admission makes me even more reluctant about telling him the truth. "It's getting late." I stand. "You should probably go."

"Yes. Of course," he says, rising. "And I apologize if I intruded." A deep blush warms his complexion, and my heart skips several beats. "I just had to make sure you were okay."

"And I appreciate your concern. Really. But I'm fine. And I'll be in the office on Monday." I rush to the door and pull it open. "No more days off for me."

"Okay." He steps into the hallway and faces me. "Good night, Azere."

"Yeah. Good night, Rafael."

I don't know what else to say. He's still standing there, smiling, making my body feel things it shouldn't be feeling. I'm curious. What's the etiquette when your one-night stand turned colleague turned father of your unborn child comes to your apartment with dinner? What's the etiquette after his knee touches yours and you basically strip him naked with your eyes? The formality of our valediction doesn't seem quite right. There's something else we ought to do, something that's more fitting, and it's not until I'm standing on my toes and leaning into him that I realize I'm doing what needs to be done, what feels appropriate.

I loop my arms around his neck and lock him in a hug, showing genuine gratitude. He showed up at my door with dinner and offered a momentary diversion when I was truly in need of one. For that, I'm grateful.

"Thank you." I whisper the words, and his arms, which have been at his sides, circle around my waist.

We hold on to each other too tightly for far too long, and when we separate and our eyes connect, it's clear something between us has come undone—the line that divides professional and personal. There was a small fragment of it before, but now, there's nothing.

"Good night, Rafael." This time, I don't delay. My wrist flicks forward, and the door swings on its hinges and clicks closed.

Just like that, he's gone. Poof. I'm the magician and he's the illusion, the illusion whose warmth clings to my skin long after he's gone.

chapter
14

There's something depressing about weddings, especially if you are single, knocked up, and used to date the groom.

It's hard to ignore that last fact with my mother watching me from across the banquet hall, her unblinking glare translating to: *This could have been you.*

She set us up two years ago, and it was one of her better matches. Sunday was a great guy who made me laugh but never made my heart skip or my skin heat and tingle or my stomach contract with excitement and nerves. And I didn't do the same for him. But he found someone who did, and she has her arms around his neck as they sway slightly off beat to Banky W's "Made for You."

She's a gorgeous bride in a fitted burgundy gown that flares just above her knees; gold and copper embroidery decorate the elaborate train. On her neck, there's a stack of coral beads that vary in length, some hitting her chest and others her stomach. Her hair, pulled into a large doughnut bun, is adorned with gold trinkets and more coral beads. She looks elegant, regal, stunning— the perfect depiction of an Edo bride.

I'm happy for her and for Sunday, who became a good friend after our relationship ended. Yet, there is something so very depressing about their wedding. Maybe it's because my life is an exact contrast to theirs.

"Azere, you okay?" Jacob, my cousin, says. "You seem off."

"Not sure what you mean. I'm just minding my business, eating my *suya*." I nibble on the spicy skewered beef while keeping my eyes on the bride and groom.

"Looks like you've got a lot on your mind. What's going on, Azere? Or is your head tie too tight?"

"My *gele* is fine, thank you."

I touch the firm material mounted on my head in the form of neat, thin pleats. Like all the female guests, I'm wearing *aṣọ ẹbí*; it is a ruby-red and royal-blue ensemble that each person has fashioned into their own unique, glamorous style. I've seen the color combination only once at another wedding. There, the colors competed with the decor. Here, it complements it. White flowers and candlelight decorate the space while crystal chandeliers cast a warm glow in the enormous hall teeming with red and blue.

"Azere, are you going to tell me what's going on?" Jacob starts questioning me again, relentless in his quest for the truth. I suppose that's what makes him a great detective.

"Jacob, it's nothing. Really. I'm . . . um . . . great." Inventing a solid lie doesn't come easy when it's intended for someone who knows me so well.

He's one of my best friends—has been since we were children. When my family moved in with his, occupying his father's three-bedroom town house, he was accepting. He was sixteen and I, twelve. He took me under his wing, educating me on things I hadn't learned in my village. The whole computer situation was especially difficult, but Jacob exercised patience during all his lessons. Over the years, he and I developed a brother-sister relationship that seemed as authentic as the real thing.

Right now, in this active space—people conversing, cutlery clinking, servers balancing platters and trying to meet the needs of each guest—I could tell him everything, and he wouldn't judge. He wouldn't lecture me or share my secrets with someone else. If I told him the truth, my secrets would become his.

"Okay. Fine," I say. "There's something I need to tell you." Our table of twelve is missing three guests—my uncle, who left to take a phone call ten minutes ago and has yet to return; my sister, who is gracefully and strategically strutting around the room simply to make her presence known and her outfit seen; and my mother, who I have lost eyes on. "I don't know how to tell you this." I lean into Jacob and lower my tone. "The truth is I'm—"

"Azere," my mother says, making an abrupt reappearance. The royal-blue lace she's wearing is radiant on her ebony complexion. She chose to go with a simple and classic Nigerian style—a *buba* and wrapper, a long-sleeved blouse and a wrap-around skirt. Her statement piece is definitely the red *gele,* which is far larger than mine. "Look over there." She sits beside me, in what was once Efe's seat, and points to the enamored bride and groom. "What do you see?"

"Um . . . Sunday and Osaro dancing."

"Azere, what I see is your age-mate, Osaro. Newly wedded and closer to giving her mother grandchildren. Meanwhile—" She gestures to me. "Here you are, using all the muscles in your mouth to chop *suya* as if there is no tomorrow."

The other guests at the table, who are neither family nor friends, but complete strangers, perk up suddenly. My utter embarrassment, the source of their entertainment.

"Azere, how long before you settle down? How long? Or do

you want to end up like Bridget Jones—single and in your late thirties? Is that the life you want for yourself? Eh?"

To my mother, *Bridget Jones's Diary* was not a romantic movie but a cautionary tale, one she often used to alert me of my fleeting youth and tragic singleness. The movie's central message of loving yourself totally escaped her, but that wasn't much of a surprise to me. After all, she was the same woman who believed Elle Woods's quest to get her boyfriend back would have been successful had she gone to culinary school rather than law school.

"Anyway." She sips from the glass she abandoned minutes ago and sighs. "Elijah told me he asked you on a date, and you said no."

She's right. Elijah called me last night—shortly after Rafael left. He apologized excessively for the past, and I forgave him because I was tired of being angry. Of course, he wasted no time and asked me out, and I said no. I have no interest in dating him, not with the current state of my life. It's just unfortunate he chose to share the details of our conversation with my mother.

"Mom, does Elijah really tell you everything?"

"I call him and we gist. And so? Is there a problem?" She waits for my answer, but my lips are sealed. "The point is, you said no. As fine and successful as that boy is, you had the audacity to open your mouth and say no. Wonders shall never end *o*." She chuckles, more out of mockery than amusement.

"Azere." Her face is straight now. "Listen to me and listen well." She holds her earlobe. "You are going on a date with Elijah. *Shebi* you're hearing me? There is no power on earth that will stop you from dating that boy."

"But, Auntie, you can't force it." Jacob comes to my defense. "She'll date who she wants when she's ready. And she doesn't want to date Elijah, and trust me, it's for the best."

Jacob is protecting me from someone he once considered a friend. They grew up together—he and Elijah—learning at the same schools, attending the same church. That's where I met him. In church. It was my first Sunday in Canada. My uncle took my family to his Pentecostal church, and there he was. Elijah. Gosh, he was beautiful. He was sixteen, and I was twelve. He had a confidence people often interpreted as arrogance. Hell, as a child, I didn't care if he considered himself a god. I just wanted to be around him—laughing with him, living in his moments, breathing in his air. And I did all those things. As a fly on the wall.

At eighteen, after years of rubbernecking and daydreaming, he finally noticed me. He started to smile at me and talk to me and touch the new curves that shaped my body. It was a progressing romance. When Jacob discovered we were dating, he gave Elijah the if-you-hurt-her-I'll-kill-you speech. I suppose Eli wasn't threatened by the speech because he did hurt me. I confided in Jacob during the ordeal, and he consoled me during the many months it took to heal. He wasn't pleased to hear Elijah was back in town, trying to spark our old flame.

"Auntie, for God's sake please leave her alone."

"Eh-heh. So, Jacob, you are now an enemy of progress. *Shebi?*"

"Auntie, of course not."

"Then why don't you want your cousin to get married and give me grandchildren? Is she not mature enough to have one child on her hip, another on her breast, and one in her stomach?"

Well, I've certainly got the latter covered.

"Auntie, all I'm trying to say is that—"

"Jacob, I doubt you have anything reasonable to say about this matter. So do me a favor and close your mouth. In fact, stuff it with food. The fuller, the better." She eyes him, hisses, and turns to me. "Azere, you are going on that date with Elijah. Whether you want to or not is of no interest to me. *Abi* you understand?

Eh-heh. Good. I'm glad we've settled it." She stands and surveys the room. "Isn't that Mama Bayowa I see? She hasn't been to church for four weeks now, but here she is at a party, shaking her big *yansh*. If you ask her to quote one Bible verse right now, she will be stammering like a *dundee*. Meanwhile, she knows all the words to these secular songs. Useless woman. Anyway, let me go and greet her." She leaves the table, smiling and dancing toward the woman she just insulted.

"Azere," Jacob says, "I hate to say this, but your mom gives me Patience Ozokwor vibes. No offense."

And there's none taken because he's right.

Patience Ozokwor is the legendary Nollywood actress who became renowned for playing the same character in multiple movies—the harsh, nagging, mean, and sometimes outright wicked mother or mother-in-law. That's the vibe my mom occasionally gives, and while it's easy to brush it off as a hilarious coincidence, sometimes, their similarities terrify me.

"Jacob, can we get outta here and go get some air? I need to talk to you about—"

"Whatever it is that's bothering you?"

When I nod, he stands and pulls out my chair.

Outside, the summer sky is bright despite night's approach. The temperature is hot, but a cool breeze breaks through the mugginess every few seconds and refreshes my dewy skin.

"So? What's up, Zere?" Jacob folds his arms over his chest, covering the embroidery on his white kaftan. "What's going on?"

"Well." I perch on the hood of his Jeep, and the hem of my mermaid-style gown hovers inches from the ground. "I'm just gonna spit it out." *Because I don't have the energy to beat around the bush.* "I'm pregnant."

There's a hint of pink against Jacob's caramel complexion as he frowns. "What? Azere, are you sure?"

"Yeah."

Now, there's a crease between his brows gathering sweat. "How the hell did this happen?"

I give him the 411 on the one-night stand turned colleague turned baby daddy, leaving out pieces of information like name and race.

"Shit," he says when I'm done. "That's insane." He blows out a long, loud sigh. "You're pregnant, Azere. Meanwhile, your mom is forcing you to go on dates. Are you going to tell her? Are you going to tell everyone else?"

"Absolutely not. I'm not telling them anything, Jacob. And neither are you."

"And what am I supposed to do with this information?"

"Keep it," I say. "Keep my secret. Like you always have."

We're silent for a long while. Jacob is clearly still processing the news.

"So," he finally says, focusing on me again, "how far along are you?"

"I'm not sure. Maybe five weeks? Six?"

"And does this guy know you're pregnant with his kid?"

"No. I haven't told him because . . . well, I don't know how he'll handle it."

"Is he a good guy? Does he care about you?"

As I consider the question, memories of the past few days come to mind—Rafael comforting me as I cry, covering for me with our clients, bringing dinner to my apartment. "Yeah." I nod. "He's a good guy. And I think he might care about me." At the admission, I smile.

"And what about you? Do you care about him?"

This time, rather than considering the question, I dismiss it, and another long moment of silence passes between Jacob and me.

The hot air thickens, flavored by the cigarette of a man swaggering past us in an *agbada* and dark sunglasses.

"So," Jacob says, "are you going to keep it?" That question adds more weight to the gravity of the situation. "Azere, what are you going to do?"

I don't answer.

"Let me rephrase that. What do you want to do? Forget about everyone else. Especially your mom. Zere, do you want to keep this baby? Yes or no."

"Yes." Tears spring to my eyes, and Jacob loops his brawny arms around me. "I want to keep it." Since getting the news from Farah, I've cried and prayed and weighed the pros and cons, and this is the decision I've come to. "I want to keep my baby." After making the confession, I cry and laugh against Jacob's shoulder.

"Azere?" He pulls back, and his gaze moves across my face, examining my teary eyes and laughing lips. "You okay?"

"Yeah. I'm good." My laughter lightens to a giggle before stopping. "I just haven't admitted that before."

"It's a huge decision," he says.

"I know. But it's the right decision for me." For the first time, I acknowledge the existence of my child by touching my flat stomach. My hand shakes. "I'm going to keep it, Jacob. Even if my mom hates me for getting pregnant out of wedlock." *And by a man who isn't Nigerian.*

"Zere, your mom has her moments, but she'll love you no matter what."

"Maybe. But she'll never forgive me."

My mother—in all her strength, patience, love, and devotion— gave my sister and me everything and asked only one thing in return: that eventually, we honor our culture and our family by marrying an Edo man and breeding his children. Of course, this request aligned perfectly with the promise I made to my father.

For so long, I was confident I could honor her request and my promise. After all, I took all the necessary precautions. In the ninth grade, I punched Michael Lee Wong for spontaneously kissing me on a dare. In the twelfth grade, I rejected Mario Rodríguez's elaborate and romantic prom proposal. In university, I denied myself a date with Andrea Casta, the sexy international student with an Italian accent that made my insides twist and flutter.

Now, my many years of precautions seem in vain due to one night. The one night I released my inhibitions and forgot my home training. One night, one mistake my mother will never forgive.

"When are you going to tell the father?" Jacob asks.

"When I'm ready."

"And what about the rest of our family? When are you going to tell them?"

"Same. When I'm ready. I'll tell them and face their wrath and, of course, deal with my mom disowning me."

"Don't be theatrical. Yes, it's going to be tough, but we'll get through this. On the bright side, I'm going to be an uncle and a godfather." He offers a wide grin that exposes his pointy canines. "Right?"

I smile and nod. "Yeah. Absolutely."

When we return to the banquet hall, the music is pulsating. Guests surround the bride and groom, dancing with them and spraying money. A flurry of dollar bills soar in the air and meander, touching the celebrants before reaching the floor. The music is loud. I feel the bass inside me like a second heartbeat. "Ayo" by Simi is playing; her delicate soprano is soulful and the beat, undeniably Nigerian. The lyrics are both beautiful and uplifting, and before the dread inside me takes over, I shuffle to the dance floor, dipping low and twisting my waist. When the band takes over and the guy on the talking drum goes at it, the crowd's energy amplifies, and Efe joins me on the floor.

For the rest of the night, I dance and laugh and force myself to ignore the pestering dread that makes me more aware of the life-changing decision I've just made and the grave consequences that will inevitably follow.

chapter
15

On Monday morning, after telling Christina about my decision to keep the baby, she cheered then proceeded to sing Madonna's "Papa Don't Preach"—a fitting song. I laughed, happy she kept things light.

I met with Farah during my lunch break, and after informing her of my decision, she gave me a detailed list of pregnancy dos and don'ts and confirmed I'm six weeks pregnant.

Now, it's after work hours, and I'm still in the office. My fingers move fast on the keyboard. When my cell phone vibrates on the desk, I stop typing and answer it.

"Hi, Mom."

"Azere, how are you? I hope you had a good day. The weather was so beautiful today."

Her pleasantries are leading up to something.

"Anyway."

It's coming.

"I wanted to remind you about tomorrow."

Getting closer.

"Your lunch date with Elijah."

And there it is.

"I hope you haven't forgotten."

"No, Mommy. I haven't."

"Good. He has night shift at the hospital this week, so he can only see you during the day. I hope you don't mind."

I'm positive it wouldn't make a difference if I did.

"So, what are you going to wear?" she asks. "Listen. I'm not saying dress like a harlot, but wear something that will show your figure. And tell him you are a great cook. Tell him you can make *ogbono* soup. It's his favorite."

"But, Mom, I don't know how to make that." It's the one Edo dish I can't get right.

"Then lie. Ah-ahn. *Abi* do you want to expose yourself and tell him all the things you cannot do?" She snorts. "Zere, in the name of the wedding I've already started planning, don't go and disgrace yourself in front of that boy tomorrow *o*."

"Planning? For what wedding, Mom?"

"The one that will hopefully happen next summer. If everything goes well with Elijah, you could be engaged before this year ends. By December, we can choose colors for the *aṣọ ẹbí*. In fact, I was thinking of purple, gold, and white for the traditional wedding and peach, gold, and burgundy for the church wedding. What do you think?"

I don't know what to say. Do I tell her the truth and completely ruin her current high, or do I let her enjoy the fantasy of me wedding Elijah a little longer—before the revelation of my pregnancy turns everything to shit?

"I love those colors, Mom. They'll look great." This seems like the safest option.

"Wonderful." Her voice is light, cheerful.

"Mommy, I have to go now, but I'll call you tomorrow."

"Immediately after your date with Elijah. Okay?"

"Okay. Good night."

I end the call and notice the office is empty. According to the watch on my wrist, it's ten minutes past eight. I switch off the computer and gather my belongings. My heels clack as I move toward the elevator. I'm familiar with the distinct chime created by my cherry-red Ferragamos, but there's another clacking that's unrecognizable. I stop walking and listen attentively, trying to determine the origin of the sound.

My ears trace the beat and my feet follow. Past rows of desks and chairs, past the elevator and the receptionist counter, my feet continue to move until they brake at the kitchen. There, under the magnifying glow of fluorescent lights, is Rafael.

He's tapping a spoon against a coffee mug. I suppose he believes he's invented a dance-worthy tune because he's swaying, tilting his head side to side and shuffling his broad shoulders. I don't want to interrupt his jam session, but I laugh, and he spins around.

"Azere." His eyes are wide, stunned. "How long have you been standing there?"

"Long enough to know you need to get some new moves." I chuckle and step into the kitchen. "Is that head-shoulder thing your only move?"

"No," he says. "Sometimes, I throw a clap or two in there."

"Aw. A clap. Total game changer." We both laugh this time, and as we quiet down, I say, "I thought you left a few minutes ago."

"I just stepped out to run a quick errand. But I've got some work to do, so I'll probably be in the office for a while."

"It's getting late. Don't you have someone to get home to? Like . . . I don't know . . . a girlfriend?" I taste something in my tone—something bitter. Jealousy.

"I don't have a girlfriend, Azere."

"Oh. Okay." I try to contain my relief, but I sigh, and it isn't quiet.

"I have a dog," Rafael says.

"Seriously? What kind of dog?"

"A toy fox terrier. His name's Milo. I spent the majority of my weekend at the dog park thanks to him." He smiles and glances over my frame—my pink lace blouse and black A-line skirt that falls on my thighs.

"How are you doing?" His wandering eyes meet mine.

"Good. Thanks again for checking on me on Friday. Even though you didn't have to."

"Azere, I wanted to." He takes a step toward me. The kitchen instantly seems small. "It was really no trouble. Actually, I wanted to call you over the weekend."

"Then why didn't you?" I ask.

"I wasn't sure how you would feel about it."

"I would have liked it. A lot." After the unexpected confession, I roll my lip between my teeth. Although embarrassed, I don't look away. I watch him. *What is he thinking?* His stare is low, and his long, dark lashes are curtains, preventing me from exploring the emotions in his eyes. "Rafael?"

The mention of his name catches his attention. He looks at me and, in rapid movements, closes the gap between us.

Finally, he touches me. His fingers reach behind my neck and pull my face to his. The emotions in his eyes—desire, greed, desperation—are lucid now. I recognize them because they're the same things I feel and have been contending with. Now, however—standing in such proximity, breathing in his air, taking in his scent, his skin pressed against mine—the urge to fight disappears.

We lean into each other, and our lips meet. I'm quick to drop the purse and coat in my hand, and he's quick to assert control.

There's a scene in *The Sound of Music* where Captain Von Trapp and Fräulein Maria share their first kiss in a stunning glass gazebo. A lot leads up to that moment—wanting glances, intimate dances, heated arguments that underline mutual attraction. When the kiss finally happens, it's slow and sweet and tender.

My kiss with Rafael is nothing like that.

With an arm around my waist, he yanks me to his chest. He kisses me deeply just like he did the night we met, but with so much more intensity, as if his technique has been enhanced by recently developed emotions.

I'm panting and quivering, and as my legs lose their function, he lifts my body and takes me across the kitchen. Objects clatter to the floor, and he sets me on a flat surface and starts undoing the buttons on my blouse, gradually revealing what's beneath.

When he touches me, heat explodes in the pit of my stomach. Sweat and goose bumps dot my suddenly sensitive skin. My breaths match the speed of my racing heart. Just like the night we met, his touch thrills me, weakens me, makes my heart manic, makes me pine for more of him, makes me reconsider the promise I made to my father. How can one touch do that to a person? How can his touch do that to me?

It does.

His lips leave mine, and I moan, pleading for their return. When they trail down my neck, kissing and licking, I moan again—satisfied. I know where they're heading and anticipate their arrival. But when they land on my stomach, anticipation instantly becomes anxiety. The haze that impaired my judgment clears, and everything hits me at once—my pregnancy, which Rafael is clueless about; my date with Elijah; my overbearing mother. The pressure, the expectations, the secret I'm keeping, the promise I've broken. I'm suddenly aware of everything, and it's all too much.

"No, no. Stop!" I shove Rafael back and take in the scenery. Spoons and forks are on the floor and so are my belongings. I don't remember my blouse coming off, but it's there—rumpled on the tiles. I look at the bra that barely conceals my breasts and then at him.

"Azere. I . . . I'm sorry."

"For what? We both did this." I dangle my feet, waving them in the space that separates me from the floor.

"I'll help you down."

"No! Don't come any closer. Don't touch me." I'm not commanding him. I'm begging, begging him to keep his distance because whenever he touches me, I lose sight of all my obligations and get carried away in his tide. It happened the night we met. It can't happen tonight. Without his help, my feet find the floor. I skim off the countertop he placed me on and bend to grab my things.

"Good night, Rafael." I turn to walk away, my clothes huddled to my chest, and he holds my arm gently.

"Azere, I . . . I . . ." He can't find the words, and I can't find the patience to wait until he does.

"This never happened." I tug my arm from his grip and rush out of the kitchen.

I'm six weeks pregnant, and I'm wondering: *When exactly can I start blaming hormones for my bizarre and irrational behavior?*

chapter
16

It never happened. Yet the memory pulses in my head, forcing me to acknowledge it, to relive it, to relish it. That night, sleep evades me. I toss, turn, and moan in recollection of his lips against mine. I allow myself to imagine what could have happened if I stayed. *What if?* I shake my head, refusing to entertain possibilities.

The next day, I'm back at the scene of the crime. Christina is heating her lunch in the kitchen. While she watches the microwave countdown, I roam idly. I inspect the various spots where he touched me and kissed me. He lowered my body onto the counter where people now gather to chat and eat. My blouse fell on the floor, and so did the spoons that now stir coffees and the forks that now pierce salads.

Hours later, in the same location, it's like nothing happened. I suppose that's the point—to leave behind no trace of us. The only evidence remains in my mind, and I wish I could expunge the memory. Perhaps even pull it out singularly like you would a loose string from a knitted scarf. Though, pulling out that one string could cause the entire scarf to unravel. Knowing this, maybe it's best I hold on to the memory. Not for my pleasure, of course. But for the sake of my sanity. I can't go messing with all the intricate strings that hold my mind in one piece. I'll keep the memory—tuck it away in a small, dusty drawer in the farthest part of my mind where it will exist quietly without disturbance.

"Azere." Christina touches my shoulder, and I turn to her. "What's with you? You seem off." Her hazel eyes shrink as she studies me. "Go on. Spill it. Tell me what's up."

"There's nothing to spill."

She isn't convinced. Her deadpan expression makes that clear. Keeping secrets from Christina is an impossible task. Why even try.

"Fine." I scan the room, ensuring our colleagues are paying no attention to us. Satisfied with my assessment, I turn to Christina and bring my lips to her ear. Within seconds of whispering, she knows everything. When I pull back, I behold her wide grin. "Christina?"

"Oh. My. Gosh." She claps and squeals, and I'm confused. "This is amazing."

"No, it's horrible."

"Zere, don't you see? Everything is working out. Think about it." She clears her throat. "You tell him you're pregnant, he's ecstatic because he's obviously into you, and you two raise the baby as a family."

"Yeah . . . I don't see it going down like that at all. What if I tell him and he wants nothing to do with me or the baby? What if he moves back to New York just to get away from me?"

"Azere, stop speculating. You won't know what his reaction will be until you tell him the truth."

"But what if—"

Arianna's abrupt appearance interrupts my speech.

"Guess what?" she says, smirking. "He's back. The hottie is back."

"The hottie?" Christina steps forward to conduct an interrogation. "What hottie? What does he look like? Where is he? What does he want?"

"He's tall, dark, and incredibly handsome. He's at the front desk, and he wants Azere. Apparently, they have a lunch date."

Christina turns to me. "What's she talking about? Who do you have a date with?"

I sigh. "Elijah."

"What? Elijah? *The* Elijah?" Her lips curl in disgust. She's likely recalling everything I ever told her about him. "Seriously, Azere?"

"He's back in town, and my mom's been trying to set us up."

"And you're actually going through with it? You're going on a date with him? Even after last night?"

"Oh. Last night?" Arianna's eyes expand. "What happened last night?"

Christina and I look at her, unsmiling.

"Right. I'll just tell him you're on your way." She struts off without another word.

"Zere, have you lost it?" Christina says, snatching my arm. "You can't go out with him. He took your virginity, then took off. That shit is unforgivable."

"It's been six years, Chris. I'm tired of being pissed about something I can't change. It happened. He apologized and that's that. Plus, my mom has been pestering me about going on a date with him. She's making me do this, Christina. I can't back out." *I want to, but I can't.* "Do you understand?"

"But what about Rafael? What about last night?"

"Last night meant nothing." I speak sternly, not only trying to convince her but also myself. "It was nothing."

"Bullshit. Zere, last night meant something to you. It's so obvious in your eyes. You're just scared to admit it because you don't want to deal with the consequences. Azere, you—"

"I should go." I tug my arm from her grip, no longer willing to hear what she has to say. "Elijah is waiting."

"Fine." She rolls her eyes. "If it was up to me, I would tell him to get a GPS and find the quickest route to hell."

And I wouldn't expect any less from her.

"But it's your call, Zere. If you wanna go, go. But after this date wraps up, what's next? You continue to hide your pregnancy from your family and Rafael and date Elijah? What exactly is your plan?"

My eyes roll skyward. I contemplate an answer but come up with nothing. "Well, I don't really have one."

"Mm-hmm. Azere, my psychic senses are tingling, and they're telling me this is all gonna blow up in your face. So figure it out before it's too late."

Her words send a chill through me, but I shake it off as I approach Elijah. He's waiting by the elevator and beams when he sees me.

"Azere. Hi."

"Hey. Sorry for keeping you waiting."

"No. It's fine. You're here now. Shall we?" He holds out his hand, waiting for mine to slip into it. "Azere?"

"Um . . ." I hesitate before finally submitting. "Sure."

The elevator arrives quickly, and we step inside. As the doors close, a hand comes between them and automatically, they slide apart to reveal Rafael.

Shit.

Our eyes connect, and then he glances at the man standing beside me, holding my hand. Offering no words, he enters the small, confined space.

It's quiet and extremely awkward. Maybe I should say something, talk about the weather. That always gets things moving. I open my mouth, but nothing comes out. We're on the fifteenth floor—five floors down from where we started—and Rafael and I stand as strangers. We've been like this all day, avoiding stares during the staff meeting, staying rooted in our offices to dodge encounters, and sending short emails instead of speaking in person. However, being close again, I can't ignore the connection that propelled me to kiss him last night. It's like a magnetic force, pulling my body to his.

"Azere," Elijah says, squeezing my hand. "Are you okay?"

"Mm-hmm. Fine." *Except I can't stop thinking about my one-night stand turned colleague turned father of my unborn child.* What's wrong with me? Last night with Rafael meant nothing. *It never happened.* I recite the phrase, but my brain doesn't accept the lie I'm attempting to pass off as truth. In the farthest part of my mind, memories rattle in that small, dusty drawer. I struggle to contain them, but their persistence outweighs my resistance. The drawer flies open, and the memories of us—Rafael and me—combust in my head like confetti.

Damn it. Who the hell am I fooling? It happened. We happened. And it was freakin' amazing. And I want it to happen again. I admit it, accept it, make peace with it, and in that moment, the steel doors slide open.

Rafael doesn't dawdle for a second. He hastens across the grand lobby and through the revolving door, leaving me behind—memories unbound and emotions amplified.

chapter
17

Rafael

For three days, I thought of what I could have done to prolong our encounter in the kitchen. I closed my eyes and envisioned several possibilities. On the fourth day—on Friday—I'm parked outside Azere's apartment building, phone in my hand, considering whether to call her. My hands shudder, nerves gradually seizing my body. After seeing her in the elevator with another man just days ago, I shouldn't be here. Is he her boyfriend? Is that why she pushed me away after our kiss in the kitchen? I shouldn't have come here, but I can't seem to stay away from her.

At the office today, after tracking her movements rather than working, I made this decision. The decision to come to her place and . . . *and what? What the hell am I doing?*

I tap my fingers against the steering wheel and search my mind for a reasonable explanation for my irrational behavior. Seconds pass, and I continue to ponder and doubt the extent of my sanity, but I don't drive away from where she is—where I want to be. It seems like there are invisible strings tethering me to her, constantly pulling me near her, working my body like I'm a flimsy puppet, making me do things I normally wouldn't. Before I can resist, I press the call button and hold the phone to my ear.

It rings, and my heart thumps.

"Hello," she answers. "Rafael?"

"Azere. Hey. How are you?"

"I . . . I'm great." I expected her to sound annoyed. But I hear it—the smile in her voice. "What's up?"

Could she really be serious about acting like nothing happened between us? It's the second time she's insisted we pretend, that we forget. The problem is, I can't pretend anymore. Nor do I want to.

"Azere, I was wondering if we could talk. About the other night." *And of course, the man whose hand you were holding.* I'm quiet, anxiously awaiting her response.

"Yeah. I think we should. Would you like to come over?"

"Actually, I'm sort of already here. I'm in the parking lot."

"Oh," she says, that smile still in her tone. "Then come up."

"I was hoping we could go out instead." Because I don't have the willpower to stay in her apartment without touching her. "If you don't have any plans tonight, I would really love to take you out."

"And where will you be taking me to, Rafael?"

"Um . . . it's a surprise."

She laughs. "Okay. Well, at least give me a dress code, so I know what to wear."

"Cocktail."

"Okay. Cool. I'll be down in twenty minutes." She ends the call, and I sigh, both relieved and thrilled.

Approximately twenty-five minutes later, she walks across the lobby and toward the glass doors in a spaghetti-strap knee-length dress. I step out of the car and march to the passenger side, watching her approach. The cherry-red fabric clings to her skin, accentuating the parts of her body that are slender and curvaceous. She isn't wearing a bra. There's a gentle outline of her nipples. *Shit.* My heart races. Does she have any idea what she's doing to me right now? Does she have any idea what I want to do to her?

"Hi." I force the word out of my suddenly dry mouth.

"Hi." She leans forward and wraps her arms around me, squeezing her body to mine.

The hug was unexpected. After recovering from the shock, I hold her and inhale her perfume. It's a soft powdery fragrance with undertones of sweet vanilla. When she pulls away, something tempts me to initiate more than a hug. It takes every ounce of resolve to let her go. We separate, and our eyes connect.

"So?" She blinks rapidly; long lashes flutter against smooth, brown skin. "What do you think? Is the dress too much?"

"No. It's perfect." With a drawn-out glance, I note where the zipper is. "You're perfect, Azere. Stunning."

"Thank you." She smiles, stroking a lock of hair behind her ear. "I love compliments."

I can't help but laugh. "I'll keep that in mind. Shall we?"

"Sure. But where exactly are you taking me, Rafael?"

"To a place where you and that dress will be appreciated." I open the passenger door. "Trust me, Azere."

"I'm not sure about that." She gives me a once-over, her red lips angled in a smirk. "But we'll see."

I fasten my seat belt and glance at her in the passenger seat, her hands resting over her knees, that slanted grin still on her face. I start the car, and as I press my foot on the accelerator, I can't help but wonder how tonight will end.

chapter
18

In awe, I watch the band play. The distinct melody of multiple instruments—the saxophone, trumpet, piano, bass guitar, and drums—intertwine and separate to create harmonies and melodies that are smooth and edgy, soulful and sensual, dark and light. Latin jazz. It's my first time listening to the genre, and I'm captivated.

Rafael has brought me to an upscale jazz club downtown. It's a stunning space. Floor-to-ceiling mirrors line the walls. Damask wallpaper interrupts the continuation of mirrors, creating an alternating pattern of reflection and gold, metallic motif. A tiered chandelier with intricate designs hovers in the center of the room—right above the dance floor. Dimmed pot lights shine over the people seated in red velvet booths. The light on the stage is sharper and allows me to observe the rapturous expressions on the musicians' faces as they play.

Slowly, the music fades, and each instrument loses its emphasis until they all die. There's a moment of silence followed by an abrupt eruption of claps and whistles from the crowd. I join the applause, and Rafael does the same. Though, he isn't look-ing at the band but at me. Unable to hold his intense stare, I turn back to the stage. The musicians are leaving, but the pianist stays. Behind a grand piano, he plays a mellow tune that isn't meant to overpower rising conversations.

"What do you think?" Rafael asks.

"I . . . um . . ." I search my mind for the right words. "Amazing. That was amazing."

Not the most original phrase, but it's impossible to form ex-pressive sentences when he's looking at me like he wants to kiss me. I wish he would. We're sitting close enough. All he has to do is lean into me slightly and his lips would be on mine. I'm ready and willing, but he doesn't make the move.

"So . . ." I attempt a conversation, hoping it will act as a dis-traction from his lustful stare and my lustful thoughts. "How has it been, living in Toronto again?"

"Good." He grabs his glass of scotch and stirs the liquid. The ice cubes in the cup clink against each other. "Really, really good." He brings the glass to his lips, keeping his eyes on me as he drinks.

"Oh. Okay . . . that's um . . . great." I shuffle ineptly in the velvet seat, repositioning myself while dealing with the discom-fort of being the subject of his attention.

"Zere." He abbreviates my name. He's never done that before, but it sounds natural—as if his lips are accustomed to the simple pronunciation. "Relax." From across the table, he reaches out and touches my clammy hand. His fingers wrap around mine.

This is a new level of intimacy between us, holding hands across the table like a couple out on a date. It should feel slightly awk-ward, but it doesn't. The gesture is as natural and unforced as my abbreviated name on his beautiful lips.

"Can I ask you a question?" he says, stroking my knuckles with his thumb. "The man in the elevator with you. Who was that?"

"Um . . ." I didn't expect that question. "Elijah. His name is Elijah."

"And who is he?"

"A friend." Well, that isn't exactly true. "We dated. When I was nineteen. But that was a long time ago. A very long time ago."

"In the elevator, he was holding your hand."

"Um . . . well . . ." I huff and sink into the velvet seat. "Rafael, do you remember the night we met when I told you my mom set me up on a date?"

"Yeah. I do."

"Remember I told you setting me up is kinda her thing—she tries and tries, hoping to get it right."

He nods.

"Well, Elijah was one of her tries."

"What?" He frowns. "Your mom is trying to set you up with your ex?"

"Yeah. That's why he was at the office—in the elevator, holding my hand. We were going on a date my mom arranged."

"She wants you guys to be together. And, of course, there's a chance because you two have history."

"No. There isn't a chance, Rafael. Elijah and I are done."

"Yeah. I don't know, Azere." He sighs and pulls his hand from mine.

He's hurt. I wish I knew what to say to make things better, to make him hold me again, but I don't have the words. For minutes, music fills the silence between us. He watches me, but my eyes travel around the room.

The band is back. They are playing something slow, sly, and seductive. On the dance floor, a few couples are swaying and grinding. When Rafael stands, I'm baffled.

"Come," he says, extending his hand with the same grace and gallantry as an Elizabethan gentleman. "Dance with me."

"I don't know how to dance to this type of music." A fast beat, I can handle. But this music requires something different from my body. It requires me to tempt and tease my partner, to ignite passion but to keep it contained all while remaining graceful. "I can't."

"Don't worry. I've got you," he says, his voice laced with conviction.

"Okay." Trust, not in my ability but in his, inspires my submission.

On the dance floor, he assumes control. His hands are on my hips, and at his will, I roll my pelvis into his—in and out—like waves touching and parting fluently. Our bodies are in perfect sync, complementing the band's tempo. I've somehow been transported into the movie *Dirty Dancing*. I'm Baby and Rafael is Johnny.

"Zere." He leans into me, and his warm breath brushes my neck. "Let's play a game."

"What kinda game?"

"Truth or dare." His lips glide along the curve of my pierced ear. "I'll go first."

He dips me, and the upper half of my body curves and sways over his arm. I dangle for a second or two, and he springs me upright. When I face him, I'm breathless.

"Truth or dare?"

I take in a gulp of air before uttering my answer. "Truth."

"Is there still something between you and Elijah?"

"No. There isn't."

"But you went on a date with him."

"No, I didn't. There was no date. As soon as the elevator opened, right after you walked out, I lied to Elijah. I told him I was feeling sick, and I couldn't go to lunch. He left, and I went back to the office."

That's the truth, and Rafael searches my eyes as if trying to ensure so. He doesn't say a word. He continues to lead our sultry dance, and I focus on him like he's some rare, unearthed treasure.

"Why did you lie, Azere?" he asks suddenly. "Why did you lie to Elijah?"

"Because of you, Rafael. My mom gave me hell for canceling that date, but it didn't matter. I couldn't go through with it because I couldn't stop thinking about you. Because the night before, I was kissing you, and it was amazing."

"Amazing?" He stops dancing. "Azere, you pushed me away."

"Rafael, it was also scary because . . ."

"Because what?" he asks.

"Do you want to know why I left your hotel room while you were sleeping?"

Of course he does. He's basically been begging for the answer.

"It's because I knew that if you woke up and looked at me and kissed me, I wouldn't leave. I would have stayed with you and disregarded every other responsibility in my life."

Because he has that effect on me. From the moment we met, he's had that effect on me. "That's why I couldn't stay, Rafael. And that's why I pushed you away. Because being with you makes me a little less aware of every single obligation in my life."

"What kind of obligations?"

"My family," I say. "They expect things from me. And, Rafael, you're a complication."

He frowns and opens his mouth, and just when I think he's going to ask how he stands as a complication, he says: "I'm sorry."

"No. Please don't apologize. It isn't your fault. You've done nothing wrong. It's just the way things are."

"The way things are." He considers the words for a moment

and then shakes his head as if rejecting them. "Do you care
about me?"

"What?"

"Do you care about me, Azere? Because I care about you. Very
much." He places two fingers beneath my chin and lifts it slightly.
"I think about you all the time. Frankly, I haven't stopped since
the night we first met. And I have no clue what force conspired
to make us meet again, but I am so fucking grateful to it. Because the best part of moving back to Toronto, the best part of
working at Xander is you, Azere. You're the best part."

"Rafael." My fingers slip into his hair, flopping the silky locks
side to side. I want to tell him I care about him too and that
lately, he's in my thoughts as well as in every one of my prayers.
I want to tell him that he has brought a sensible chaos into my
life that has inspired me to reenvision my future. I want to tell
him that I'm carrying his child and already I love it more than
anything or anyone. But instead, I gather a fistful of his hair and
pull his head forward. His lips touch mine, and I control the
ardent kiss. When he takes over, I'm breathless.

Right now—his hand secure on my waist, our breath min-
gling, our tongues intertwining—temptation seems too hard to
fight. It stupefies me, makes me senseless to everything but him.

"I believe it's my turn," I say, panting. Our lips part but remain close enough that we inhale and exhale each other's
breaths. "Truth or dare?"

"Dare," he says, his voice hoarse.

I take in the setting—the people dancing, chatting, drinking
under the beam of low lights—and look at him. "I dare you to take
me home and do everything you wanted to do to me that night
at the office."

In an instant, he's guiding me through the crowded dance floor.
He takes care of the check and then leads me out of the club.

In the car, before pulling out of the parking spot, he kisses me but pulls away before either of us can enjoy it. "Soon," he says.

Soon. The only word capable of containing me as he focuses on the road.

When we arrive at my apartment complex, he parks the car and looks at me, a thrill in his eyes. He leans forward, presses his lips to mine, and the word *soon* becomes an unbroken promise.

chapter
19

In the jam-packed elevator, we stand apart. I'm desperate to touch him, but strangers fill the space between us. The anticipation is exhilarating and causes the pulse between my legs to intensify.

On the eleventh floor, we slither through the huddle of laughing, chatting people. As we walk down the hallway, we remain apart. At my door, I fumble with the key before inserting it into the lock and pushing the door open.

He takes me into his arms the instant we're inside my apartment. We kiss and stumble down the corridor, banging into the walls and rattling picture frames hung on nails. We make it into the bedroom and kick off our shoes. As he unfastens the zipper at the back of my dress, I release the buttons on his shirt, revealing a sculpted chest layered with a light sheet of hair. The shirt lands on the floor, and the dress loosens, the spaghetti straps gradually falling off my shoulders and exposing more of my brown skin. At the full reveal, Rafael tenses—his jaw locks in a square and his temples pulse.

When my back sinks into the duvet, I think of Rose in *Titanic*, lying naked before Jack as he sketched her. Rafael isn't capturing my likeness with charcoal, but his unhurried gaze shows he's taking mental snapshots of the curves that frame my body and the fullness of my breasts and the length of my neck and even the slant of my collarbone that sticks out too sharply. This—me lying naked and untouched and him looking over every inch of me with hungry eyes—is the most erotic moment of my life.

Finally, seconds or maybe minutes later, he makes a move. He kneels at the end of the bed and pulls my legs apart. "Do you know how long I've wanted this, Azere—how long I've wanted you?" His lips press along my inner thigh, gradually moving higher and then stopping. He licks me once, and I moan. Twice and I quaver. Thrice and I sob. When his tongue finally slides inside me, I grip the edges of the bed. My hips buckle, and his hand lands on my stomach and keeps me in place. As he continues licking and sucking, gathering my juices and flavors into his greedy mouth, his hand on my stomach inches high. He cups my breast, takes an erect nipple between two fingers, and tweaks it hard. The combination of multiple sensations sends me screaming, pleading, crying as a climax builds and implodes.

"Rafael." My voice is raspy, heavy with desire. "Please." Even in this state—spent, limp from the pleasure he's selflessly given—I'm not satisfied. I won't be until I've felt every inch of him inside me. "Rafael." I groan, arching my back against the bed.

"You taste so good." There's a sensual playfulness in his eyes as he licks his lips. "I'm reluctant to stop, but since you're so eager . . ." He stands and drops his pants. Through his white boxer briefs, the bulge at his pelvis is apparent. When his boxers come off, my eyes expand, astounded and ecstatic, as I take in his size.

There's a shiny wrapper in his hand, which he pulls apart. As

I watch him roll the latex over his considerable length, my heart flutters rapidly.

He aligns his naked body with mine, the weight of his hard chest against my soft breasts. "I've been distracted for days now. I can hardly function right. And it's all because of you, Azere." He kisses me. "Now, here you are. So beautiful. So fucking perfect."

Slowly, he eases into me. His hardness fills me, his length hits every fraction of me. His rhythm is impeccable—shallow thrusts followed by a sudden plunge and his name falls out of my lips, mixing with soft moans and rough breaths. His mouth comes over my nipple, grazing it with the sharp edges of his teeth, tasting it with the tip of his wet tongue, and sucking on it with the whole of his warm mouth. His actions send me into a frenzy, and I dig my toes into the duvet and my nails into his back.

In one swift movement, with very little effort, he hooks an arm around my waist and mounts me over him. His eyes encourage me to take control, and I do. With my hands propped on his chest, I begin a slow up and down pace. My round breasts, glazed with sweat, bounce as I move; Rafael cups them and rotates his palms against their softness and fullness. When I change maneuvers, shifting my hips back and forward, he groans. I relish the control he's given up, but it doesn't last.

In another swift move, I'm on my back and he's on top, pinning me down with his strength. He takes hold of my leg and lifts it high, placing it over his shoulder. My flexible body settles comfortably into the new position, and he moves faster, traveling further, reaching a spot no man has ever reached before.

Oh. My. Gosh.

My skin tingles as pressure and pleasure build and build. I'm spent, but despite my drooping lids, my stare doesn't waver and neither does his. I don't shy away from his blue eyes that are so intense, so saturated with emotions. The moment is so sincere and intimate, it solidifies our connection and amplifies all the sensations we're experiencing until long, loud, winded moans erupt from both of us.

I gasp, trying to catch my breath, and he drops on his back and draws my feeble body over his. Slowly, our forceful pants fizzle out.

"Azere," he says, stroking my braids, "look at me." I can't find the strength to do that, so he lifts my chin gently until our eyes lock. "I need you to understand something."

"Mm-hmm."

"This is not another one-night stand."

"Okay. Then what is this?" I watch his lips for an answer.

"More," he says. "This, you and me, it's more."

"More."

He nods, and I smile.

"Okay, Rafael."

He holds me against his body, my ear pressed to his chest, his fingers working along the length of my braids. Tonight, right now, there is nothing beyond these four walls. There are no obstacles, no weight of obligation, no heartfelt promise linking the living to the dead. There is no prejudice. Every path has been paved, every door open, every mountain reduced to dust. Stars realign in our favor. The universe revolves around us.

His hold tightens, and we lay in the dark, fostering a connection so deep, it's as if a needle and thread are stitching our hearts together.

chapter
20

In the morning, sunlight slips through the lace curtains and draws shadowed patterns on Rafael's serene face. Under the duvet, his arm is around my waist, securing my naked body to his. He's tired. I am too. Various interruptions kept us from sleeping through the night. First, his hardness against my backside jolted me from sleep. The next interruption came a little past three—approximately an hour after the first. In the dark, my lips found his, and I drew him out of sleep.

After that session, we couldn't sleep. With me nestled at his side, he asked to hear the story my father used to tell me—the one about the cruel king who falls in love with a kind palace maid.

"Story, story . . ." I chanted. I waited for a response and realized he didn't know it. "You're supposed to respond, story."

He frowned, puzzled.

"It's a Nigerian thing. As children, it's what we recited before telling a story. It's how my father told us stories."

"Okay." He nodded. "Is there more to it?"

"Yeah. I say, 'Once upon a time.' And you respond, 'Time, time.' Got it?"

"Got it."

"Okay. Story, story . . ."

"Story." He even got the rhythm right.

"Once upon a time . . ."

"Time, time."

I told him the romantic tale, and he listened attentively, and a little after four, when the story ended, we fell asleep.

Now, according to the clock on my vanity, it's 10:15 a.m. He's probably exhausted, but I want to wake him anyway. I have the strangest urge to sing him a morning lullaby, something hushed and mellow that will gently lure him awake. It's a pity when that urge is overpowered by another—the urge to vomit.

In my stomach, nausea writhes like snakes in a pit. The sickening sensation intensifies. Vomit rises. Chunks of food scrape my gagging throat. I roll off the bed and run to the bathroom. After shutting the door, my head comes over the toilet bowl. The substances tickling my throat surge through my mouth again and again. After every release, I'm light-headed.

"Zere." Rafael is at the bathroom door. "Are you okay?" There's concern in his disembodied voice.

"I'm fine." Lies. My head is throbbing and my vision is blurry.

"Zere, you don't sound fine."

"I'm totally fine. Just chilling on the bathroom floor, doing a little puking. It's really no big deal."

"I'm coming in."

Before the knob twists open, I turn the lock.

"Azere, open the door. You're sick. I'll take you to a hospital."

A wave of morning sickness doesn't warrant a visit to the hospital. Because it's my third time experiencing the illness this week, I know rest is the only remedy.

"I just need to sleep it off. That's all," I tell him. "You should go home."

"I'm not leaving."

And I don't want him to. Not after last night. But he can't see me like this—frail and nauseous with chunks of vomit probably at the corners of my lips. He would likely want to know why I'm sick. And what would I say? What answer would I give to divert him from the truth? How would I look into his eyes and lie? After last night, I can't lie to him, and I'm certainly not ready to tell him the truth.

"Rafael, just go. Please."

"All right. Okay." Disappointment lowers his pitch. "I'll check on you later. I'll bring lunch."

"You don't have to do that. Besides, I won't be home later. I'm going to my mom's. I gotta mow the lawn."

"Mow the lawn?" Outrage spikes his pitch. "Azere, you can't do that. You're sick."

"I'm fine. Don't worry about me." I huff and with that sharp release of air comes a sudden release of vomit.

Rafael is banging on the door, demanding I let him in. My head is over the toilet bowl while I puke. Not the post-sex morning I envisioned. I imagined snuggling with him for at least an hour, then wearing his shirt as we made breakfast—him flipping pancakes and me cutting fruit. Lastly, I imagined us sitting at the table, eating from each other's plates, sharing kisses between each mouthful. Alas, that is not the case. Not even close.

"Azere."

I've stopped barfing, and he's stopped banging.

"Are you okay?"

"I'm fine, Rafael. You should get going. I'll call you later."

"When you return from mowing your mother's lawn?"

"Yeah. I have to. It's how I help her out." I didn't give up the chore when I moved out because my mother couldn't do it, and Efe was too much of a princess to attempt yard work.

"Azere, how far away does your mother live?"

"Not far. She's in Etobicoke."

"What's her address?"

"Fifteen Baneberry Crescent. Wait." I shake my head slightly. "Why are you asking?"

"No reason," he says.

"Um . . . okay. Then I guess we'll talk later. I'll call you when I get back. Okay?"

"Yeah. Sure."

I listen to the sounds that follow his compliance—feet stomping to the bedroom, clothes scuffling over body parts, and the front door creaking shut. He's gone, and I wilt on the cold tiles and fall asleep.

When my eyes open, I don't care to check how much time has passed. I go to bed and curl under the duvet. On the verge of another nap, my phone vibrates. After seeing the caller ID, I consider not answering before finally accepting the call.

"Good morning, Mommy," I say into the phone.

"Good morning?" She isn't exchanging greetings. Her tone is sarcastic. "Azere, it's one in the afternoon."

How long was I out?

"Azere, I've been calling you for over an hour."

"I'm sorry. I was asleep."

"You promised to cut the grass and rather than keeping your promise, you slept in and sent someone instead. What kind of nonsense is this?"

"Sent someone? Mom, what are you talking about?"

"Azere, there is a white man cutting my grass. He said you sent him."

"What?" I sit up and press the phone closer to my ear. Maybe I heard wrong. "Mom, what did you just say?"

"Zere, are you deaf? I said a white man is currently cutting my grass."

"Who? Who is he? What's his name?"

"Um . . . um . . ." She takes far too long to answer, and I tick with impatience. "Rafael."

No. No. No. This can't be happening.

"Azere—"

"Mom, don't talk to him. Please, please, don't talk to him," I say, leaping out of bed and sprinting to the bathroom. "I'm on my way. Okay? I'm coming."

I end the call and turn on the showerhead. Cold water turns hot, and I enter the bathtub for a quick rinse. I'm not going to my mom's house smelling like barf and sex, especially since the man who sexed me up is there, doing and saying who knows what.

Christina warned me about this. *Everything is going to blow up in your face.* Those were her exact words.

And she was right.

chapter
21

Driving up to my mother's house, I see Rafael in a white T-shirt and blue jeans. He's snapping garden scissors over the shrubs that line the walkway, trimming any outgrown leaf threatening their round structure. The scene is surreal.

I pull into the driveway and park. He's fixated on his unassigned task and doesn't notice me staring through the car window. I'm livid. I have every right to be. He took steps he shouldn't have without my consent. For crying out loud, the man is at my mom's house, grooming her lawn with precise focus like it's his livelihood.

Why is he doing this, working under the searing May sun, performing a task that wasn't assigned to him, a task that seems beneath his elegant exterior?

Though, right now, he doesn't look so elegant. His windswept hair dangles above the strip of sweat that lines his brow. His white T-shirt, drenched with perspiration, has turned transparent and is sticking to his chest. Even though I'm pissed, I find myself biting my lip and lusting a little. It's hard not to, but the question still remains: *Why is he doing this?* I step out of the car and approach him, ready for an answer.

"Rafael." I stand in front of the shrub he's trimming, and his eyes lift and meet mine. "What the hell, man?" It's uncharacteristically hot for late May. Only seconds out of the air-conditioned car and my skin is already going damp from the heat. I ignore the icky unpleasantness and focus on my interrogation. "What do you think you're doing?" My voice isn't angry, but it's curt and peeved.

"Azere." He inspects my face, and his expression hardens. "You should be resting. What are you doing here?" he says irately, as if I'm the one guilty of an offense.

"Excuse me. What am I doing here?" Aghast, I release a breathy explosion of jumbled words. "This . . . this . . . um . . . ugh . . . is my mom's house. What the hell are you doing here?"

"I'm mowing the lawn. Well, I'm done now." He looks at the cut grass, and my gaze follows his.

Okay. I'll admit it. He's done a superb job. Clean, straight stripes align the short grass—a style I have never been able to achieve. It's a good job, but it still does not excuse his behavior.

"Rafael." My voice is gentle now; there's no hint of irritation. "Why did you do this?"

"You were sick." He drops the garden scissors on the grass and dusts his hands over his jeans. "You couldn't do it, so—"

"So you drove over to do it yourself. And that's why you asked for my mom's address." *Unbelievable.* "Rafael, do you realize how crazy this is? Not to mention inappropriate, weird, extremely creepy, and—"

"Okay," he says, throwing up his hands in surrender. "Okay. You're right. I overstepped. I'm sorry." He thrusts his fingers through his hair, making each wavy lock fall backward.

"You were sick, Zere. I did it so you wouldn't have to—so you could rest." His stare drops to the grass. "I really didn't mean to overstep any boundaries. I guess I wasn't thinking. I'm sorry. It won't happen again."

The grand gesture is one of the most pivotal scenes in romantic movies. It's a moment meant to accomplish one or all of three things: prove one's love, earn a lover's forgiveness, or win back a lover's affection. There are many variations of grand gestures—the last-minute race to the airport where the hero stops the heroine's departure, the big song number where the hero serenades his love interest, or the public apology followed by a heartfelt declaration of love.

In the movie *Brown Sugar*, the grand gesture occurs when Dre calls the radio during Sidney's broadcast and publicly admits he's in love with her. His exact words: "Sidney, I have loved you from the first time I laid eyes on you. And I love you still. You're my air."

In my complex story, there isn't a sentimental speech. There's just a man grooming my mother's lawn. It's a simple act—understated in every sense, and yet, I am floored. This man labored in the smothering heat so I would be spared any discomfort. Someone watching might not understand the significance of this gesture or see how grand it truly is. I, though, see it clearly.

"Rafael." I touch his cheek, and his beard stubble prickles my palm. "Look at me." He obeys, and I reward him with a smile. "I stand by what I said before. This is crazy. But it's also thoughtful. Very thoughtful. Thank you."

He smiles, and remorse leaves his eyes. "How are you feeling?" He takes my hand that's on his cheek and presses it to his lips, kissing each pointy knuckle.

It occurs to me that my mother could be near. I should step away from Rafael, but then he wraps an arm around my waist and pulls me into him, and I forget the threat. "I'm feeling better," I tell him. "Just a little tired."

"In that case, let me take you home and put you to bed. And

when you're rested . . ." His lips brush the shell of my ear as he whispers something in a foreign language.

"Wow." I look up at him, marveling. "I didn't know you speak Spanish. What did you say?"

He translates, and after comprehending, I wilt over his chest, weak from his words. Though, when the front door squeaks open, I regain both my bearings and my wits and jerk away from him. And in that exact moment, my mother walks through the door and comes down the porch steps.

"Azere, you finally decided to show up," she says, balancing a glass of water on a stainless platter.

"Um . . . yeah." I clear my throat while eyeing her and Rafael. "Good afternoon, Mom."

She doesn't return the greeting. She walks to Rafael and presents the platter to him. When we spoke on the phone, she was upset about the white man who was cutting her grass. Now, she's serving him.

What changed her mind?

"Look at the great job you did." My mother smiles, admiring the neat lawn. "You are amazing."

"Thank you." Rafael takes the cup, and his fingers smear the drops of moisture dotted on the glass.

"Azere has been cutting this grass for years, and she has never done it like this. Look at those straight lines. Beautiful."

I roll my eyes, and I'm grateful she doesn't notice. "Well, he's done now. He should get going."

"Going?" My mother looks at me—shocked and confused—as if I've sprouted a second head. "Going where?"

"I don't know. To his house?"

"No, he's staying." She turns to Rafael. "Right? Because Jacob is expecting you in the backyard."

"Jacob's here?" I blurt.

"Yes *o*. With your uncle. They are barbecuing. Rafael is going to join them."

My eyes bulge. "What?"

"Azere." My mother studies me. "Are you okay?"

When I nod, she doesn't probe further.

"Well, I have something on the stove." She turns and walks toward the house. "Rafael, we'll talk about your fee later!"

"Fee? Rafael, what's she talking about?"

"Your mom thinks I'm a landscaper." He takes a sip of water. "She wants to hire me for the summer." He laughs, but I don't find the humor in the situation. "And so does your uncle."

"You met him too? You met my family?"

"Yeah. Wonderful people. Very hospitable. Especially your mother."

Yeah, until she finds out who you are and what you mean to me.

"Rafael." My breaths quicken, coming through my mouth in short, shuddery explosions. "You have to leave. Right now."

"Why?"

"Because—" As I'm about to offer an explanation, Jacob makes a sudden appearance and plants a kiss on my cheek.

"Hey, cuz. How you doing?"

"Great. Just great." I fake happiness with a tight-lipped smile. "Didn't know you were coming by."

"Yep. Just firing up the grill. I see you've met Rafael, the only landscaper I know who drives an LC 500." He turns to the car that's parked on the curb and smacks Rafael's shoulder like they're buddies. "We still going on that drive later?"

"Absolutely," Rafael answers. "Just say when."

They slap their hands together, then bump fists.

I watch their interaction utterly perplexed. *What the hell is going on? Are they friends now? When did this happen?*

"So you still coming to the back?" Jacob asks. "I've already got the grill going."

"Um . . ." Rafael looks at me, seeking permission.

"Unfortunately, he—"

"Azere!" Again, I'm interrupted. This time by Jason Carter, the kid I used to babysit. He swaggers toward me, his pants hanging a little below his waist. "Hey, sexy." He ignores the grown men in my company and gawks at me, licking his thin, chapped lips. "I smelled barbecue, saw my girl, and knew it was gonna be a good day. How about some sugar, babe?" He leans into me with puckered lips.

"Boy, what is wrong with you?" my cousin says, smacking Jason's head.

"Hey!" He glowers at Jacob and rubs the spot where he's been hit. "Can't a man show his woman some love?"

Rafael is observing with amusement. Again, I don't see the humor in the situation, especially since I'm focused on the black Mercedes-Benz pulling to the curb. The windows are tinted, but I have an idea who's inside. My subconscious tells me to take off before this scenario gets more complex. It's good advice, but I stand stagnant, concentrating on the pavement, watching black Nike sneakers step out of the car and move toward me. I'm not surprised when sturdy arms seize me in an embrace.

Elijah.

His biceps curve against my body, one around my back and the other around my waist. This is how he used to hold me—possessive and secure. Over his shoulder, Jason is scowling as he regards the nearness of Elijah and me. To my right, Rafael is doing the same.

When Elijah's arms fall from my body, Jacob clears his throat, signaling for his attention. "What the hell are you doing here?" he asks, disdain heavy in his voice.

As Elijah holds Jacob's flinty stare, something unspoken transpires between the former friends. Tension rises, making the hot air more unbearable. When Elijah finally gains the good sense to look away, I exhale.

"Azere's mom invited me," he says. "She said she's hosting a family barbecue and wanted me to attend."

"Well, since you aren't family, you have no business here. Leave."

"Look, Jacob. I don't want any trouble." There is a humility in Elijah's tone, a silent plea that makes him appear vulnerable. "I just came to see Azere. That's all. And if she wants me to leave, she can tell me that herself." He looks at me. "Zere, what do you want?"

Four pair of eyes—Elijah's, Rafael's, Jacob's, and Jason's—are on me, all expecting something distinct. This reality is too messy. In need of an escape, I close my eyes, and another version of my reality instantly begins to play out.

I'm in an off-the-shoulder sequin gown. Three men, dressed in tuxedos, stand before me—Jason, Elijah, and Rafael. There's a red rose in my hand they look eager to possess.

"Who will Azere pick?" Chris Harrison, the host of *The Bachelorette*, appears. He speaks while strolling toward a camera. "Will she try her luck as a cougar with Jason, the perverted boy next door? Or will she choose Elijah, her first love and the man who took her virginity, then shattered her heart into a million pieces? Or will Azere take a chance at a happily ever after with Rafael, her baby daddy and the non-Nigerian man she vowed never to date? Find out next week on the most dramatic episode in *The Bachelorette* history."

Calls of my name pull me out of the reverie. My eyes flutter open, but a sheet of haze curtains my vision. Faces are smudges of colors that spiral. My lightweight head droops. Equilibrium is declining. Arms come around my body, but I'm not sure whose they are. There are voices around me, but they aren't lucid. There is a world beyond my deteriorating mind, but I am detached from it. Darkness overtakes my consciousness, and I am insensible to colors and senses and life.

chapter
22

My eyes open, and I push past the mist impairing my vision. Soon, faces take form. My mother, my uncle, Efe, and Jacob are standing, observing me. Concern and fear distort their faces, making their brows furrow and their lips shrivel in deep-set frowns.

"Zere." My mother steps forward, and I recoil from her outstretched hand.

"What's going on? Where am I?" I take in the setting. White walls, polyester sheets atop the rigid bed I'm lying on, the grip of bandages holding the IV catheter injected in my forearm, and the mild stink of disinfectant. *I'm in a hospital.* "What happened?"

"Azere, you fainted," my mom says. "I tried . . . we tried." She sniffs and sobs. "We couldn't wake you. I thought . . ."

"Mommy, please don't cry. I'm okay." *Am I? What about the baby?* With my mother's support, I rise to a sitting position and touch my stomach. "Where's the doctor? I need to speak to a—"

Before I complete the sentence, a woman in a lab coat enters the room. There's a clipboard in her hand and a stethoscope around her wrinkled neck.

"Hello, everyone," she says. "I'm Dr. Lois Clark." She studies the paper on the clipboard. "Azere Izoduwa." She looks at me and smiles. "How are you feeling?"

"I'm fine. Tell me what's going on."

"Sure. But first, let's take this out." She disconnects the IV catheter injected in my arm and discards it in the waste bin.

"Now. Where were we?" She glances at my family. "Azere, would you prefer us to have some privacy? Maybe they should wait outside."

"Absolutely not," my mother snaps. "She is my daughter. We are her family." She gestures to the squad. "You can speak freely. Isn't that right, Zere?"

I should say no. I should ask them all to leave and allow the doctor to deliver my news privately, but my mother's strict stare indicates that isn't an option. So I exhale and nod, giving the doctor liberty to speak and most likely expose my biggest secret. I'm terrified. After the revelation, everything will change. Nothing will be the same again.

"Okay." She pulls silver-rimmed glasses from her face, showing the puffy bags beneath her fatigued eyes. "You fainted because your blood sugar levels were extremely low. When was the last time you ate something?"

"Um . . ." I had a salad and some chicken wings for dinner yesterday—a few hours before Rafael came by. Today, I ate nothing to replace the food I puked. "It's been a while."

"Well, in your condition that isn't sensible. You have to—"

"I'm sorry," my mother interrupts. "In her condition." She frowns. "What condition?"

"Um . . ." The doctor glances at my mother and then at me. "Well . . . um . . ."

"I'm pregnant." The confession makes my mouth bitter and my heart palpitate and my eyes water. "Mom?"

She doesn't respond. She gapes at me. Her dark eyes are blank with no emotions evident to decipher.

"Maybe I should give you all a minute," the doctor says, backing toward the door. "I'll be back later."

"Wait!" I call out. "The baby. Is it okay?"

"Everything looks good. We'll talk later."

Upon the doctor's exit, I refocus on my family. They aren't doing so good. Jacob, already informed of my status, is calm. My sister, however, has both hands over her gasping and cursing mouth. My uncle is breathing hard, pumping air into his large chest and releasing it rapidly. My mother hasn't stopped staring at me.

"Mom?"

"Azere." Finally, she speaks. "Tell me you are joking."

"No." I tug on the hospital gown, separating the cotton fabric from my sweaty neck. "I'm pregnant."

"But you're a virgin, saving yourself for marriage."

"No. I'm not."

Initially, I planned to stay celibate until marriage. My mother's numerous lectures about the importance of celibacy convinced me the devil would drag me to hell the moment I had premarital sex. The whole idea scared me, but then Elijah came along, and I got pulled into a whirlwind of emotions and hormones. After losing my virginity, remaining celibate seemed pointless. I dated and, when I felt a deep connection with someone, had sex. It wasn't frequent, but it happened, and I always thought I could keep my sex life from my mother. Today, unfortunately, she's found out in the worst possible way.

"So, Azere, you are pregnant?"

I nod. "Yes, Mommy."

"Jesus Christ of Nazareth!" She throws her hands on her head and wails, calling on her maker to intervene. "Help me o!"

"Auntie," Jacob says, "please calm down." He wraps an arm around her shoulders and tries to soothe her, but she shoves him away.

"Calm down for what?" she yells. "Calm down for what? Or have you not heard the news? Your cousin is pregnant. Pregnant and unwed." Now, she's jumping and wailing. "What will people say? Who else will they blame but me, her mother? What will I tell the pastor? What will I tell my prayer group? How will I face the world? Zere, you have ruined me. Prepare my grave. Because I am dead. You have killed me."

The dramatics of a Nigerian mother is nothing, nothing compared to that of an Academy Award–winning actress. Viola Davis, take a seat and behold my mother.

"Itohan," my uncle says, stepping forward. "Calm down. Right now."

Instantly, my mom's antics mellow. Her wails reduce to shrill whines, and instead of jumping, she bounces on her toes.

"Azere." My uncle turns to me. "You are a grown woman, so I will not interrogate you about your personal life and the decisions you make—no matter how stupid they are. You're pregnant. Okay. The only question I have is, who is the father?"

Now, my mother stops bouncing. She waits for the answer like everyone else in the room.

"Um . . . well . . ." I look at the closed door and then through the slim slice of glass that exhibits a view of the hospital hallway, and I see Rafael. He's out there, pacing with his head low and his hands stuffed in his pockets. Knowing he's near somehow eases my nerves.

"Azere, answer me before I lose my patience," my uncle says, irked. "Who is the father of your child?"

"He is. He's the father." My family's gaze follows mine.

"The gardener!" Efe says, a hand to her chest. "You slept with the gardener?"

"He's not a gardener." Their eyes are on me again. "He's my coworker."

"Your coworker?" my uncle says. "And he came to your mother's house under the guise of a gardener? To do what? Make a fool of us? What kind of rubbish is all this? What kind of game is he playing?"

"Uncle, it's not like that."

"Then what is it like, Azere?"

"It's complicated."

"Then un-complicate it."

"Okay. Well, he . . . um—"

"Azere," my mother interjects. "Just wait. Just hold on one minute because I am misunderstanding something. When you looked through the door and said, 'He's the father,' were you looking past the gardener and actually looking at Elijah?" I suppose she hasn't digested the information I've offered. "Because Elijah is also standing out there. You were looking at Elijah, correct?"

"No, Mom. I wasn't. Rafael is the father of my child."

"Jesus!" She staggers back like she's about to collapse, but my family and I know she's being theatrical. "Zere." She springs upright again. "You slept with a white man."

"Mommy, he's actually Spanish."

"Will you shut up your mouth! What difference does that make? Eh?" She switches to Edo, lifting her hands to the ceiling and speaking to my father's ghost. "Come and see what your daughter has done o! Come and see how she has shamed you! Come see the disgrace she has brought on your name!"

"Mommy, please. I'm sorry. I—"

"Don't get involved with a man who is not Nigerian, who is not Edo." She speaks English now. "Azere, that was the last thing your father asked of you and the one thing I begged of you. And yet you did." She wipes away falling tears, and when her eyes clear, disappointment, shame, and disgust are evident in them. Those emotions are directed at me. "You are not the daughter I hoped for. If your father were alive, I am sure he would say the same."

Those words hit me like a knife, and I clench my chest, sustaining the pain rippling through me.

"Itohan!" my uncle protests her harsh words. "Be careful. Don't say anything you will regret."

"The only person who should have regrets is Azere." She bunches her long dress in her quivering hand and hastens to the door.

"Itohan!" My uncle trails after her and together, they leave the room.

Upon their exit, Rafael and Elijah enter.

"Azere," Rafael says, stepping to my bedside, "what's wrong?"

"Are you okay?" Elijah speaks next, also stepping to my side. "Your mom stormed out of here. What's going on?"

She didn't tell them. My mother left furious but quiet, and I am so grateful. This time, her hysterics were kept to a minimum—contained within the walls of this room. Next time, she won't be so gracious. All her anger will be directed at Rafael. Before that happens, I have to tell him the truth. He deserves to know.

"Everyone leave. Everyone but Rafael."

They don't move. They're all standing still, eyes set on me.

"Efe. Jacob. Elijah. Get out. Now."

My sister resists, but Jacob pulls her out. Hesitantly, Elijah follows.

"Azere, what's going on?" Rafael asks. "What did the doctor say?" Gradually, his complexion turns ashen. "Are you okay?"

"Rafael, I . . . I need to tell you something." My voice shakes as the truth works its way out the confines of my dry mouth. "Remember the night we first got together?"

"Yeah. What about it?"

"Well, um . . . I . . ."

"You're what, Azere? What's going on? You're scaring me."

"Rafael." I grip the sheet underneath my body. "Because of that night, I'm pregnant. With your child."

chapter
23

Rafael

What the fuck?

Azere's confession is still ringing in my ears, but it hasn't settled in my head because it's far too absurd.

I stand from the chair I've been sitting in, and she sniffs and wipes her wet eyes.

She cried after revealing the news and continued as I staggered into the chair. I remained seated for a few minutes, totally dumbfounded and unable to speak or look at her. Still, nothing has changed. I can't talk to her and can barely look at her. Within minutes, everything between us has changed, and it's all too much. I'm battling disbelief and confusion and outright shock.

I need to get out of here.

I head for the door, and on the verge of wrenching it open, her voice trembles and breaks around my name. I halt, and my forehead falls on the closed door.

"I don't understand. We used protection, Azere."

"Well, it didn't work." She sighs. "It's yours, Rafael. I swear. I haven't been with anyone else since."

It's strange that I believe her instantly. Her confession is no longer ringing in my ears, but settling in my head as truth, and I have questions.

"When did you find out you were pregnant?"

In a shaky voice, she explains. As she speaks, an unexpected emotion crops up. Anger. I spin around, scowling.

"You've known for over a week and you said nothing!"

How could she do something like that? We spent the night together. We were intimate in more ways than one, and she kept a secret of that magnitude from me.

"Why didn't you tell me last night?"

"Because . . . because I thought you wouldn't want this. I thought it would be too much for you."

"Well, you thought wrong, Azere."

"Did I? Do you really want a kid you never planned?"

Seconds pass, and I don't reply. The answer is on the tip of my tongue, but for some reason, perhaps fear, it doesn't fall.

"Listen," she says. "I've already decided. I'm keeping it. I want it." She shuts her eyes, pushing back tears. "I won't ask you to make the same decision or take on the same responsibility. You can walk away . . . if . . . if that's what you want. I'll understand. You didn't ask for any of this. It was supposed to be a one-night stand—no strings attached. But then this happened."

"Exactly. This happened. And I'm not just going to walk away." I'm vocal again, expressing my intentions regardless of fear. "Azere, there's no way in hell I'm walking away from you or my . . ." I clear my throat. I clench my jaw. Tears gather underneath my eyelids, making them heavy. I look at her and look away. "My child." *My child*. The words rattle something deep inside me, and my knees go weak. I stumble backward, into the chair I sat in minutes ago. My shuddering hands come over my eyes and tears pool in them.

"Rafael." She shuffles off the bed and rushes to me. "I know it's a lot." She squats at my feet. Her hands move over my legs, up and down, attempting to soothe me. "And I'm sorry I didn't tell you. I'm so sorry. I was scared. I was so scared and confused. But you're right. I should have told you sooner."

She believes I'm upset because of the secret she kept, but there's so much more to it. Maybe I should explain that to her. But what will she think of me once she learns about my past? Will she consider me broken, damaged, irredeemable? Will she still want me? I don't know, but I can't risk losing her. She means too much to me, so I'll bear the baggage of my past silently—like I always have—and build something new with her.

"Azere." I rub my face, ridding it of tears. "I'm just a little overwhelmed." I look down at her, eyes bearing more worry than they should in her state. "But I'm supposed to be strong. For you."

"We can take turns," she says. "Next time, it's my turn to have a breakdown. You can be strong for me then."

"Okay." I nod, smiling. "Deal."

"Rafael." She searches my eyes. "Are you all right?"

"Come here." I take her hands and jerk her toward my legs. "Sit."

She settles in. Her small frame curves against mine, and her ear rests over my beating heart as if she needs proof I'm breathing, that I'm okay.

"Azere, I'm scared," I admit. "Scared out of my mind."

"Me too, Rafael."

"This is crazy."

"Insane."

"Zere, I'm not walking away."

She lifts her head and looks at me. "I don't want you to." She exhales as if relieved by her admission. Again, her ear finds the spot on my chest where my heart thumps the loudest.

We sit like this for a long while, my arms keeping her secure, her presence soothing my angst.

"Rafael," she whispers. "Last night, when you said more, you didn't have this in mind. This is a lot."

"Yeah. It is." It's more than I could have ever imagined, but there's a joy that emerges when my hand falls on Azere's stomach. "We'll get through this," I assure her. "Together."

"Yeah." Her hand comes over mine. "Together."

chapter
24

It's Sunday, a day after the disclosure of my pregnancy. I'm at my mom's house. My uncle has summoned everyone for a family meeting, including Rafael. He's sitting beside me, holding my hand under the dining table.

"Are you okay?" he asks.

"Yeah." I'm not. My family are a panel of judges, and I'm awaiting their judgment. What will it be? Will my mother disown me? Will my uncle strangle Rafael? He's shooting him a baleful glance that indicates he might. This is a disaster. I emit a burst of air, and my back slacks, leaning into the chair.

Dinner—salad, baked chicken, *jollof* rice, and fried plantain—is on the table. Opposite Rafael and me, Jacob and Efe sit side by side. My uncle is at the head of the table, glowering at the space across from him where my mother should be. We've been waiting for her to appear for ten minutes. The wait has been long and unnerving.

"I'll go see what's keeping her," Efe says, pushing her chair back. As she stands, the rubber soles of slippers tip-tap toward the dining room, signaling my mother's approach. "I guess she's coming." Efe attempts to retake her seat but pauses midair and gawks. "Shit," she murmurs.

My stare trails hers, and my stomach drops at the sight of my mother.

Oh my God.

I know she's angry, but how could she go this far? She's wearing a black *buba* and wrapper, the same traditional attire she wore to mourn my father.

For six months after his death, she wore these clothes—put them on every day like they were her uniform. We weren't permitted to laugh briefly or live momentarily without the reminder of our loss. Even as we prepared to leave Nigeria, she packed variations of black clothes in her suitcase because it was what our tradition demanded of a widow—to never forget, to honor her husband in the most tragic form, to wear her misery like it was her sole identity.

When she finally wore colors, the burden of our loss became lighter. Now, looking at my mother, dressed in black, the weight of my father's death comes back like a hammer to my head. Past pain resurfaces and I lose my breath.

"It's okay," Rafael whispers into my ear. "Breathe, Zere. Breathe."

His hand draws circles on my back, and I meet his stare and slowly catch my breath.

"There you go." He kisses my forehead. "You're okay."

"Itohan!" my uncle says, lunging to his feet. "What is the meaning of this?"

"Ah-ahn. What do you mean?" She's acting coy, like she's done nothing wrong.

"Itohan, why are you dressed like this?"

"Isn't it obvious? I am in mourning, of course."

"Mourning?" He's probing for a response I don't want to hear.

"I am mourning my daughter. Azere." Her voice is hard and cold, not even a hint of emotion to humanize it. "As of yesterday, she is dead to me."

I turn to her and speak Edo, asking why she's doing this.

"Because you are a disappointment, Azere," she responds in English, and I'm sure it's because she wants Rafael to hear every insult she throws at me. "I am ashamed of you. You are not the daughter I raised."

"Mommy, I understand you're angry and disappointed. I totally get it. But how could you go so far? How could you wear those clothes, the same clothes you used to mourn Baba?" I rub my teary eyes. "You knew what that would do to me."

"And you knew what this"—she gestures at Rafael—"would do to me. If you cannot take my feelings into consideration, why should I take yours?"

And that's all I can tolerate. "Okay," I say, standing. "We're leaving." I nudge Rafael, and he stands as well.

"Azere." My uncle turns to me. "Sit down."

"Uncle, no. I can't do this. We're leaving."

"Sit! Now!"

His thunderous voice makes me squeal. Quickly, I retake my seat, and Rafael does the same.

"Itohan." He turns to my mother, and his forehead creases, skin folding and overlapping as he scowls. "Change your clothes into something appropriate and rejoin us."

She opens her mouth to protest, but words don't come out. Perhaps the resolve in my uncle's eyes has rendered her mute.

"Go and change, Itohan. Right now. I do not want to repeat myself."

Her exit isn't delayed.

In her absence, no one speaks. Minutes later, when she reappears, it's in a colorful short-sleeved dress made of *ankara*. She enters the dining room and sits in the chair opposite my uncle. Still, no one speaks or attempts to eat the food spread out.

"Well, I've lost my appetite," my uncle says. "Anyone still willing to eat?"

Silence.

"Well, then. Efe, please clear the table."

My sister stands and gathers bowls and cutlery. Jacob assists her, and they take the food into the kitchen.

"Let's get straight to this matter." My uncle clears his throat. "Rafael, in Nigeria, when a situation such as this occurs, both families come together to discuss a solution. I'm disappointed neither one of your parents could make it to this meeting."

"My family is currently in Europe, sir."

"I expect to meet them when they return."

"Yes. Of course. Absolutely."

"All right." My uncle traces the goatee that frames his lips. "Now, as we all know, Azere is pregnant. How does this news strike you, Rafael? What has been your reaction?"

"It was a shock. It was a complete shock. But . . . um . . ."

"But what?" Tonight, my uncle has no patience, and I'm sure that's partially due to my mother. "Listen, Rafael. These children, Azere and Efe, are not my nieces. They are my daughters. Their father left them in my care, and they are my responsibility. I will do anything for them. I will die for them. And please believe I will kill for them."

Where the hell did that come from? My uncle isn't a violent person. Though, he has been giving Rafael a look that's contrary to his nature. Must be an intimidation tactic.

"So, Rafael," he continues, "when I ask you a question concerning my daughter, be blunt with me." His voice is harsh as he demands clarification. "What exactly do you want? Make your intentions transparent to me and my family."

Efe and Jacob enter the dining room and take their seats.

"Well." Rafael's eyes move around the table, meeting my mother's eyes and Jacob's and Efe's and, finally, my uncle's. "I care about Azere very much, sir." He squeezes my hand. "She's brilliant, passionate, stubborn, gentle, kind. I could tell you all the reasons why I adore her, but I guarantee you, we'd be here all night.

"Yes, this pregnancy was a complete surprise, but I want it. I want our child. I want to be with Azere. We didn't plan for this, but we can't plan every aspect of our lives. Can we? We just have to deal with the unexpected and hope for the best."

"And this, her pregnancy, is your definition of the best?"

Rafael turns to me. "I know it might not seem like it right now, considering the circumstances. But one day, this child will be a source of joy rather than a source of concern and anger and frustration."

I can't wait for that day.

"Damn," Efe says, sniffing. "That was so sweet." She wipes her wet cheeks and snorts.

Jacob brings his arm around her shoulders and comforts her.

"I'm sorry." She cries into his shirt. "Carry on, Rafael. Keep on talking."

"Yes, *o*. Keep on talking. Carry on with this stupidity," my mother snaps. She hasn't spoken in a while. I thought, maybe, she was listening to Rafael and reconsidering her stance. No such luck. "I, for one, will not take part in this rubbish." She stands and marches out of the dining room.

"Mom." I try to go after her, but Rafael holds my wrist. "I have to talk to her."

"I'll come with you," he says, standing. "We'll do it together."

"No. Stay." I push his shoulder down, forcing him to sit back down. "I have to do this alone. But I'll be okay, Rafael. Promise."

Gradually, his hold slacks. "Okay."

"You two." I look at Efe and Jacob. "Be nice to him."

"You don't have to worry about me," my sister says. "He's already won me over. Now, go." She flicks her hand, shooing me away. "Talk to Mom. I'm sure she's got lots to say."

That's exactly what I'm afraid of.

chapter
25

In the kitchen, my mom stares through the window. The ocher shades of dusk bleed through the blinds, painting the white tiles with an orangey glow.

"Mom."

She says nothing. Seconds pass, and she doesn't respond or turn to me.

"Mommy." I run a hand over the granite countertop; the cold surface sends a shiver through me. "Please look at me. *Lahǫ.*"

"When your uncle said he would bring us to Canada, your father was happy. He could die peacefully, knowing we would be taken care of. But even so, he was scared." Finally, she turns around. "Your father was an intelligent man. He knew Canada was a world apart from ours. He was scared you and your sister would become so integrated in its ways, you would forget our ways.

"He was scared our culture and heritage would become diluted and you would lose yourself. And maybe in a sense, lose him. That was why he asked you to make that promise. A promise you have broken."

"I'm sorry, Mom." Guilt weighs my eyes down. "I'm so sorry."

For a long while, it's silent. My mother paces around the kitchen then stops abruptly. "Do you want to be with him?" she asks. "Do you want to be with Rafael?"

I'm afraid to answer.

"Azere, do you want to be with him? Speak."

"Yes," I whisper. "I do."

"*Nawa o.*" She shakes her head. "At least Efe has the good sense to date a man who is Edo."

She's referring to Mike, my sister's best friend who also doubles as a mock boyfriend. I won't expose Efe's ruse. I'll just endure my mother's rebuke.

"Meanwhile, you want to be with an *oyinbo.*" She clenches her jaw, her features hardening. "Azere, you are slowly losing yourself in this country—forgetting your culture. It's a huge shame."

"But Mom, do you think it was easy to move here—to fit in without losing some aspect of our culture?"

"Azere, please. Just stop all that nonsense." She flicks her eyes over my frame—up and down—then hisses. "Are you the only person who immigrated to this country? Didn't I also come? Didn't I also go to school here? Didn't I also build a career and a life here?"

"It isn't the same thing, Mom. You were older. You went to an adult learning center where most of the students were just like you—Nigerian immigrants. When you went to university, most of those people were with you—in the same program." She was constantly surrounded by people who shared the same experiences as her. I didn't have that. "Mom, it was far more difficult for me."

"Azere, I am not blind. I know the culture here is different, but you accept that challenge and remember who you are, where you come from. It is very possible to do just that. So, please. For God's sake, don't tell me all that rubbish. I don't want to hear it."

She never did understand or care to understand what it was like for Efe and me to move to Canada. Efe was ten. I was twelve. In Nigeria, I had already established a clear understanding of who I was. There was never any question or doubt until I moved to Canada.

When I first entered my sixth-grade class, at a school where the majority were Caucasians, the difference between myself and my peers became apparent. There was a clear definition of normal, and I didn't fit it. The kids wore T-shirts, jeans, and sneakers. I wore my favorite dashiki dress and brown strappy sandals. The kids spoke fast; their Canadian accent and slang made me feel inferior. At lunch, they ate sandwiches cut in neat triangles. My lunch of yam pottage made eyebrows raise and noses scrunch. The kids were cruel. And the only way to stop their cruelty was to conform. It was a survival mechanism—alter the way I speak, so I don't stand out; ask for a turkey sandwich for lunch, so the smell of Nigerian food doesn't attract attention and notify people of my difference; wear Levi's jeans and an American Apparel T-shirt, so I fit in with the group of girls who are finally starting to like me.

My mother didn't understand the struggle of trying to reconcile my heritage with my new environment at such a young age. She didn't understand I had to survive middle school and high school, not as a Nigerian but as a Canadian. To her, I compromised and lost parts of my identity. To myself, I made room in my life for two distinct worlds. I redefined myself—created a new identity. And my mother resents me for that.

"Azere, you came to this country a Nigerian. Thirteen years later, you are barely that. What do you think will happen when you date or even marry a man who isn't Nigerian? Will you lose more of your culture? Will you still know who you are, where you come from?"

I don't speak because I don't know the answer. *What will*

happen if I date a man who isn't Nigerian? I ponder, and silence hangs in the tense atmosphere.

"Azere, you can't be with him. You cannot be with that man."

"Mom, Rafael is a good man."

"Elijah is better. And he cares about you. Despite the news of your pregnancy, he still wants to be with you. He told me so yesterday."

"Wait. What?" I'm trying to make sense of her words. "Elijah . . ."

"Still wants to be with you, Azere. So, end things with Rafael."

"I'm pregnant with his child, Mom."

"And so? We'll tell everyone the baby is Elijah's. Hopefully, it won't be too fair. But if it is, we'll say we have a half-caste in our family and the child took its likeness."

It's a disgusting, deceitful scheme, and I consider agreeing to it just to please her. I would do anything to please her. I would do anything, anything but this.

"No." I shake my head vigorously. "No, Mom," I say it firmly. "That's insane. I'm not doing it."

"Azere, think about this carefully. Consider it."

"There's nothing to consider. I'm going to be with Rafael, and we're going to raise our child. Together."

"Azere—"

"Mommy, I care about him. And I swear, I didn't mean to. It just happened. And if I could, I would get rid of those feelings." I would pluck them out of my system like splinters from my skin. "But I can't. And I'm sorry I've disappointed you. Mommy, I am so sorry. But I've made my decision. And it's Rafael. I choose him."

"You choose him." She lifts her chin and looks down at me. The disdain in her dark eyes is so vile, she almost doesn't look like my mother. "You imagine a future with him. Okay. Fine. But ask yourself this: How much more of yourself, of your culture will you lose to accommodate him in your life?"

The question has more weight than I expect; it sinks deep into my mind like a rock sinks into water.

How much more of yourself, of your culture will you lose to accommodate him in your life?

"Answer, Azere."

"I . . . I . . . gotta go." I attempt to march off, but she snatches my arm.

"Azere, I will only say this once. If you don't do as I have asked, I am no longer your mother. And you are not my daughter. Do you understand?"

"Mommy, please. Please. Don't do this. I'm pregnant. With your grandchild. I need you—more than ever."

"If you are with that man, then I cannot have anything to do with you. I cannot be your mother, Azere. I won't."

I knew it would eventually come to this—to her disowning me. But I still wasn't prepared for the gut-wrenching feeling.

I'm doing the right thing. I must believe that even though I'll no longer have a mother who claims me as hers. *I'll no longer have a mom.* That truth hits me hard, and tears gather at the rims of my eyes. *I'm doing the right thing.* "Okay." I blink back the tears and nod. "Fine. If that's what you want, then . . . then okay."

Slowly, she releases her grip. I walk ahead, toward the kitchen door, but something stops me. Maybe it's the rebellion that caused me to reject my mother's request or maybe it's the anger and bitterness of hearing her deceitful scheme. Maybe it's a combination of all three elements—rebellion, anger, bitterness— twisting inside of me like a slowly ascending tornado. Whatever it is, it makes me spin around and glare at her.

"By the way, Elijah, the good Christian man you want me to marry, took my virginity at church camp."

Her eyes bulge and her jaw drops. The exact reaction I was hoping for.

"Yep. We had sex in a tent in the woods. It's ironic because it was right after your session on abstinence."

My mother's face morphs into a combination of rage and disbelief. I expect her to say something, but she doesn't. She's speechless.

But I'm glad that for once, I wasn't.

chapter
26

At home, I soak in the bath Rafael prepared for me. I'm not sure what possessed him to fill the freestanding tub with warm water, bath oils, and a lavender-scented bubble bath. As I sat on the couch, staring into space and recalling the conversation with my mom, he was doing this. He knew exactly what I needed, and I didn't have to ask.

"How are you doing?" he says, poking his head through the door.

"Good."

"Are you sure?" He steps into the bathroom. "Do you need anything?"

"No. This is perfect." I especially like the mountain of bubbles that puff above water level and stop at my shoulders. "Thank you." I want to show gratitude by smiling, but my lips are fixed in a firm line.

"Do you want to tell me what happened with your mom?" He walks to the tub and hovers over me. During the ride home, he didn't ask what had happened, clearly understanding I wasn't ready to talk. Now though, his curiosity is at its peak. He bends down, kneeling on the checkered tiles so his eyes are level with mine. "You can tell me, Azere."

But I can't, because I am ashamed of my mother, ashamed of the things she said. I can never repeat them to him. I'll offer another explanation—one that's the truth but not so harsh on the ears.

"Rafael, it's just that she wants me to be with a Nigerian man—marry him, have his children."

"And that's why I'm a complication. Isn't it? That's the reason you fought being with me. Because I'm not Nigerian."

"Yeah."

"Your mom wants you to be with a Nigerian man. Like Elijah."

I nod.

"Yesterday, I saw the way he looked at you."

"There's nothing between Elijah and me—not anymore. I promise." My hand emerges from the water, breaking through the mold of foam. "You have nothing to worry about, Rafael." I take his hand and bring it to my lips. Gently, I plant kisses on his palm. "I want to be with you."

He's relieved by my admission. His crinkled brows lose their stiffness, and his breath relaxes.

"Rafael." I clear my throat, making way for the awkward question I'm about to ask. "Have you ever dated a black girl?"

"Yeah. I have."

"And your parents, your family were okay with it?"

"Yeah. Of course. As long as I'm happy, they are too."

It's unfortunate my mother doesn't share a similar notion.

We're quiet for a while. When the tension elevates, I reach for the buttons on his shirt and undo them. "Get in," I say.

"Sorry to disappoint." He smiles faintly. "But I won't fit."

"Oh." I examine the length of the tub. He's right. The ceramic basin won't contain his tall stature.

I sulk until an abrupt series of bangs at the front door reminds me of the takeout Rafael ordered an hour ago. Considering dinner was opted out of tonight's gathering, I'm starving.

"I'll get the door." He presses his lips to mine, a brief kiss before standing. "You get dressed." He grabs a towel off the rack, hands it to me, then leaves the bathroom.

On the couch, after eating three slices of pizza and a Caesar salad, my head falls on Rafael's lap. It's a few minutes short of midnight, a few minutes short of the end of May and the start of a new month. I'm drained, but something keeps me from sleeping—curiosity, the need to know more about the father of my unborn child, the man who I chose over my mother and father.

"Rafael." I'm drowsy, barely holding on to consciousness. "What kind of movies do you like? Please don't say"—a yawn cuts off my sentence—"sci-fi."

"No, I don't like sci-fi."

Thank God. "What's your favorite movie?"

"You're tired, Azere. Get some rest. You can ask me all the questions you want later."

"Okay."

I doze off quickly and settle deep in my subconscious. I dream about everything—dying fathers and wailing mothers, wedding bells and screaming babies, snow and blood, red sand and cinders, love and regret. It's not a peaceful sleep, as my fears and desires manifest as one twisted, bittersweet dream. When my eyes open and his signature scent fills my nose, I'm grateful for where I am and who I'm with.

"Rafael, will you stay the night?"

"Yeah. Of course."

"Wait." My head snaps up. "What about Milo?"

"He's with Jenny, the dog walker and sometimes sitter. I wasn't sure how today would play out, so I made arrangements in case you needed me."

"That was really sweet of you." I throw my arms around his neck, locking him in a tight embrace. "Thank you." I pull back and watch him, study his eyes. "You're a good man, Rafael." A smile ticks at the corners of my lips, but the thought of my mother stops it from spreading. "I wish my mom could see that. I wish she would give you a chance."

"Give her time, Zere. She'll come around."

I highly doubt it. Tonight, I went against my mother's command. It almost felt like going against my nature. I suppose it would after so many years of being compliant.

In Nigeria, my sister and I were raised to obey our elders. While Efe rebelled, I stayed in line. I tried to set the example. I tried to make our parents proud by any means. I was the obedient daughter when my father asked me to make a promise I didn't quite understand. I was the obedient daughter when my mother perpetuated that promise and forced me into multiple unsuitable relationships.

In the movie *Ella Enchanted*, Ella's fairy godmother bestows upon her the gift of obedience. But the gift is more like a curse, especially when Ella is ordered to kill the man she loves. Faced with such a dilemma, Ella finds the strength to free herself from the curse and to be disobedient for the first time in her life. As a result, she saves herself, saves the man she loves, and secures her happily ever after.

Will the moment of rebellion I experienced tonight set me on the same path to a happily ever after? I don't have the answer, but looking at Rafael, I'm hopeful. And when his lips caress mine, I ignore my mother's nagging, disapproving voice that's resonating in my head and focus completely on Rafael.

chapter
27

Rafael

It's hard not to ogle Azere when she struts around in those heels, commanding the attention of every single person in the conference room.

Today, we're having a meeting with the team working on the FeverRun campaign. All eight of them—copywriters, graphic designers, web developers, and artists—sit around the table that's piled with papers, tablets, laptops, and cups of coffee. One after the other, they direct questions at Azere, seeking her opinion and waiting for her direction. She doesn't delay any of her responses. She answers questions quickly, gives orders and deadlines, and explains to each member of the team what she expects of them. The confidence she's projecting is incredibly sexy. I'm tempted to pull her on my legs and kiss her. I push the distracting thought aside and refocus on the meeting. Though, my attention veers off again when I notice my colleagues' stares darting between Azere and me.

Earlier this week, when we told HR about our relationship and our status as expecting parents, we knew the news would circulate gradually, finding its way into everyone's ears until accuracy was lost, the truth distorted to suit each's own outlook. There were questions—some voiced with an air of humor and others expressed with squinting, shifting gazes. Nick from production took the former.

"Damn. You move fast, man," he said yesterday morning as I filled my cup with coffee in the kitchen. "You didn't just get booed up. You practically became a family man." He laughed, then frowned, smacking his lips as if he suddenly gained an intolerance for the taste of his laughter.

"You know, I asked her out once. Well, I wanted to but . . ." He dropped his head and shrugged. "She probably would have said no anyway. Arianna told me she's only into black guys, but . . ." He raised his head and gave me a once-over. "How the hell did you two happen? How did you manage to—"

Annoyed, I walked away before he could complete the sentence.

"When do you think it will all stop?" Azere asks after the conference room clears out, leaving only the two of us. "I just want things to go back to normal."

"It will," I assure her. "Just give it some time—a couple more days. Everyone will get bored and start talking about something else."

She nods, but the wrinkle between her brows proves she isn't convinced. Since the fallout with her mother a month ago, work has been her anchor to normalcy. It isn't anymore, and I feel responsible for that. I insisted we tell HR about us, and she agreed, despite being hesitant. She wanted to keep our budding relationship safe, nurturing it within the confines of our homes, allowing no additional negativity to stunt its growth. The attention from our colleagues seems to pose the threat she feared.

"Azere." I walk to her, reducing the distance between us and caring very little about the audience beyond the glass walls. "Don't let this bother you. Things will get better." I take her hand in mine. "I promise. Okay?"

She bobs her head slowly and then briskly as if suddenly gaining more confidence in my words. "Yeah. Okay. It has to."

"It will."

She exhales, expelling all the tension in her body and relaxing her posture. "So." There's a liveliness in her eyes that wasn't there seconds ago. "Are you still making me dinner tonight?"

"Of course."

"Want me to bring anything?"

"Just an appetite." I lean into her, my eyes on her lips. "You know, I really want to kiss you right now."

"Unfortunately, that can't happen." She looks through the glass. "Don't wanna give them something else to talk about. So, save that kiss for later." She steps back and moves toward the door, her laptop pressed to her chest. "See ya."

"By the way," I say before she leaves, "the meeting went well. Despite all the staring, you did an incredible job managing the team. You were brilliant, Azere. As usual."

Her brows bend slightly as she considers me.

Did I say something wrong? While reassessing my words and tone, she shrugs and marches to me.

"Oh, screw it. They're already talking, so to hell with it." She wraps an arm around my neck and plants her plush lips firmly on mine.

Shock grips me, tensing my shoulders, but then another emotion takes over, heating my insides and loosening my lips. My tongue strokes hers. I love the sensation. I savor her taste, crave more of it, and then she pulls away unexpectedly, shocking me again.

"I'll see you later." A coy smile lifts one corner of her lips.

"We'll continue this then." She steps through the door and struts to her office, ignoring our colleagues who undoubtedly caught the brazen display of affection.

It takes a moment for my heart to fall back to its routine rhythm, for my mind to be centered again, for reality to become more vivid. Reality fades when Azere kisses me and touches me and I do the same to her. Emotions disorient me, temporarily preventing me from seeing what we have, in such a short time, become—a couple expecting a child.

I'm going to be a father.

The news stunned my family more than it did me, especially since they believed I wasn't dating. Frankly, I had no intention to date. I was minding my business in a hotel lounge when I saw Azere drinking alone at a bar. Her mere presence highlighted all the inadequacies in my life and made me utterly aware of the loneliness I had forced myself to grow comfortable with. There was a clear definition of happiness I had boxed away. Azere made me want to open that box and reclaim all the contents within it. When I explained this to my family via Skype, omitting the one-night stand, their expressions altered from shock to a mixture of happiness and relief—relief that I had a fresh eagerness for life, that I was gradually reverting to the man I used to be. Though, even with their relief, they were concerned the relationship was moving too fast.

It's a rational concern. In such a short time, so much has happened. Azere and I have become so close, so dependent on each other. Most nights, we fall asleep in the same bed. We share meals, laugh together, exist in such proximity, it's as if our individualities are merging to form one idea—a family. That's what we are—me, her, Milo, and our unborn child, who I already love more than words can express.

A family.

Things *have* moved fast. However, I'm confident that no matter what path Azere and I took—whether we first met at Xander
or bumped into each other on the street, whether we dated for
months or years—we would have eventually ended up just as we
are, a couple expecting a child.

There's nothing to support this. It's just a feeling, an un-
founded certainty I have grown to rely on.

chapter
28

My reaction is always the same.

The elevator that leads to Rafael's penthouse slides open, and my eyes expand as blue skies and the harbor come into view through the large windows that wrap around the open-concept living space. I've stayed here a few times now, but I still gape with fresh interest.

Clinging to the duffel bag in my hand, I step out of the elevator and look from the elegant sitting room to the sleek, modern kitchen where Rafael's chopping bell peppers with the swift precision of a culinary mastermind.

When he looks up and sees me, he smiles. "*Mi cariño.*"

Perplexed, I frown. "What does that mean?"

He wipes his hand and extends it to me. "It means my darling."

"Oh." The term of endearment hits me in all the right places. "I like it." I take his hand, grip it tightly, press it to my chest. Does he feel it—my heartbeat quickening? Does he understand he's the reason?

"You look beautiful."

I assess my attire. "Really? I'm in leggings and a T-shirt and my hair is—"

"I stand by my statement, Azere." He inches to my lips, observing my expression before finally kissing me.

It's here again—that feeling, the one that tingles my insides and makes me less aware of everything else and utterly enthralled by him. Will it ever go away? Will time eventually dilute it, make it less potent? I'm scared of what will happen then. Will I still stand by my choice when the sweetest phase of our relationship—the newness and awe—becomes dulled by routine and the consequences of choosing him are no longer possible to ignore? And in that case, will I still consider him the right choice or a mistake? It's a lot to consider—too much to consider right now, so I don't.

"Dinner smells amazing," I say when his lips leave mine. "What are you—"

Movement against my ankles causes me to look down.

"Milo!" I crouch and pet the toy fox terrier. "Hey, buddy." He wags his tail as I stroke his neck.

"I think he loves you more than he does me," Rafael says, looking down at us.

"Oh. I'm certain he does. Don't you, Milo?"

Right on cue, the dog barks as if voicing his agreement or disagreement. Though, I hear what I want to hear.

"You see? Told you he loves me more."

Rather than disputing my interpretation, Rafael laughs until a frown pinches his lips downward. "Is that your overnight bag?"

"Um . . ." I glance at the bag beside my feet that's crammed with clothes and toiletries. "Yeah."

"So, come tomorrow, you'll pack all your things in there again?"

"Yeah. Like I always do. What's the problem?"

"It's just that I . . ." He shakes his head and turns away. "Forget it. Dinner will be ready in a few minutes." His attention returns to the chopped peppers; he tosses them into a salad bowl along with cucumbers and tomatoes and then drizzles olive oil over the colorful assortment of fruits and vegetables.

"Rafael." I stand, depriving Milo of a belly rub. "What's going on? What's on your mind?"

"We can talk about it after dinner, Azere."

"I'd rather we talk now." I stand in front of the oven and prevent him from reaching the handle. "What's wrong?"

He dishevels his hair and huffs. "It's that overnight bag, Azere. I've told you, you don't have to lug it around like baggage every time you stay over. You can leave your things here. I'll give you a closet if you want."

"That isn't necessary, Rafael."

"Of course it is. You're not some random girl who's in and out of my life. You're my girlfriend. You're going to be the mother of my child. Azere, you have a place in my life and in my home. That bag makes me feel you're not totally settled with me—like you don't want to root yourself in my life."

"Rafael, that isn't true."

"Then stop with the bag, Azere. This place is big enough for us." His hand falls on my slightly protruded stomach. "For the three of us. Move in with me, Azere."

Shocked, I flinch and take an unsteady step back, away from him. I look at the space I've created and then at his confused eyes that are trying to interpret my reaction. "Rafael, um . . . moving in together is a big step."

"And so is having a baby. Things between us are already moving at an unconventionally fast pace, so why not? We already spend so much time together—at your place, at mine." He takes a step toward me. "Azere, I care about you, and we're having a baby. I want us to raise our child under one roof—together. As a family."

A lukewarm smile touches his lips, an imploring one that doesn't compare to when he really smiles and his dimples deepen and his eyes glint. "So? What do you think? Will you move in?"

The answer is heavy on my tongue, making it difficult to voice what is, in fact, a refusal. "Rafael, um . . . I—"

Just as I conjure the words and the nerve, his phone on the countertop rings, cutting off my sentence. I'm more than grateful for the interruption. With any luck, I'll have a moment to weave together an answer that lacks the sting of rejection. If that's possible.

"Your phone, Rafael." I nudge my head toward the device. "You should get it."

"Azere, we're in the middle of something."

"What if it's an important call?"

After considering what I've said, he grabs the phone and looks at the screen. "It's just my sister. I told her you were coming over, and she mentioned calling. She wants to talk to you—say hi. But we can do that another time."

"No. Let's do it now." I haven't spoken to any member of his family. Maybe the connection I make with them will prove that I am fixed in his life, that I'm not going anywhere. "I'd like to say hi to her. It's about time we got acquainted."

Reluctantly, he answers the call. "Hi, Selena." He listens then nods. "Yeah. She's right here. Hold on." He extends the phone to me. "Just a warning, she can be a lot."

I take the phone and clear my throat. "Hi, Selena. It's Azere."

"Tell him I heard that." She laughs, clearly not bothered by her brother's assessment.

The conversation between Selena and me is casual and pleasant, a brief introduction that lasts two minutes and ends with her promising to come to Toronto before the birth of the baby. I hand the phone to Rafael just as mine rings. When I pull it out of my purse and look at the screen, my chest tightens.

Elijah.

The last time I spoke to him was in the hospital, when he and my family discovered the truth. Since then, he's called a few times, but I haven't answered. He wants to be with me—my mother said so herself. Maybe that's why he's calling—to tell me himself, to convince me to end things with Rafael. The phone is still ringing in my hand, still presenting me with two options—accept or reject. I surprise myself by sliding a finger across the screen and holding the device to my ear.

"Hello?"

"Azere! Finally!" He releases a loud huff, and it's not a melodramatic act meant to imitate relief, but the real thing. I note the way strain steadily eases from his voice until his pitch reverts to its normal state. "I've been trying to reach you. How are you?"

"Um . . ." Rafael is talking to his sister and pulling browned potatoes out of the oven. I walk to the terrace, slide the glass door open, and step out. "I'm fine, Elijah." Out here, his name means nothing—the sound of it, each syllable, is just another chord in the city's bustling chorus. It isn't singled out and taken into severe consideration like it would have been inside with Rafael at earshot. "How are you?"

"I'm fine, Azere. Though, I've been worried about you. I spoke to your mom, and she said—"

"Please, Elijah. I don't want to talk about my mom and the things she might have or might not have said to you."

The line grows silent. He breathes deep and heavy as if taking more effort than usual to accomplish the simple task. "Azere, why are you with him? Is it because you're pregnant?"

There's an appropriate reaction that should follow Elijah's questions—one that would comprise shouting and cursing. Considering the insensitive, intrusive, offensive inquiry, I am fully entitled to that reaction. Though, the impulse to backlash doesn't rise. Looking at the view beyond the iron railing—the lake snaking through glistening high-rises and sailboats drifting in the distance—I sigh and offer an answer free of spite.

"No, Elijah." Maybe this is what he needs to hear, so he can move on. "I am not with Rafael because I'm pregnant with his child. I'm with him because I care about him. Very much." I look through the glass door, into the penthouse where Rafael is setting the dining table. Our eyes connect and even with the tense conversation we were having minutes ago, he smiles—no anger or resentment straining the extent of his lips. "Elijah, I'm happy. Rafael makes me happy. That's why I'm with him."

He expels a long, brash breath as if something has popped and deflated inside him—hope, maybe.

I end the call and return inside where there is an appetizing spread of food on the table. "Rafael, this looks amazing." I bite my lip while gaping at the perfectly bronzed whole chicken. "Another of your grandmother's recipes?"

"Yeah." He unties the apron around his waist and places it on the kitchen counter. "You know, when I was a kid, my family would spend every summer with her in Spain." He walks toward the dining table, Milo trailing him. "It's funny because whenever she would make my siblings and I help her in the kitchen, Max and I would always throw a fit. We called it child labor." He chuckles at the memory. "But *Abuela* always said cooking was a labor of love." He looks at me, smiling, and pulls out a chair. "She was right."

We eat the delicious meal, laughing and discussing many things but the topic of living together. Later, on the couch, while he rubs Milo's ear, I babble about the movie *The Age of Adaline*.

"It's really good, Rafael. Trust me. Have I ever picked a movie you didn't like?"

"Um . . ." He considers briefly. "No. You haven't. And I was very skeptical about *Tangled*."

"But you loved it. Didn't you?"

He reclines into the couch and draws me over his chest. "I don't know what you're doing to me, Azere. But, yeah. I loved an animated movie specifically targeted at children."

"Relax. I won't tell anyone it's your favorite movie of all time." I clap my hand over my mouth, stifling a giggle. "I'll just keep it between us—don't want you getting picked on at the playground."

"Oh. You think you're funny, don't you?"

I shake my head, but a burst of laughter breaks through my lips. The sound becomes thicker and richer only because he's joined me.

Ten minutes into the movie, after our laughter has stopped, he looks down at me snuggled at his side and says, "Whenever you're ready, *cariño*."

And that's it. The conversation about living together doesn't extend past those four words. It's a relief. The sweetest phase of our relationship—the newness and awe—can still be preserved, safeguarded from being dulled by the routine of living together. And I know it's only temporary—this time when we are still learning about each other and obsessing over each other. Soon, the mist will fade, things will become clearer, the fact that my mother has disowned me will have a stronger sting, and the fact that I have broken a promise to my father will leave me guilt-ridden. Any day now, I'll feel the full effect of choosing Rafael. But I don't want to think so far ahead. I'll just relish this moment, even as it slips through my fingers like sand.

chapter
29

In most romantic movies, there's a montage that depicts a couple's progressing relationship with a series of heartwarming, tear-jerking, *aww*-worthy scenes. Usually playing along with this collection of scenes is a soundtrack, something upbeat or mellow but equally sentimental. In the montage that illustrates my last three months with Rafael, the song playing is "My Darlin'" by Tiwa Savage.

In this montage, Rafael and I are snuggled on the couch, snacks sprawled out on our legs while we watch a romantic movie. In the next scene, he's teaching me how to do the bolero, a traditional Spanish dance that's slow and sensual. I'm not very good at it, but he's a pro. We're cuddling in bed in the next scene, discovering and rediscovering each other. I tell him about my childhood, my village, my late father, and the promise I made. He tells me about his childhood too—his parents, his siblings, and his time in Spain. In the next scene, we see our baby for the first time via ultrasound. Our teary eyes connect and then our lips. In the next clip, we're at the office. It's the middle of the workday, and we're hiding out in the stairwell, making out like hormonal teenagers. He's made dinner in the next scene—gazpacho and chicken paella. I'm scarfing down the food because it tastes so damn good. He laughs because I've somehow managed to get soup in my hair and on my nose. In the last scene, we're making love over rumpled sheets. Right after, he holds me in his arms and whispers the sweetest things.

Of course, in most romantic movies, another scene follows the montage. In this scene, the bubble the love interests have been sheltered in tears slightly and reality slips through like a slow-acting poison, gradually destroying everything they thought was secure. In the movie *The Notebook*, it's when Allie takes Noah to meet her parents, and her parents—being wealthy and high-class—deem Noah unworthy of their daughter. In my case, it's when I'm at Pottery Barn shopping for the baby's nursery, and I realize I haven't spoken to my mother or seen her in three months. She should be here with me, shopping like the mother-daughter duo in the store who are laughing and picking out things together. The daughter, probably the same age as me, keeps asking her mother questions.

"Should I get this, Mom? Will the baby need this? Mom, how often will you visit when the baby comes?"

In my culture, after giving birth, a woman experiences the traditional postpartum care known as *omugwo*. During this period, the new mother gets pampered by her mother who moves in for a few months after the baby is born and handles all the household chores. The new mother is only allowed to feed the baby, relax, receive visitors, and sip lots of pepper soup. In my village, I witnessed many women experience this with their mothers. It's only just occurred to me that I won't have the same privilege. My mother won't be there for me in any capacity when I have this baby. As that hint of reality slips into the bubble I have been sheltered in, tears sting my dry eyes, and I release Rafael's hand.

"You okay, *cariño*?" He looks at the space I've created between our bodies and at me. Over the past months, he's learned my habits. In such a short time, he's become an expert on me. He can tell when something is wrong. "What is it?"

I miss my mom. Even after everything she said and did, I miss her. I'm ashamed to admit it, but I miss receiving her approval. For the first time in my life, I don't have it. I don't have my mom, and it's killing me. I should tell him this, but I can't. I don't want him to feel guilty or responsible for our falling-out.

"I like this one." I rush to a crib and run my fingers along the interior fabric. "It's beautiful," I say, attempting to avert his attention from me. "What do you think? Do you like it?"

"Um . . ." His stare stays on me before moving to the crib. "Yeah. Sure. Do you want it?"

"I'm not sure yet. Plus, Christina's coming. I want her opinion."

"Okay." He comes to my side and reclaims my hand. "Let's look around." He takes me through the store, stopping at cribs and dressers, asking the salesperson questions I never thought to ask. He's good at this baby stuff. He's been reading tons of books, conducting research online, and signing us up for prenatal classes. I didn't even know that was a thing.

As we inspect the features of a bassinet, the mention of Rafael's name makes our heads snap up. A white couple, likely in their late fifties, stand in front of us. They smile, and wrinkles rim their elated eyes.

"Rafael," the woman says. She pulls a lock of silver hair behind her ear, exposing the pearl necklace around her neck.

"Oh my God," Rafael says.

He smiles at the couple, but it isn't the routine gesture aimed at politeness. There is something else underlined in the stretch of his lackluster smile; I can't detect what it is. He releases my hand and leans into the woman for a hug. The moment is intimate, and during its duration, I don't exist in Rafael's world. When he finally pulls away from her, he turns to the man and offers a handshake that conveys its own hint of intimacy.

"It's so good to see you both," he says, withdrawing his hand. "What are you doing in Toronto?"

"Visiting friends," the woman answers. "We were walking down the street and saw you through the window display. We had to say hello."

"Yes," the man says, pushing his glasses to the bridge of his long nose, "it's been far too long."

"It has," Rafael agrees. "I . . . I've wanted to reach out. I just . . ."

"It's okay. Really. It's fine. We understand." The woman nods and finally notices me, standing in the background, twirling my braid futilely. "Oh," she says. "Hi."

Rafael follows her gaze, and by retaking my hand, he invites me back into his world. "This is Azere," he says. "Zere, this is John and Anna." He doesn't follow the introduction with an explanation of who they are.

"Hi." I extend my hand to each of them for a handshake. "Nice to meet you." When my withdrawn hand falls on my round stomach, a recently adopted reflex, Anna's eyes drop.

"Oh," she says, studying my body. She looks at Rafael, and though her lips are sealed, her tear-glossed eyes ask him a question he answers by nodding.

"Oh my God. That's amazing." Tears wet her cheeks, but she grins widely. "I'm so happy for you, Rafael. So happy."

"We both are," John adds, smiling. "Honey." He turns to Anna. "We should get going."

"Of course." She leans into Rafael, plants a kiss on his cheek, and steps back.

The couple say nothing else. Hand in hand, they walk past the arrangements of displayed furniture and through the exit.

Now, Rafael is quiet. He stares at the space they occupied as if they're still standing there. I don't want to interrupt any thoughts or emotions he might be working through, so I stand as I did moments ago—separate from his world.

When minutes pass, approximately two, he blinks sharply and continues to inspect the features on the bassinet. It's as though John and Anna never appeared.

"Rafael?" I examine him. "Are you okay?"

"I'm fine."

"Who were they—that couple?"

"Just family friends."

"Okay. Family friends. Do you want to elaborate on that?"

He says nothing.

"Do you expect me to act like that encounter was normal? That lady was crying, Rafael. Why? Who were they?"

"Azere, I already gave you an answer. There's nothing more to say."

"Hey." I touch his cheek and direct his face to mine. And there it is, in his eyes, that deep, eerie void I detected months ago. Some days, his eyes are lively and filled with so much joy, but occasionally, that void returns. And I'm reminded Rafael is haunted by some great pain he refuses to share with me. "Why won't you talk to me? You never talk to me."

"We're talking right now, Azere."

"You know what I mean, Rafael. Whenever I ask you about New York, you shut me out. You went to university there. You lived there and worked there for years, but you never talk about it." I stroke his cheek, the area where his sideburn meets his newly grown stubble. "Did something happen while you were there? You can tell me, Rafael. You can tell me anything."

"Azere." For a second, it looks like he's going to speak, going to tell a truth I've waited so long to hear. But then he turns from my touch and refocuses on the piece of furniture. "Nothing happened in New York. There's nothing to tell." He squints as if trying to prevent the truth from leaking out of his unconvincing eyes.

He's not the only one who's been paying attention. Over the past months, I've learned his habits as well. For example, whenever he lies to me, he squints. Like he's doing now, like he did when he pretended to love the awful chocolate cake I baked, and like he did last month when I found a picture of a woman in his home office.

He was taking a shower, and I was looking through some work documents and needed a pen. In his office, I opened a drawer and stuffed my hand under the layers of files. Rather than the length of a pen between my fingers, I held the cold rim of a picture frame. Curious, I pulled it out and there she was—an exceptional beauty with warm olive skin, rouge lips, emerald eyes, and wavy black hair. The image was stunning and far too perfect, so I assumed it had come with the frame. However, Rafael's reaction made me reconsider.

When he entered the office and saw me holding the silver frame, his entire persona changed. The muscles on his crimson face tightened. When he pulled the picture from my grip, his fingers shuddered. His voice swelled as he ranted about privacy and respecting boundaries. Hours later, after the confrontation, he came to me on the balcony. He apologized repeatedly. After offering my forgiveness, I inquired about the identity of the woman.

"No one," he said, squinting like he's doing now. "No one. She's no one."

Honestly, that was the moment reality slipped into the bubble I had been sheltered in—the moment I realized Rafael was keeping secrets.

"Hey, guys." I'm not sure when Christina arrived, but she's standing in front of Rafael and me. The tension between us must be apparent. "Sorry I'm late. I got caught up in something."

"It's fine," I say, my eyes fixed on Rafael. "We haven't started shopping because we got caught up in something too."

"Well . . ." Christina clears her throat. "Looks like y'all are still caught up in it." She takes a step back. "Maybe I should give you guys a minute . . . or five. Maybe even ten." She's still moving.

"No need," Rafael says. "I have to make a call." He pulls out his phone and marches off.

"Okay . . ." Christina comes to my side and joins me to watch his hasty exit. "What was that about? What just happened?" She drinks from the Starbucks cup in her hand, staining the white lid with purple lipstick, and looks at me expectantly. "Go on, Zere. Tell me."

After sucking in a deep breath and releasing it, I tell her about the encounter with John and Anna.

"Damn." She puffs and the scent of coffee escapes her mouth. "That's shady as hell. Why didn't he just tell you who they were? What's up with him?"

"Seriously, I don't know." I shrug. "Rafael isn't being honest with me. He's keeping something from me. I've given up so much for him. My mother has disowned me, and he can't even give me the truth." Tears prick my eyes. "It's the end of August, Chris. I haven't spoken to my mom in three months. Three. Months. I tried to reach out, but she blocked my number. Whenever I call, it doesn't go through. I even dropped by the house, and she wouldn't let me in."

"I thought your uncle was gonna talk to her."

"He did, and so did Efe and Jacob. They all talked to her, begged her. It didn't make a difference."

"Then give her time, Zere. Maybe when the baby's born, she'll come around. Babies have a way of bringing people together. Trust me." She takes my hand and squeezes it. "Have a little faith in your mom and in Rafael. Okay?"

"I don't trust him, Chris." I rub my frowning brows, pushing them to rest straight. "He's keeping things from me."

So many things. I think of last month when he had to visit Xander's New York branch. Initially, he wanted me to come along. Though, at the last minute, he changed his mind. When he came home a week later, he was different—distant. He hardly spoke to me or touched me. Something was terribly wrong, and he wouldn't tell me what.

"Azere, listen to me. Don't hassle Rafael about secrets. If he's keeping something, he'll tell you when he's ready. Everyone deals with things differently. Just give him some more time. Be a little patient."

I don't think that's possible, but I don't tell her that. "Sure. I'll be patient."

"Good girl. Now, let's build my godchild a nursery." She pulls me toward the direction of an oval-shaped crib. "Have you seen anything you like?"

"A few. But we're not buying anything today—just looking around."

"You know, you could get all this stuff for free if you let me throw you a baby shower."

"No baby shower, Chris. I already told you. I don't want one."

"But why not?"

"I just don't. Okay?" I face her, ensuring she sees the seriousness in my eyes.

"Okay. Fine. No baby shower."

The ride home with Rafael is quiet—no music from the radio, no words spoken. As he pulls up to my apartment building, he glances at me.

"Do you want me to stay?"

He's never asked before. He's always stayed, knowing his place was with me. Today, I suppose he's uncertain where we stand and so am I.

Rafael is keeping secrets. Where does that leave us? Where does that leave me? Do I hold on tighter, find ways to mend the cracks, or do I let go and let things fall apart?

chapter
30

I make a decision.

I don't let go. I strain myself, holding every piece together, patching what's broken with insincerity so things don't fall apart. I do it for my baby. I do it for Rafael. Because I care about him.

We don't talk about what happened in Pottery Barn almost two months ago. We bury it, suffocate it under the loads of other things we refuse to discuss. I act like everything is all right. It isn't. I don't tell him I miss my mother. I don't tell him about the guilt I feel for dishonoring my father. I don't tell him how much I distrust him. I act. I'm good at it.

"This won't take long," Rafael says as we ride in the elevator heading to his penthouse. "I just have to grab something, and then we'll be on our way."

We were meant to go from my apartment to a restaurant. His sister is in town, and we planned to meet her for lunch, but Rafael's detour to his place has put us fifteen minutes behind schedule.

"What exactly do you have to get anyway?" I turn to him, waiting for an answer and notice how rigid his posture suddenly is. "Rafael, are you okay?"

Just as I ask, the elevator stops on his floor. Though, the ping that usually sounds as the doors slide open becomes overpowered by a loud and abrupt eruption of the word *surprise*.

I flinch and grasp Rafael's arm. As my heart thumps, I turn to the crowd inside the penthouse and see the faces of my family, friends, and colleagues.

What the hell?

"Welcome to your baby shower!" Christina squeals and sprints to me, a toothy smile on her freckled face. "We got you, right? You didn't see this coming. You had no clue."

No. I had none whatsoever because I made it very clear to Christina that I didn't want a baby shower. Yet, here we are.

Rafael takes my hand and leads me out of the elevator. If he hadn't made the move, I would have remained inside, waiting for the doors to close.

"Azere!" Efe maneuvers past the people that surround me, Jacob behind her. "Uncle couldn't make it because something came up at work, but he sends his love and a really nice gift." She smiles and gestures to the living space that's bright with pastel colors. "So? What do you think? Do you love it?"

There are clusters of helium balloons at every corner, streamers and banners hanging from the high ceiling, a flower arch positioned at the balcony door, and towers of cupcakes and French macarons all with the pale, whimsical color scheme. The gender-neutral decoration is undeniably beautiful and perfect because Rafael and I have decided we want the sex of the baby to be a surprise. If I had wanted a shower, I would be ecstatic right now, but that isn't the case. I didn't want any of this. And as I stand amid well-wishers, the reason becomes more apparent.

"Well?'" Efe says. "Do you love it?"

There's that question again. I certainly can't answer with the truth. "It's great." I force a smile. "Perfect."

"It was a team effort. I helped, and so did Jacob and Christina, and, of course, Rafael."

I turn to him, hoping irritation isn't obvious on my face. "So your sister isn't in town."

"Actually, she is. And so is my mom." He nods his head toward two women making their way to us.

We've spoken via Skype a few times, so I recognize Selena immediately. She has dark, close-cropped hair that frames her small face perfectly and the same delicate, understated beauty as Audrey Hepburn—if Audrey Hepburn's style personified Gothic chic. She's petite, but her presence invades a room. It isn't only about her appearance—the short, black dress with bell sleeves and floral embroidery, the antique and definitely expensive Victorian-style choker around her neck, her scarlet-red lips, and liner-rimmed doll-like eyes—it's her unspoken conviction that seems to demand attention.

"Azere! I can't believe I'm finally meeting you." She locks me in a tight hug. When she pulls back, she holds my shoulders and examines my face and then my frame—the white long-sleeve dress that flares at my knees and puts my baby bump on full display. "Gosh, you're gorgeous. Pregnancy definitely suits you."

"Thank you." I take the compliment to heart. "You're sweet. And it's so great to finally see you in person."

My attention veers to the poised woman beside Selena—her wavy black hair specked with strands of grays and her blushed cheeks lined with gentle wrinkles. "You must be Rafael's mom." I extend my hand, but she doesn't take it.

"I've heard so much about you." She smiles, broad and genuine, and leans into me, offering a warm and affectionate hug much like her daughter's. "It's such a pleasure to finally meet you," she says, tightening her hold.

"It's nice to meet you too, Mrs. Ca—"

"Call me Isabel."

Isabel. In my culture, it's considered disrespectful to call elders by their first names. Sir, ma, auntie, uncle—these are appropriate titles. And if an elder is your significant other's parent, the title automatically gets upgraded to mom or dad. But she wants me to call her Isabel, not even Mrs. Castellano. So I do.

"It's so wonderful to meet you, Isabel."

"Likewise, dear." She steps back and runs a hand over her burgundy cocktail dress, smoothing any wrinkles that might have formed during our embrace. "Rafael's father and brother are still in Spain, but they'll be back next week. We should all have dinner then, get to know one another more intimately. How does that sound, Azere?"

"Good." I nod eagerly. "That sounds wonderful." Maybe getting to know Rafael's family will bring some transparency to him. I hope so, but I try not to dwell on that. I'm more focused on maintaining a smile for the duration of the party.

I introduce Efe and Jacob to Isabel and Selena, exchange pleasantries with guests, nibble on snacks even though I lack an appetite, partake in the games Christina organizes even though I'm not interested, open gifts with forced enthusiasm, and remind myself to keep that smile in place.

"Excuse me," Isabel says, standing, a glass of champagne in her hand. "Can I please have everyone's attention?" At her request, the music stops and so does the chatter and laughter. "For those who I haven't had the pleasure of meeting, I'm Isabel, Rafael's mother." She scans the open space and finds her son in the kitchen, standing with Jacob, a beer in his hand. She watches him deeply as if seeing something only a mother can perceive.

"The truth is, I haven't seen Rafael this happy in a very long time. And I can only credit his happiness to one person." Her eyes shift again and land on me. "Azere." She beams. "I don't think you'll truly ever understand the joy you've brought to my son's life and to my family. Words can't express how excited I am to be a grandmother.

"It's a role I will take seriously, just as my mother did with my children. They spent many summers with her in Spain. She taught them so much about our culture. I look forward to doing the same with my grandchild, showing him or her what it means to be a true Spaniard." She raises her glass. "So cheers to Azere for giving me the opportunity to be a grandmother."

Everyone raises a glass and *cheers* resounds around the room. The music, chatter, and laughter resumes. Isabel approaches me, smiling, but the firm smile I've been sustaining withers. Gradually, tears gather at the corners of my eyes. Blinking doesn't push them into my sockets; they're on the verge of falling, and the sob tickling my throat is on the verge of breaking free. I turn away swiftly, maneuver past the crowd, and climb the floating stairs that lead to the second floor.

"Azere, what's going on?" Christina trails me into Rafael's bedroom, sprinting and then slowing once at my heels. "Where are you going? What's the problem?"

"You are, Christina!" I spin to face her, my hands shuddering at my sides. "I told you I didn't want a baby shower. I made that very clear. Didn't I?"

"Well . . . I . . . um." She cocks her head and studies me, confusion apparent in her assessing stare. "I didn't think you actually meant it, Azere. I thought you just didn't want to deal with the stress of planning one, so I did it. I planned everything, and I thought you would love it."

"Seriously! You thought I would love this?" I rub my temples and breathe slow and deep, soothing myself. I don't want to say or do anything I might regret. "Christina." My voice is leveled, collected. "Go downstairs. Look around. Rafael's mother is there. Where's mine? Where's my mom, Christina?" Tears pour out my eyes just as a rough sob breaks through my lips. "She should be here—with me. But she isn't. She isn't here."

"Azere. Honey." Christina makes a move to hold me, but I avoid her touch. "Efe told her about the baby shower. She invited her, but she . . . she refused to come."

Of course she did. That's exactly why I didn't want a baby shower—a celebration where my mother's absence would be overly apparent, where I would feel it more gravely, where it would be a question in the minds of my guests. Arianna has already asked, and my answer lacked all the elements of a good lie.

"While Rafael's mom is giving a heartfelt speech about being a grandmother, mine is MIA." I wipe my wet cheeks and sniff. "This is exactly why I didn't want a baby shower, Christina. Because I knew she wouldn't come." I lift my shoulders in a weak shrug. "Why couldn't you just listen to me? Why?"

"Azere." She buries her face in her hands, digs her fingers into her hairline, and groans. "I'm sorry. I thought . . ." She looks at me and shakes her head. "No. I wasn't thinking. I messed up. I'm so sorry, Zere."

Her somber expression appeases my anger, but not the other emotions. "Christina, I know your intentions were good, but . . . but . . ." Tears flood my eyes again, and my throat tightens. "I just need to be alone right now. Tell everyone I'm sick or something." Before leaving the room, Christina gives me a quick hug, conveying once more how sorry she is. I squeeze her tight. She's a good friend. This situation is just so impossible.

Curled atop the king-size mattress, I wipe my eyes while thinking of Isabel—how her presence made me painfully aware of my mother's absence, how the mention of culture during her toast made me slightly nervous. She plans to teach my child what it means to be a Spaniard. *A true Spaniard.* What will that mean for my culture—what place will it have in my child's life? Will my child get a chance to visit Nigeria, or will he or she spend the summers in Spain as Rafael did? When the door cracks open, I stop pondering and sit up.

"Azere, are you okay?" Efe hurries to the bed, concern causing her brows to unite. "Christina said you were feeling sick."

"It's nothing." I clear my throat and relieve the strain in my voice. "I'm feeling better now."

"Okay. Good." She sits on the edge of the bed. "Well, the party is over. I told Rafael I'd check on you while he sees everyone out." She squints and inspects my face. "Are you sure you're okay? It looks like you've been crying. What's wrong, Azere?"

Everything. But I can't tell her that. She's my baby sister. I don't want to bother her with my problems. "Nothing's wrong, Efe. Everything is fine."

"Mm-hmm." She doesn't believe my answer but also doesn't dispute it. She sets her lips in a firm line and turns her attention to the abstract painting above the upholstered bedframe. "Do you remember when we were younger and Auntie Ivie used to visit?"

I frown at the absurd question. "Of course I remember." Probably even more than she does.

Auntie Ivie, my mother's younger sister, lived in Benin City and would come to the village once a month to visit us. She would ride into our compound on an *okada*, her legs on either side of the driver, her skirt hitched to her thighs, revealing too much of her swarthy skin. She could have easily worn a longer skirt, but she liked the attention—the admiration from the distracted *okada* driver, the judgmental glares from the village women passing by, the rebuke from my mother. It all fed something in her—the desire to be the exception, to be the *but* in every sentence.

"Every other girl wants to get married and have children, but Ivie wants to go to the city and make money," my mother would rant. "Every other girl will dress like they have home training, but Ivie will dress like a common harlot. When elders are speaking, every other girl will be silent, but Ivie will put her mouth in every matter even if it does not concern her."

Auntie Ivie was a rebel in her own right, and Efe connected with her for this reason. They were alike. They both had a defiant nature that made them fall out of line and say and do what they shouldn't. I didn't have that.

"Do you remember what Auntie used to say about you?" Efe asks. "She used to say you don't speak your mind enough—that you hold too much inside."

I remember that.

"One time, she said something I'll never forget. She said, 'Azere, if you accidently swallowed poison, you would smile, pretending everything is okay rather than open your mouth and ask for a cure.'"

I remember those words coming from my aunt. They hurt now just as they did then. As I attempt to scold Efe for repeating them, she presses a finger to my lips.

"Azere, the point I'm trying to make is that you're hurting. I know you are." She drops her finger. "Look. I like Rafael. He's a great guy, but I know the decision to be with him wasn't easy. I know you're dealing with a lot, so why are you acting like everything is perfect?" She holds my hands. "Azere, I'm here. Talk to me." She looks at me intensely, trying to persuade me with her honey-brown eyes when the door opens and Rafael steps inside the room.

"*Cariño*." He comes to the bed and presses his lips to my forehead. "Are you okay?"

Turning away from my sister, dismissing everything she said and everything Auntie Ivie said years ago, I look at Rafael and do what I've done for months. I act like everything is all right. I strain myself, trying to hold every piece together even with the toll it's gradually taking on me. I do it for my baby. I do it for him. Because I care about him. But above everything else, I do it because I'm afraid to admit that I might have made a mistake by choosing Rafael.

chapter
31

Rafael drives up to a large gate that slides open and reveals a clear path enclosed by manicured grass. He drives along the curvy route, nearing a majestic French provincial-style mansion.

When he said his parents live in Bridle Path, an upscale neighborhood in Toronto, I expected extravagance but not to this extent. A flurry of nerves tickle my stomach. I reach for my head and twirl a braid around my finger.

"You okay?" Rafael asks, parking the car a few feet from the front door.

"Just a little nervous."

"Don't be. You've already met Selena and my mom, and they love you. My dad and Max will too. Trust me."

That's the problem. I don't trust him, but I don't voice my reservations.

He steps out of the car and opens the passenger door. His sultry stare moves over me. "You look really beautiful by the way." The crisp October air makes his breaths appear as puffs of feathery mist.

"Really? Even like this?" I signal at my protruding stomach. "Six months pregnant with a belly the size of a basketball?"

He crouches and leans into me. "Azere, you're beautiful—perfect. I don't deserve you." He pecks my lips. "I feel like I've cheated someone who's truly deserving of you." Another peck. "But you're mine now, and there's no way in hell I'm ever giving you up." He leans in for another peck, and I hold his head in place and kiss him fiercely as if I can taste those sweet words on his velvety lips.

"So," I whisper, breaking away. "We should probably go inside."

"Right." He sighs. "You still nervous?"

"Yeah. Just a little."

"Okay. How about you hold my hand and don't let go until we step out of that house. I'll be your support, and you'll be mine. Just in case Selena starts to drive me crazy." He extends his hand, waiting for me to seal the agreement. "Deal?"

"Yeah." I smile and nod. "Deal."

We shake, and he helps me out of the car. We walk to the double doors hand in hand, and after Rafael pushes the bell, an elderly woman, brown-haired and fair-skinned, pulls the door wide open.

"Good evening, Rafael," she says, smiling. "And who is this lovely lady?"

"Hi, Beth." He enters the house and draws me in along with him. "This is Azere."

"Hi," I say. "Nice to meet you."

"Likewise."

Rafael rolls my coat off and places it on Beth's extended arm. He does the same with his coat. And it registers. She's the maid.

Well, damn. How much money do these people have? A hint of intimidation crops up, but I suppress it with a shitload of confidence.

When Beth leaves with our coats, I turn my attention to the twin staircase that curves against white walls. The interior is a flawless depiction of contemporary elegance. There's a crystal chandelier hanging over the grand foyer; its design, long and slim, resembles drops of rain ready to cascade. The decor follows a simple color scheme—black and white. The absence of every other color creates a sophistication that lacks warmth.

When Rafael squeezes my hand, I notice Selena and Isabel approaching us; two men—who I presume are Rafael's brother and father—follow behind them.

Fifty Shades of Grey. A scene from that movie comes to mind—the one where Christian introduces Ana to his family. It went something like this, in a house somewhat like this one, with a man just as handsome and enigmatic. Now I wonder if this night will end as Christian's and Ana's did.

Will Rafael let me in just a little? Will he let down his guard and tell his secrets? Will he at least whisper them to me like Christian did to Ana while she slept?

At this point, I'll accept anything.

"Azere!" Selena throws her arms around me and squeezes. "So good to see you again." When she pulls away, her mother offers the same affectionate greeting.

"Azere." Rafael gestures to the striking older man. "This is Gabriel, my father."

"It's so nice to meet you, Mr.—"

"Please," he says, taking my outstretched hand, "call me Gabriel." A dark mustache extends to a beard that neatly frames his jawline and lower cheeks. If he wasn't smiling, his stern features, which are much like Rafael's, would have made him appear intimidating.

"And this is my brother."

"Hi." Máximo pushes past his sister and steps forward, flashing a smile that displays his pearly teeth. With an argyle cardigan over a blue button-up, beige boat shoes, and slick, dark hair parted precisely, it's obvious he's of the prep school/ivy league breed. He presents his hand in a formal manner. "I'm Max. It's nice to meet you, Azere."

"Likewise," I say, shaking his hand and noting the slight facial similarities between him and Selena, his fraternal twin.

Dinner follows the introduction. Under the table, Rafael and I continue to hold hands while being the center of attention. With the intimate setting the baby shower didn't offer, his mother and sister ask about my job, my interests, my family and our move to Canada, and they seem sincerely interested in the answers.

"So," Selena says, stabbing a slice of tomato with a fork, "right now, you two live separately, but that's going to get complicated once the baby is born. Are you guys going to move in together?"

Rafael tenses up. He hasn't brought up the topic since that day at his place, but I see the request in his eyes every time I pack and unpack my overnight bag. I see it now as he turns to me, a gentle furrow between his brows.

We're in a committed relationship and are expecting a child. It makes sense to live together, especially now when all the gifts from the baby shower are in his penthouse, in a beautifully lit room that would make the perfect nursery.

Moving in together. The act seems so permanent, and it scares me more than I'm willing to admit. Maybe Rafael was right. Maybe I don't want to completely root myself in his life.

"So," Selena continues, "are you guys going to move in together? Hopefully before the baby is born?"

"Selena, they'll live together when they're ready. Now, stop pestering them." Thankfully, Isabel shuts down her daughter's inquisition. "Now, on to something I've been dying to know. Have you two thought of any baby names?" Unfortunately, she begins her own. "I was thinking Ximena if it's a girl and Mateo if it's a boy. Such beautiful names."

She wants to name my child Ximena or Mateo because it sounds beautiful. In my culture, names aren't chosen because they sound good. Names always bear a significant meaning and are either a prayer or a prophecy. Azere means "a child born for a remarkable purpose." Efe is short for Efesona, which translates to "there is no greater wealth than this." We don't give names on a whim. We believe a child's name is their crowning glory. As such, we put a lot of thought into it. But how do I explain this to Isabel without offending her? If she were Nigerian, I wouldn't have to.

"I also like the names Matías and Catalina or—"

"Um . . . I would like to give my child an Edo name. If it's a boy, Esosa. It means 'God's gift.' And if it's a girl, Amenze. It means 'a river that's calm and brings order to chaos.'"

"They're beautiful names," Isabel says, smiling. "But you must understand our side of the family won't recognize those names."

And my family won't recognize or understand Ximena or Mateo.

Baby names that reflect our two cultures—it's something Rafael and I have discussed casually. Clearly, we need to discuss it in depth. Separate from his family.

"What about the name—"

"Okay," Rafael says, interrupting his mother. "Why don't we talk about something else?"

"Yes. Why don't we?" Selena agrees, turning to me. "Azere." One eyebrow lifts off its base in a pronounced arch. "I'm curious. What in the world is a girl as fabulous as yourself doing with my bore of a brother?"

The question makes everyone laugh.

"Seriously. Give me a little insight because I don't get it. Why are you with Rafael?"

"Well . . . um . . . he's a pretty cool guy."

"A pretty cool guy?" Selena shakes her head. "Nope. That doesn't work for me. Please elaborate."

Everyone at the table, including Rafael, seems just as interested in my elaboration. They're a nosy bunch, prying into my personal business just as my family did when Rafael visited. Back then, all those months ago, he confidently and sincerely expressed himself to my family. I owe him the same courtesy.

Smiling, I turn to him. Things aren't perfect with us, but what makes being with Rafael easy is recalling all the reasons why I care about him. "He has a good heart," I say. "He's selfless. His confidence isn't arrogant or offensive. He makes me happy. My career, my dreams matter to him.

"He supports my romantic movie addiction. He is already obsessed with our unborn child. He talks to my stomach far too much, but it's the cutest thing. Rafael is . . . he's amazing."

"You're pretty damn amazing too, *cariño*." He leans into me and presses his lips to mine.

Momentarily, I forget his family is present. The world around me dissolves. I swear his saliva is laced with some venom that penetrates my system and renders me delirious and half-witted. Whenever he kisses me, no matter how brief, reason eludes me, and I forget I'm kissing lying lips. Even now, I struggle to resist the effect of his kiss. My attempt is unsuccessful until someone coughs. Finally, Rafael sets me free, and the world comes into focus again.

"Oh my God." Embarrassed, my cheeks turn hot. "I'm so sorry."

"It's okay," Isabel says, laughing. "That was—"

"Totally adorable!" Selena shouts.

"He's obviously crazy about her," Max adds. He takes a sip of red wine from the goblet in his hand. "Haven't seen him with puppy-dog eyes since Sofia."

The instant Max utters the name, everyone falls quiet. Even the silverware stops clinking against the china. All eyes are downcast except for Gabriel's. His features harden as he regards Max with a censoring glare. He says something in Spanish, his tone gruff. I don't understand what he's said. I don't understand why the atmosphere has suddenly changed. I look to Rafael for answers.

"Who's Sofia?"

He says nothing.

"Rafael?"

He doesn't meet my gaze, and that's when my heart races.

"Who is Sofia?"

"His wife," Max answers. "Sofia was Rafael's wife."

No one makes a sound as I turn to Rafael and wait for his explanation, his defense, his denial—anything. But he doesn't utter a word, so I do the only thing I can while dining with his upper-class family. Under the table, I pull my hand from his and continue eating with a stoic expression keeping my face straight.

chapter
32

When I step into my apartment, he's behind me. When I pull off my shoes, he pulls off his. My coat comes off next, and so does his. When I walk into the living room, he mimics my steps, and I halt. I look at him for the first time since Max revealed the truth—a truth Rafael kept from me for months, a truth he didn't even bother explaining during our extremely quiet ride home.

"Rafael, you can't stay here tonight. I don't want you here. Please leave." I hurry to my room, not caring to read the expression on his face.

"Azere, wait. Please." When I enter the bedroom, he grabs me.

"No! Don't touch me!" I wrench my arm from his grip and shove him back. "A wife! You were married!" Tears drop, dampening the mold of mascara on my lashes. "How could you keep something like that from me?"

"I thought . . ." He tightens his jaw. "I didn't know how to tell you."

"Okay." I rub my wet eyes and mascara residue accompanies tears, painting my hand black. "Then tell me now. Tell me everything." My anger, intensified by pregnancy hormones, is passing. "Who is she? Is she the woman in the picture?"

"Yes."

And he still has a picture of her stashed away. Why? Does he still love her? I'm not prepared for the answer. "What happened between the two of you? How come you're no longer married? Tell me."

"Azere, I . . . I can't. I'm sorry." A deep blush tints his white skin. "Just let it go. Please."

"You're keeping things from me. I know you are. And this happens to be one of them. You can't ask me to just let it go. That isn't fair, Rafael."

"Zere, I'm not asking." He expels a shaky breath and ruffles his hair. "I'm begging you. Please. Just stop."

I have never seen him like this. Pain and dread are apparent in his watery eyes and trembling voice. Maybe I shouldn't push any further. Maybe I should just let it go, but I have so many questions. One especially keeps coming to mind. I have to ask it.

"What's her ethnicity? Sofia. Is she like you, Spanish?"

"Yeah."

"Of course." He was with someone who fit him perfectly, while I am a puzzle piece being forced where it doesn't belong. "She was perfect for you, and I bet things were so much easier with her."

"Zere, I don't understand. What are you talking about?"

"Tonight, your mother and I almost got into an argument about baby names—Edo or Spanish. At the baby shower, she made a speech about taking our child to Spain." The recollection makes me anxious. "Rafael, I'm starting to wonder where my culture will stand in our child's life. Will it be secondary or maybe nonexistent while yours is front and center?"

"Of course not, Azere." His voice is soft, soothing as he tries to reassure me. "That will never happen."

"But what if it does? How am I sure you won't impose your culture on our child and push mine to the sidelines? How am I sure you won't eventually do the same to me?"

"Azere, I'm not imposing my culture on you." He edges toward me, a small step. "But we'll have to learn how to compromise. I'll learn and adopt some of your culture and you'll learn and adopt some of mine. For the sake of our child and our relationship, we'll compromise and make it work."

"I've compromised enough."

I've been compromising for thirteen years, rearranging things so I can exist in two different worlds. Now, he wants me to exist in a third—his. I can't do that. And maybe I'm being unreasonable and even selfish, but I'm terrified—terrified that adopting Rafael's culture will put me at greater risk of losing my mine. After all, my mother warned me of the possibility.

How much more of yourself, of your culture will you lose to accommodate him in your life?

The question she asked me months ago buzzes in my head like a fly trapped in a jar. I consider it deeply. Next, I recall the heartfelt promise I made to my dying father and the disappointment in my mother's eyes when she learned I was pregnant with Rafael's child. Last, I close my eyes and envision the life I meticulously planned as a child—simple, uncompromising, and with a man whose heritage was similar to mine. After all this, I look at Rafael and gather the courage to say what needs to be said.

"I can't do this anymore." A long breath gushes out my mouth, deflates my chest and makes my shoulders slump. "I've been trying, Rafael. For months, I've been trying to hold things together, but it's all become too much." Tonight—right now—is the breaking point. "I can't do it anymore. I can't be with you."

"What?" He freezes momentarily, regards me, then shakes his head firmly. "No. Zere, you don't mean that."

"Yeah. I do. You want me to compromise, but what will happen once I do? Will I adopt some of your culture and lose some of mine? Will I eventually stop eating Edo food? Will I stop speaking my language? Will I eventually forget who I am and where I come from?

"Rafael, that was my father's greatest fear. That was why he asked me to make that promise. A promise I broke by being with you, by choosing you. I made a mistake. This—us, you and me—it's a mistake."

Within seconds, I've said everything I've been harboring and mulling over for months. Yet, I'm not certain if those words are genuinely mine or my mother's.

"Rafael." I can't hold his stare. I can't look at his dejected eyes and confront what I've just done to him. "I'll see you at the office and at doctor appointments, but that's it. If you want to check on me for any reason, use a phone. You can't come over. When the baby is born, we'll figure out a shared-custody arrangement. Now." I suck in air and release it. "Leave. Just go. I'll pack up all your stuff and have it sent over."

For a long while he's dazed. He says nothing, and then he blinks sharply. "Azere, honey, you're just upset. I understand. We'll sleep on it and talk in the morning. Okay?" He takes off his wristwatch and tosses it on the dresser like he usually does before going to bed.

"What the hell are you doing?"

He pulls his tucked shirt out of his pants.

"Stop it, Rafael. I want you to leave."

He undoes the buttons.

"You're not listening to me!"

"Because you're being ridiculous!" He slams his fist against the dresser, and I flinch. "You're making irrational decisions and quite frankly, acting insane. And I know you're upset, so I'm going to stay. I'll sleep on the couch. Hell, I'll sleep on the balcony if you want. But I'm not leaving." Resolve toughens his voice. "Tomorrow, we can talk and figure this out. Or you can ignore me if you want. And whenever you're ready to talk, whether it's tomorrow or next week or next month, I'll be here. I'm not leaving, Azere. I'm not leaving because I'm in love with you." He sighs, and his voice is soft again, vulnerable. "I love you. So much."

I don't realize I'm crying until tears overflow, spilling down my chin and hitting my chest. Those words. He's never said them before, and hearing them makes me both ecstatic and miserable. It's the best thing he's ever said to me, but it's the last thing I need to hear right now.

"Rafael." My hands tighten to fists that shake at my sides. I'm fighting the urge to reach out to him, to kiss him. "I need you to listen to me. We can't be together. Okay? Apart from the differences in our cultures and the fact that you've been keeping things from me, I've been dealing with the guilt of disappointing my parents. I've been dealing with the fact that my mother has disowned me because I chose you. It's been killing me, Rafael. So, I can't be with you anymore. I just can't do it. I am so sorry."

"But I—"

"Rafael, you need to respect my decision. You need to leave. If you don't, I'll go instead. I'll stay in a hotel until you're gone."

He doesn't say a word. He must be frustrated and hurt, but his face is suddenly blank, and it reveals nothing. His eyes are cold and hard like the opaque sheet of ice that conceals the depths of a lake. He walks to the front door and puts on his shoes and coat.

"Don't forget Milo," I say. The dog is sleeping on a cushioned mat adjacent to the sofa. "Please take him."

Rafael doesn't object. He scoops Milo into his arm, pulls the front door open, and walks out.

In bed, curled in the same spot Rafael usually sleeps in, I cry hard until I'm panting and clutching my chest. It hurts. It hurts so bad. There's a grip around my heart, squeezing the life out of it until it's a shriveled, raisin-like thing.

Maybe I made a mistake. If it hurts this much, maybe it's the wrong decision. I should go to him, talk to him, fix this. But I quickly recall the reasons why I can't do that, why I can't be with Rafael even though his absence is tearing me apart.

chapter
33

The worst part about being without him is going home—going home to silence, to dinner alone, to an empty bed. The best part about work is him. Knowing he's close loosens that grip around my heart.

This morning, I saw him briefly as he walked toward the elevator. We greeted each other as civil colleagues would and that was it. It's currently 7:30 p.m. on the same day, and he hasn't returned to the office. When we were a couple, he would tell me where he was off to, what clients he was meeting, and what business he was conducting. I'm no longer entitled to that information.

I'm working late tonight. I've worked late most nights since our breakup. Four weeks and two days—that's how long it's been. I miss him. Terribly. But I immerse myself in work. It's a distraction that offers the perk of seeing him.

In the office kitchen, I look through the window while waiting for the electric kettle to boil water. The trees that decoratively align the sidewalk are bare now—all bony, dainty branches covered with fresh snow, courtesy of late November. When someone enters the kitchen, I give up the view and spin around.

"Hey, Arianna. You heading out?"

"Yeah," she says. "It's getting late. Plus, I have a date tonight." She walks toward me in her usual style—body straight, one leg falling in front of the other, and hips swaying from side to side. "Looks like it's just gonna be you here. Heading home anytime soon?"

"Yeah. In about an hour. I've got some stuff to finish up."

"Cool." She turns to leave, but pauses and faces me again. "By the way, is it just me or do things seem a little off between you and Rafael? You guys don't seem too couple-like these days. Trouble in paradise?"

Of course the dynamics of our relationship have changed since the breakup. Among many things, we no longer have lunch together, nor do we arrive and leave work together. I'm sure my coworkers have noticed. Though, the only person aware of the breakup is Christina. No one else knows. No one else asks or pries except for Arianna, who has no boundaries and who would thrive with a career as a gossip blogger.

"So?" she persists. "What's going on between you two?"

"How about you mind your business, Arianna? You must have enough going on, seeing that you have a date and there's a run in your pantyhose."

"Oh shit!" She gawps at her legs, mortified. "I gotta go. I might have an extra pair in my car." She leaves in a hurry, not moving in her usual style.

"Have fun on your date!" *Well, that worked out better than planned.* I fill a cup with hot water and while ripping open a bag of peppermint tea, approaching footsteps resound. *Great. She's back.* "Forget something, Arianna?" I turn around, but it's not my nosy colleague at the entrance. It's someone else. Someone I never, ever expected.

"Hi, Azere," Elijah says, wearing his signature side-slung grin. "Arianna left, but she told me where to find you. How are you?"

"Um . . . I'm okay." But more than anything, I'm confused. "Elijah, what are you doing here?"

"I'm sorry for just showing up like this, but I really needed to see you." His eyes land on my stomach, which swells in a white cashmere sweater. "I went by your apartment. You weren't there. I figured you might be here." His eyes meet mine again. "Can we talk?"

"Talk about what?"

"Well, I saw your mom today," he says. "I went by her place. She asked me to come over. She wanted us to talk. About you."

"Excuse me?" *What the hell?* My mom won't even talk to me about me, but she talks to Elijah. Wonderful. "What exactly were you two discussing?"

"She told me you ended things with Rafael."

I shared the news with Efe. She shared it with our mother, but that hasn't changed the status of our relationship. She's still shutting me out.

"Zere, I'm sorry about the breakup."

"Seriously?" I arch an eyebrow. "Are you really?"

He contemplates before speaking his truth. "No. I'm not. Because I want to be with you." He inches toward me until there's no space between us. "I love you, Azere. I always have, and I'm very certain that will never change. We always talked about having a family. Well, we still can. We can be a family—you, me, and this baby, who I will love because I love you. I'll make you happy, Azere."

I don't think he can, but us together will make my mother happy. She'll forgive me if we're together and that means more.

"We don't have to rush, Azere. We could take things slow until you're ready." He holds my cheek in the curve of his large palm. "I'll be patient for as long as you need."

He's too close. His scent is suffocating me, his touch is repulsing me, his presence is creating angst rather than soothing it. Just when I can no longer tolerate the discomfort of his nearness and I'm ready to shift away, footsteps echo.

The brisk strides get closer, and within seconds, Rafael appears at the door. As he takes in the scene before him, his eyes well up with emotion. Quickly, I shift away from Elijah, and he becomes aware of Rafael too. All three of us stand in the kitchen, regarding each other.

It's quiet. Not the still, peaceful type. Nope. Definitely not that. Or the uncomfortable, awkward type. Nope. We're way past that. This kind of silence mounts tension upon tension; it makes the thin, almost indivisible hairs on my skin spike up, it makes my stomach tighten and heart thump, it makes me sweat and brings me near close to pissing myself. This kind of silence sends an intense shiver through me.

"Get the hell out!"

I'm not sure whose voice that was. Rafael's lips moved, but that wasn't his elegant, collected tone. That, what I just heard, was guttural. I don't know how to associate it with Rafael, but he speaks in the same chilling, unrecognizable voice and all doubt leaves my mind.

"Get out now," he says, eyes on Elijah, "or so help me God . . ." He rolls his fingers into fists and marches forward.

"Rafael." I call for his attention, but his predatory stare doesn't waver from his target. "Stop." He doesn't listen, so I stand in front of Elijah, my body preventing Rafael's rising fist from advancing. "Stop this. Right now." I touch his arm—my fingertips against his warm skin. It's the first bodily contact we've had since our breakup. His eyes, hard and livid, flick to mine. I hold his stare and gently push his arm down.

"Azere, I'm gonna go." Elijah is calm, and I'm so grateful. "I'll call you later." He flexes the muscles in his jaw, regards Rafael with a condescending sneer, and leaves.

Upon his exit, I switch my attention to Rafael. I'm not sure what's going on in his head, but the rage in his eyes is disappearing and quickly being replaced with a deep sadness.

"You said there was nothing between the two of you. Remember that?"

I nod. Like a damn fool, I nod.

"Obviously, that isn't true. So, what's the truth, Azere?"

"Rafael." I can't hold his gaze. I turn away, staring at the view through the window—bleak night dotted with streetlights and falling snow. "Elijah is . . ." *He's the man my father hoped for. The man my mother approves of. The man who will earn me her forgiveness, her acceptance.* "He's the man I was always supposed to be with. I'm sorry."

chapter
34

Rafael

The hardest part about loving Azere was knowing she wasn't 100 percent mine. Throughout the course of our relationship, I knew her mind and her heart were divided. With me, she was half happy and half in love. The other half of her was bound by obligation. That half ended our relationship and chose another man.

"Rafael. I'm so sorry."

"Do you love him?" I hate that I even have to ask this. "Do you love Elijah?"

"Um . . . I . . ." She shuts her mouth.

"Do you want to hear my theory?" I watch her intently as if trying to navigate the blueprint of her mind. "I think you only want to be with Elijah because of your parents." The two people she's been conditioned to obey. "Azere, for years, you've been restricted by them—dictated to by one and haunted by the other. You've put their desires ahead of yours. If you keep living like that, you'll never be happy. You'll be miserable. All your life."

My last words must have had an effect because tears fall quickly, soaking her cheeks and reddening her eyes. I hate seeing her cry. Hurting her isn't my intention, but my candor is necessary. This is my rescue mission. Though, unlike the fairy-tale–themed movies she once made me watch, there are no dragons to slay or evil queens to overthrow. In this case, the damsel stands as her own obstacle. So rather than using a sword or a life-restoring kiss, I use words, hoping to wake her from the obligation-induced trance she's been in for years.

"Zere, you have this strength you aren't even aware of. I see it all the time. Your strength, your spunk, your audacity, your sharp tongue are the best things about you. They make you a great leader, they make you a great friend, they humble me. Maybe it's time you show this part of yourself to your mother. Maybe it's time she sees the daughter who has been hiding from her."

As I leave, walk away from her, my movements are slow, hoping she might reach out and stop me. I exit the kitchen, wait for the elevator to arrive, step inside. The doors slide toward each other, the view of the office gradually disappearing until there's only a sliver of space and then, there's nothing.

She didn't come. She let me walk away. She let me go.

My body shakes as if strained, unable to contain my heartbreak. Everything I'm feeling pours out of me—tears through my eyes, a growl through my mouth.

I'm angry at her, but I'm angrier at myself.

The future I imagined with her is gone, and I know I'm partially to blame. She wanted the truth, and she deserved it, but I couldn't give it to her. I tried so many times to force the words out of my mouth, but I couldn't do it. The chance that she would see me differently scared me. It terrified me. So here I am, without her or the strength and optimism to hold on to us or the possibility of a better ending.

chapter
35

For the first time in months, I'm looking at my mother, talking to her, eating with her. This new development occurs because of Elijah. He's the pass that grants me full access to my family.

When my mother called me a week after Elijah came by the office, she cut straight to the point—no pleasantries.

"Elijah told me he spoke to you," she said when I answered the phone.

"Yes. He did."

"And what did he say?" she asked even though I suspected she knew.

"He wants to be with me."

"And you don't like his offer?"

"I didn't say that."

"Then what are you saying, Azere? He told me you wanted time to think. Think about what? Eh? You have a second chance with Elijah, and you want to squander it."

"Mom, I just need time."

"Azere, in your condition, despite your stupidity, a man wants to marry you. In fact, he is not any ordinary man *o*. He is a medical doctor, an Edo man, a man your father would have proudly approved of. Yet you are contemplating your answer." She scoffed. "If you are trying to *shakara* or play hard to get, don't *o*. The time for that has already passed. At this point, you should be playing easy to get.

"Anyways. This conversation has taken longer than I wanted. In fact, it has exhausted me." She sighed long and loud as if truly fatigued. "Azere, let me simplify things for you. If you choose Elijah, I will forgive your past stupidity. You can even rejoin the family in time for Christmas. But if you choose that white man, things will be as they have been for months. I will not be your mother, and you will not be my daughter. Simple. The decision is yours."

A few days after that conversation, I had dinner with Elijah at Khao San Road, a Thai restaurant we used to frequent. Halfway through my bowl of green chicken curry, I leaned into the table, narrowed my eyes, and studied him.

"Elijah, why do you want to be with me?" I asked. "I don't get it. I'm having another man's baby. And even though Rafael and I are no longer together, we're always going to be connected because of our child. Why deal with all of that? Why not just move on—find another girl with a lot less baggage?"

He opened his mouth and then closed it as if he knew he couldn't give the routine *I love you* as an answer. "Azere, when I learned you were pregnant, I tried to move on. When you told me you were happy with Rafael, I tried even harder. But I . . . I just couldn't do it." His voice thickened with emotion, and he looked away, his gaze wandering aimlessly before settling on me again. "Azere, during those years when I was away, when we didn't talk, I still believed that somehow, we would end up together. I suppose that was the mistake I made, thinking you wouldn't carry on with your life. You did." Tears touched the corners of his eyes. "If I had handled things differently back then, we could be married right now with a child or two. Just like we wanted. Do you remember, Azere?"

I nodded, recalling the life we had planned, a life forged into existence by naivety, hope, love, and a certainty that we would be together forever. I craved it, the simplicity of that life—the knowledge that I would have made my parents proud, that nothing would have been threatened or compromised.

"I made a mistake back then," Elijah continued. "And I know I'll make another if I don't fight for you and for us—for the family and the life we can still have. This is me fighting, Azere."

"Elijah." The sincerity in his eyes was spellbinding, alluring. I was tempted to give in to him, but I couldn't. "I'm not over Rafael." It was only fair to tell him the truth. "I still care about him."

He frowned and considered what I had said. "Um . . . okay. Then we'll take things slow. Will that be all right?"

"Yeah. Slow. Very slow—be friends first. Just friends."

"Yes. Of course." His lips stretched until a wide smile made the corners of his eyes crinkle. "We'll take things as slow as you want, Azere. No problem."

Unfortunately, things aren't moving at a pace I would like because only two weeks later, we're sitting side by side, having Christmas dinner with my family. My mother, thrilled about the decision I had made, extended an invitation to Elijah, and he accepted without hesitation or consideration for the word *slow*. I glance at his hand on my shoulder. It seems strange there—out of place. I wiggle, shrugging gradually until it falls off.

"It's so great to have the whole family together," my uncle says. He reclines into the chair and rubs his stomach, which almost looks as round as mine. "It's been so long since we've all been together."

"Yes, *o*. To God be the glory. Azere finally came to her senses.

Praise God." My mother eyeballs me. "You and that *yeye* man."
She bends her lips. "Nonsense. But you and Elijah." She smiles.
"Perfect. Your father would be pleased."

"You can't please someone who's dead," Efe mutters.

"Yes, but you can honor them."

"And dishonor yourself." She stabs a slice of *moi moi* with her
fork and coats it in tomato stew. "Because that's what she's doing."

"Efe." Jacob says sternly. "Stop." For my sake, he's trying to
keep the peace just as I begged him to before showing up with
Elijah. "Can we just enjoy the meal?"

It's quiet again. We eat and drink, and then Efe clears her
throat. Immediately, I know the peace at the table is in jeopardy.

"I'm just trying to understand how we're all sitting here, acting like everything is okay when—"

"Efe." I hold my sister's gaze. "Please. Stop it."

She glares at me, shaking her head. Then she pushes her
chair back, stands, and storms out of the dining room.

chapter
36

I bang my knuckles against my sister's bedroom door. Three
knocks and she doesn't answer. Rather than attempting the
fourth, I twist the knob and push the door open. She's lying
facedown on the bed with her head under a heap of pillows and
stuffed animals.

"Efe." I sit on the edge of the queen-size bed. The linen on
the mattress is carnation pink, matching the walls and most
of the stuffed animals mounted on her head. Thankfully, the
white furniture—a dresser, nightstand, and chaise longue—
dilutes the heavy dose of pink in the room.

"Azere, go away." The mountain of plush fabrics muffles her
voice. She says something else but it's inaudible.

"Okay, let's talk." I swat her butt playfully. "Come on." I swat
it harder this time, and her head jerks up. Pillows and stuffed
bears fly up, landing on the bed and the floor.

"Are you trying to further flatten my already flat ass?" she
says, pouting.

"Oh, please." I roll my eyes. "You have a great ass."

She props up on her elbows and turns to view her round behind that bulges in blue jeans. After an inspection, she nods,
agreeing with my statement.

"So," I say. "Dinner. What was that about?"

"That was me calling you out on your bullshit. That was me
speaking for you because apparently, you forgot you have thoughts
and desires separate from Mom's."

"I'm aware of all these things, Efe."

"Are you?" She shuffles on the bed and switches to a sitting
position. "Because it doesn't seem that way. You're here with
Elijah, the man Mom chose for you, when your heart isn't in it."

"Who says my heart isn't in it?"

"I've been watching since you came through the door with
him. He touches you in the slightest way and you cringe. He
turns to you and you turn from him. I don't even think you've
made eye contact with him all evening. Instead, you find ways to
occupy yourself—checking your phone, reading the label on the
salad dressing bottle." She's calling me out on the gestures I
performed subtly, hoping no one would notice. "You didn't act
this way when Rafael came over."

"Efe, don't even go there."

"Well, I'm about to."

"Then I'll leave." I stand, and she snatches my wrist before I
can move further. "Let go."

"No. Talk to me. What happened between you and Rafael?
Huh?" Tugging my hand, she forces me to sit. "Why did you guys
break up? You never gave me the details."

"It's complicated. I don't wanna talk about it, so drop it."

To my surprise, she obeys. She lets me dwell in silence for a
short while.

"You know, Rafael came over a few times," she says when
seconds pass.

"Wait." I shake my head, clearing it of any trivial data to make way for this major, mind-blowing information. "What? He came over here, to the house?"

"Yeah. Over the past months, since the day you left with him and Mom shut you out, he's been coming by."

"Coming by?" I gather a fistful of bed linen and rumple it in my heating palm. "To do what?"

"To speak to Mom," Efe says. "To apologize."

"Apologize. For what?" *He did nothing wrong—nothing at all.*

"His exact words: 'If I have disrespected you or your family in any way, I sincerely apologize. It was never my intention.'" My sister nods. "Yep. Then he told Mom he cared about you. He promised to take care of you and the baby—to protect, provide, honor, love, all the good stuff."

Tears touch my eyes. "And what did Mom say?"

"Trust me, you don't wanna know."

Of course. "Why didn't you tell me he was coming by?"

"He asked me not to. Nothing good ever came from it, so he thought there was no point telling you."

I'm speechless.

"He loves you, Azere," Efe says, yanking on a stuffed bear's flimsy ear. "He really, really loves you. Like . . . like Christian loved Satine in *Moulin Rouge!* Like Jack loved Rose in *Titanic*. Like Winston loved Stella in *How Stella Got Her Groove Back*. Like—"

"Okay, okay. I get it," I say, laughing. "I get it." And I do because she's communicated using the one thing I truly understand. Love stories. "I get it."

"Then throw one back at me."

"Like . . . like Westley loved Buttercup in *The Princess Bride*."

"Aha!" She claps. "You got it." We laugh but not enough to forget ourselves and our current discussion. "Zere, do you love him? Do you love Rafael?"

Rather than answering, I roll my lips into my mouth.

"Fine. Don't talk. But I know you don't love Elijah. You did. Once. But that was a long time ago. Plus, he broke your heart."

"How do you know that?" I never told her a thing about Elijah—the relationship or the falling out.

"I've always known. I know you two dated." Her top lip curls upward like she's about to snarl. "I know he took your virginity then bailed like a little bitch."

"Seriously, how the hell do you know that?"

"Back in the day, I used to eavesdrop on all your conversations with Jacob," she says. "Usually by pretending I was listening to my iPod."

A mischievous thrill sparks in her honey-brown eyes. She's proud of herself.

"I had no choice. I had to." No apology, no regret. "Zere, we're two years apart, but you've always treated me like a child. You never tell me about your problems. You've always just turned to Jacob and then later, Christina. Meanwhile, I've always been your baby sister and never your friend."

"Efe, that isn't—"

She grimaces, and I close my mouth.

"You didn't even tell me you were pregnant. You told Jacob and Christina. I'm your sister, Azere."

My younger sister. The two years that separate us in age means she's more vulnerable than I am. Because of this, I never wanted to burden her with my issues or ask her to be the keeper of my secrets. I always thought it was my responsibility to care for her, to protect her. But maybe that was the notion that put distance between us.

"Efe, I didn't mean to hurt you. It's just that in my mind, you're a—"

"I am not a child, Azere," she says, her voice thick with conviction. "Disregard my collection of stuffed animals and consider other facts. I'm twenty-three. I'm in law school, and I'm hella smart."

"This is true."

"Good. Because I want you to take me seriously. And I want you to tell me stuff or I'll be forced to tap your phone."

"Eavesdropping no longer good enough for you?"

"Nah. I've changed levels. Met some people at school who are very skilled. If you know what I mean. I currently have many resources at my disposal." She flips her shoulder-length hair and winks at me.

I'm not sure if she's joking, but I crack up, and she does too. The laughter is so intense, tears sprout to my eyes. I wipe them away, but they spring out again. The new batch streams down my cheeks. My laughter is no longer genuine. I can't remember what I found so funny, but I remember the pain that's been clawing at my heart for days. It's here now, provoking more tears.

"I miss Rafael," I confess. "So much."

Efe, suddenly silent, stares at me.

"We were supposed to spend the holidays together." My awkward mixture of chuckles and sobs continue. "I even got him a present. One of those World's Greatest Dad mugs. It's cheesy as hell, but he would have loved it." When Efe holds me, the laughter stops and I just cry.

"It's okay," she says, rubbing my back. "It's okay, Azere."

"No. No, it's not. Nothing's okay."

"Zere, can I give you some advice?"

I nod, bobbing my head against her shoulder.

"Now, I know this is going to sound harsh, but consider it a necessary harshness." She releases me and meets my stare. "Azere, you gotta pull yourself together and figure your shit out."

"What?" Not the advice I was hoping to hear.

"Seriously, Azere. You have to figure out what you want. Forget about Mom and Dad. For once in your life, stop trying to please them. If you want to be with Rafael, be with him." She takes my hand and squeezes it—not gently but firmly. "I know it hasn't been easy, especially with everything Mom has put you through, but you have to find the strength to stand by your decision. Even when things are difficult. Do you understand?"

"Yeah. I understand."

The problem is, I'm not sure how to do that.

chapter
37

Christina's Christmas gift to me is a weekend getaway to Muskoka, a vacation destination in the heart of Ontario's cottage country. She insisted I need to relax before the baby arrives, which, according to Farah, is the eighth of January. I'm totally prepared. I've assembled the nursery, read a few baby prep books, and even attended a few prenatal classes—solo, of course. Christina is right. I do need to unwind. I deserve it.

On Friday, the day after Christmas, we make the two-hour drive from Toronto, eating Timbits and listening to a Beyoncé playlist. As we near her parents' cottage, I look through the window and past the silver lining of a frosted lake where there's a cluster of fir trees. The lush forestry is rooted at the base of craggy, snow-hooded mountains that peak and slope.

As I admire the scenery, something stirs inside me—something familiar but distant. I recall a childhood spent fetching water from streams, harvesting cassava with my father on our farm, climbing trees to pluck fruits, playing soccer atop red sand and dust. This panorama, secluded from the city, reminds me of that time, and I smile.

The car curves into a steep pathway. As we travel farther down the route, past more clusters of shrubs, a cabin comes into view. The rustic and refined pine lodge occupies an immense amount of space. Sunlight shimmers over the snow sprinkled on the high rooftop. Smoke emits from the stone chimney and meanders whimsically in the air. The charming view is like something out of a winter postcard.

"And we're here," Christina says. She parks the car and unfastens her seatbelt. "I'll get the bags. You head for the door."

"All right." I zip up my parka and step out of the car. After inhaling the fresh air and releasing it in a gratifying sigh, I walk on the ridged cobblestones that pave a curved path to the front door. Before reaching my destination, the door opens. I freeze on a stone tablet and gawk at the couple standing under the doorframe. "Auntie. Uncle," I say, acknowledging Christina's parents.

"Hello, Azere," her mother says, chipper.

"It's been such a long time," her father adds. "How've you been?"

"Great. Just . . . um . . . great." I turn around and glare at my friend, who has two duffel bags in her hands and one over her shoulder. "I didn't know you guys would be here."

"Really?" her mother asks. "Christina didn't tell you?"

"I did, Mom. She must have forgotten."

"Right." I turn to her parents and force a smile. Unfortunately, it doesn't compare to the genuine ones on their faces. "I totally forgot."

"Well, come inside. It's freezing." She steps aside and ushers us into her warm home. Christina shuffles behind me, balancing the bags like an inexperienced bellhop.

"I'll take those." Her father, a handsome man with sand-colored hair and hazel eyes, takes the bags. "I'll put them in your rooms." He turns down the lengthy corridor, and his wife follows behind him.

"What the hell, Chris? You told me we were gonna spend the weekend stuffing our faces and binge-watching *Skinny Girl in Transit*. You didn't tell me your parents were gonna be here."

"Well, we're still gonna watch *Skinny Girl in Transit* because I'm obsessed. But first, we have to talk to my parents for a little bit."

"Talk to your parents about what?"

"Zere, you broke up with Rafael. And even though you're doing who knows what with Elijah, you miss him. You're miserable."

"Christina, what exactly is your point?"

"My point is, you want to be with Rafael. But from where I'm standing, there are two reasons why you're not with him. One, you're a puppet and your mom's your master. Two, you believe being with someone outside your ethnicity will make you less of a Nigerian—a notion I believe was somehow planted into your brain by your mother." She rolls her eyes. "Anyway, I can't help you with the first reason. That's something you gotta man up and do on your own. But I can help you with the second reason. This is me helping."

"By having me spend the weekend with your parents?"

"Zere, my parents have been in an interracial relationship for twenty-seven years. Did I mention they're happy? Like seriously, they still make out. I've caught them. Many times." She shudders.

"So, what? You want me to take a glimpse into their happily ever after?"

"Sure. You could do that. But you could also talk to them." Her hand drops on my shoulder. "Zere, when my mom was twenty-five, she was in the same position you're in now. She was a Nigerian woman in love with a man who wasn't Nigerian."

"I never said I was in love with Rafael."

"Yeah. Sure." She scoffs. "Whatever. Anyway, my mom wanted to be with my dad. Her family wasn't having it. They were scared she would marry outside her ethnicity and lose her heritage. I think it's a fear lots of immigrants face, you know?"

"Yeah. I know."

"Anyway, my mom's parents were gonna disown her. They gave her an ultimatum—them or my dad."

"And she chose your dad."

"Yeah. On the day she was supposed to marry someone else."

"Wait." Now, I'm interested. "What exactly happened?"

"She was walking down the aisle to the groom her parents approved of. She ended up going through the emergency exit. Sounds like a rom-com, right?"

I nod eagerly. "Yeah. And why are you just telling me this incredibly interesting story now?"

"Well, we don't really talk about it. I'm only making an exception because I want you to see that my mom chose my dad even when it wasn't convenient."

"Because truth is, love is hardly ever convenient." A honeyed voice resounds in the corridor.

Our heads spin to Christina's mom. Her slender physique doesn't fill the sweater dress that exposes her long legs. She's beautiful. I've always admired her features—the stunning shade of her coppery-brown skin and the black locks that twist and puff above her head like an abundance of dark clouds.

"You girls should get cleaned up," she says, approaching us. "When you're rested . . ." Tenderly, she strokes Christina's hair flat, but the coils spring wild again. "And when we've had dinner"—she focuses on me—"we'll talk."

AFTER DINNER, WE ALL SIT IN THE SUNROOM. THE BLAZE IN the stone fireplace creates a cozy ambiance. Christina's parents nestle under a thick quilt. My snuggle buddy is Christina. We share a wool blanket and look through the floor-to-ceiling windows, enjoying the sight of dusk shimmering over the frosty lake.

"I love it here. It's so beautiful," I say, bringing a cup of hot chocolate to my lips.

"That's the greatest thing about this place," Christina's dad says. "The scenery." His attention moves to his wife. He pulls the quilt over her legs, depriving himself of its comfort.

"Twenty-seven years," I say. "That's pretty impressive. How do you make it work?"

They both turn to me, but it's Christina's mom who speaks.

"Love, patience, respect, trust." That isn't the answer I was hoping for, and she realizes it. She leans away from her husband and sits up. "Acceptance," she says. "We're different. Obviously. But I accept his differences, and he accepts mine." She tucks a dark curl behind her ear and searches my eyes. "Christina tells me you've been struggling with the fact that Rafael isn't Nigerian. It's been a little difficult."

"Yeah." I place the cup of hot chocolate on the table and pull the plush blanket to my chest. "Auntie, I tried. Believe me. I really did. But there was always this voice in the back of my head, reminding me we were too different." *Reminding me of what I could lose by being with him—my culture, my identity.* That same voice constantly reminded me of the promise I had broken.

"And whose voice was that?"

I don't answer.

"Mine was my mother's," she confesses. "Her voice was always in the back of my head, telling me it could never work because I was Nigerian and Frank was Italian."

"But you chose him. And the voice—your mother's—wasn't it

still there, tormenting you, making you feel guilty?" I speak from experience.

"The day I walked out the church instead of down the aisle, it stopped. I decided to listen to my voice, not my mother's. And my voice told me Frank was the one." Her eyebrows draw together as she studies me. "What about you, Azere? What is your voice telling you?"

I'm quiet, but Christina speaks on my behalf.

"Azere is still trying to find her voice," she says. "She had it once. Walked out of a kitchen instead of a church, but it was equally empowering. But somehow, sadly, she lost it again."

I don't reprimand her because she isn't being malicious. She's being honest. The rebellion I felt months ago was brief. Yet, it prompted me to speak up, to stand up to my mom, to take what I wanted despite the consequences. I was that girl for a moment in my life. I wish I could be her again.

"Auntie, did your family forgive you? Did they forgive you for choosing him?"

"Eventually," she says. "Years after the runaway-bride fiasco. When Christina was born, I sent them a picture. They wanted to meet their first grandchild. Forgiveness came slowly after."

"Told ya," Christina gloats. "Babies have a way of bringing people together. I was the glue that mended my family."

"Yeah, they were in love with Christina. At first, they tolerated Frank because of her. Slowly, they got to know him." She looks at her husband, and her lips turn up in a smile. "Now, they love him too."

"What about your family, Uncle? Were they okay with you marrying a Nigerian?"

"My family in Canada was fine with it. But my family in Italy, my grandparents, didn't approve. They love Christina. But Grace, not so much." He rubs his wife's shoulder. "They're old.

They've lived in a small village their whole lives and are set in their ways."

"But Mom, *bisnonna* is warming up to you," Christina says. "Last time we went to Italy, she was pretty cool. You spoke Italian and totally impressed her."

She speaks Italian. Interesting. "What about you, Uncle? Do you speak Edo?"

"*I ghuan khere,*" he says. Translation: I speak a little.

I'm amazed.

"Don't look so surprised, Azere," Christina's mother says. "We've been together for years. It's only normal we learn about each other's culture—I take on some of his, and he takes on some of mine. Doing that doesn't mean he's any less of an Italian and I'm any less of a Nigerian. It just means our world expanded, became richer."

Perhaps that was Rafael's intention, and I was too scared and naive to envision it.

"I was excited to learn about Frank's culture because I loved him. Azere, do you love Rafael?"

My lips are sealed, confining the answer like it's the content in Pandora's box.

"You're scared to admit how you feel because the consequences are grave—be with him, lose your mom. I get it. But if you really love him, you shouldn't let anything get in the way. Especially your mother's voice."

During my relationship with Rafael, that voice was relentless. It confused me and controlled me. However, after listening to Christina's parents, I'm inspired to resist that ever-present voice.

That night, before getting ready for bed, I reach for my phone and compose a text message.

Rafael. Can we talk?

I hit Send before I change my mind.

Delivered. That appears under the message I've sent.

Minutes pass. Hours pass. No response.

In bed, a little after two in the morning, I check my phone.

Read. That appears under the message I sent over five hours ago. And yet, no reply.

chapter
38

I spent two days in Muskoka, sipping hot chocolate by the fire-place, enjoying the stunning landscape, and watching Christi-na's parents with a renewed hope for Rafael and me. Sunday morning, as Christina drove us back to Toronto, I ignored the fact that Rafael hadn't answered my message. At home, without my best friend, ignoring that fact proved difficult. And that's why I'm here—in a private elevator that will soon open to reveal Ra-fael's waterfront penthouse.

Just as my anticipation peaks, the double steel doors part. I step out of the elevator and look from the sitting room to the kitchen.

"Rafael?" I move to the balcony where he often sits, even when it's cold. I attempt to slide the glass door open, but light footsteps make me whirl around.

"Azere," Selena says, smiling. "Hi." She rushes forward and hugs me. "It's so good to see you."

"You too, Selena." I hold her tight. Over her shoulder, Rafael stands with his hands in his pockets, his face deadpan.

"What a pleasant surprise." She pulls back and turns to her brother. "Right, Rafael?"

He says nothing—not a word, and his face remains straight.

"Anyway." She turns to me. "You actually came at the perfect time. We just finished setting up the nursery. Wanna see? Come. I'll show you." She takes my hand and leads me to the second floor. Rafael trails a few feet behind us, taking his time on the floating stairs. When we reach the third door on the floor, Selena claps and squeals. "I present to you Baby Castellano's nursery." She turns the knob and pushes the door wide open.

The first thing that comes into view is the wall decal that's in the form of a massive tree. The tree's leafy branches curve over the crib; its white color pops out against the gray wall and complements the subtle hints of turquoise that decorate the room.

"You did this?" I turn to Rafael behind me.

"We did this," Selena corrects. "I was the interior decorator, he was the handyman."

"It's beautiful." I step into the room and further examine the space.

On one wall, there's a shelf hosting an array of stuffed animals and a second shelf with towels, diapers, and blankets. Silver picture frames with paintings of baby animals—an elephant, a lion, a giraffe, and a zebra—cover another wall.

"You did an amazing job."

Selena accepts the compliment with a wide grin, but Rafael is still sporting his stoic expression. The tension between us can't be mistaken for anything else. I consider cowering and leaving, but heavy breathing and the pitter-patter of little paws make me perk up.

"Hey, Milo." The small dog enters the room with his tail wagging. He approaches me, and I bend down, as much as my round stomach will allow, to pet him. "Did you miss me?" He licks my hand, and I giggle. "I missed you too, boy."

"Selena." Rafael clears his throat. "Can you give me and Azere a minute?"

"Um . . ." She looks from her brother to me. "Yeah. Sure."

"And take Milo."

"Okay." She heads to the door and calls for the dog, promising him treats if he follows. He accepts the bribe and trots off, and Rafael and I are left alone.

It's beyond awkward. It has been since he walked in on Elijah and me. At the office, we interact only when it's necessary, and our conversations are short. He makes it to every doctor's appointment but converses with Farah far more than he does with me. Maybe whatever he felt for me is gone now. After everything, I wouldn't blame him.

"Azere, what are you doing here?" His voice is firm and flinty.

"I wanted to see you." My voice is small and weak in comparison to his. "I sent you a text message. You read it. I know you did. And you said nothing."

"I was busy putting the nursery together."

"Right." I focus on the ivory rug. "Well, I thought . . . um . . ."

"You thought what?"

I wish his tone would change. Maybe into something light and sweet as it often was whenever we were done making love.

"I thought we could talk. About us."

"*Us.*" He says the word as if it's completely foreign to him.

"Yeah." I muster the confidence to meet his hard stare. "Us as a couple."

"Azere, you stood in front of me, looked me in the eyes, and told me you wanted to be with another man. You picked him. We aren't a couple."

"Rafael, I know that. But I was with Christina's parents this weekend. And we talked. And I thought . . . maybe . . . me and you . . . could . . . could . . . um." *Damn it.* I have all these words I want to say, all these emotions I'm dying to express, but there's a muzzle on my mouth. There's something hindering me from being vocal.

"Azere, why are you here?"

"Because I . . ." When I open my mouth, when those two words fall out, his eyes brighten in anticipation of what I'm going to say. Though, when that invisible muzzle claps over my mouth again, his eyes dim with disappointment, frustration, hurt. So much hurt.

He turns away as if he can't bear to look at me. "I think you should leave."

"Rafael." I'm taken aback. "You don't mean that." I want to reach out and touch him, but maybe my touch no longer has an effect on him. Maybe everything he once felt for me has drained from his system.

"Azere, listen." He faces me again. "No matter what happens between us, we're going to be great parents." Tears gleam in his eyes, and I swear a piece of my heart chips away. "You'll be the mother of my child, and I'll be the father of your child. But that's all we'll ever be to each other. Nothing more."

"Rafael, don't—"

"Nothing more, Azere. I just can't. Okay? I don't have it in me. Not anymore." His pitch deflates. He sounds so defeated. "So, please. Just go."

But I can't. Not yet.

"Rafael, I know I messed up. But you can't put the blame solely on me. We were together for months. I gave up so much for you, and you kept so many secrets. How do you think that made me feel?" I search his eyes. "It made me feel alone. It made it easier to regret my choice and to focus on the ways I felt I had let my parents down. Your secrets did that. So, whether you choose to accept it or not, this is on you too."

And that's all I permit myself to say. Any other words will come out amidst sobs and squeals. I hurry down the stairs and to the elevator. The doors slide open and I enter. I won't cry—not here, not when there's a security camera he has access to. I'll sustain my breaking heart for a minute more.

chapter
39

Rafael

"What the hell happened, Rafael?" Selena looks from the closed elevator to me. "Azere ran outta here looking like someone had taken an ax to her heart. What the hell did you do?"

"Selena, don't start." I head to the kitchen and she follows.

"Seriously." She bounces in front of me, preventing me from opening the refrigerator. "What happened? Talk!" There's so much authority emanating from her. Even as her brother, it often takes me a moment to reconcile her small stature with her audacious character. "Rafael!"

"It's really none of your business, Selena. So just stop." I leave her in the kitchen and move toward the grand piano that separates the dining space and the living space. I run my fingers over the keys and play a few notes from Mendelssohn's "The Venetian Gondola," a melody I learned as a child. My fingers move fast, determined to drown out Selena's high-pitched nagging. Though, when she reaches for the fallboard, I retreat before the lid hits my knuckles.

"Don't ignore me, Rafael." With the classical music gone, she has no reason to raise her voice. She's soft-spoken. Maybe she even believes her gentleness will coax an explanation out of me. "I'm pretty sure Azere wanted to get back together, but then she left on the verge of tears. What did you do?"

"I did us both a favor. Things wouldn't have worked between us." My explanation, short and simple, will hopefully end her interrogation.

"Says who?" She isn't satisfied with my curt answer. "Rafael, says who?"

"I just know it. Okay? She wants to be with that other guy. She chose him. She chose him over me." I shake my head, trying to dispel the painful memory. "Do you have any idea how that felt? I'm not putting myself through another round of that. No. Besides, I was better off without her."

"Better off?" Selena's thick brows bend in a deep scowl. "You think your life, post Sofia, was better?"

Sofia. That name speeds up my heartbeat. Sweat seeps from my pores, gathering between the creases on my tense forehead.

"Rafael, it's been three years. Three years. Sofia died. And you've been closed off ever since." Her pink lips pout and tremble. "And I'm sorry you had to go through that. I'm sorry that experience broke you. I'm sorry that for three years, you've been a ghost—here but not really here, detached from the living.

"But as you mourned your loss, our family mourned you. You have been lost to us for three years, Rafael." Tears touch the corners of her grieved eyes. "You came back a few months ago. Do you remember the day you called us—me, Mom, Dad, Max? Do you remember that day? You told us Azere was pregnant." Now, tears flood her eyes. "For the first time in three years, I heard you laugh. It was brief, but you laughed. Azere did that. You were dead, Rafael. You were a ghost, and she breathed life into you. Don't you see that?"

Of course, I do. After Sofia, I became numb. The pain of losing her and the guilt that came with it did something to me, took something from the depth of my core. Though, every single moment with Azere restored what I had lost. With her, I was smiling and laughing again. With her, the emptiness inside of me slowly began to fill. With her, life had a different flavor; it was sweet and I wanted to savor every moment. Azere revived me gradually until one day, I looked in the mirror and saw the man I used to be.

"Rafael, don't delude yourself into thinking you're better off without Azere. Because you aren't, and you know it."

I bob my head, agreeing with my sister.

"Rafael, you love her. Don't you?"

"So much." The words rush out, as if they've been hanging on the tip of my tongue just waiting to fall. "I love her so much."

"Then you have to fix this, Rafael. I understand you're scared. You don't want her to hurt you again. That's totally understandable. But I'm asking you to risk it. Risk getting hurt on the chance that you might get a lifetime of happiness." She leans forward and wraps her arms around me. "Because you deserve it, Rafa. I don't know anyone who deserves it more."

My arms wind around her too, and we hold each other like we did three years ago when I experienced the greatest loss of my life.

"You have to go to her. Talk to her."

"After today, she probably hates me. What do I say?"

"Don't worry. It'll come to you."

And it does.

I have to tell Azere the truth—reveal every secret I've kept, completely bare myself to her, and see what she makes of me.

chapter
40

As I pull into my mother's driveway, my heart palpitates. My attempt to step out of the car is miserable. I stumble on a crack in the pavement but catch myself before my body meets concrete. I'm a mess. The safe arrival from Rafael's place to my mother's is a miracle.

On the porch, I twist the doorknob. It's unlocked. I enter the house and scan the space. It's late in the evening. Efe isn't home, but my mother is. Her car is in the driveway.

"Mom?" She isn't in the living room or in the kitchen. "Where are you?"

Honestly, I'm not sure why I'm here. Christina's place should have been my destination. Though, when I left Rafael, I got in my car and drove straight here. Maybe it's the child in me, running to mommy after getting hurt. I'm uncertain what comfort she can offer in this situation, but maybe she'll just hold me. That would be enough.

With a hand on my stomach, I wobble down the hallway. At my mother's bedroom door, I don't knock. I don't call her. I simply open the door. That's all I do. And that's the moment a crack ripples in the already strained glass that's been sustaining my chaotic life. That's the moment my whole world shatters.

"Mom?"

She's in bed with him. My uncle. Their naked bodies are half-exposed, half-hidden by white sheets. She was kissing him when I walked in, unaware of my presence until I spoke. Now, she's hurriedly pulling sheets over her bare body, covering parts of herself he has no right seeing or touching.

"No." I shake my head. "No."

This is a dream. She wouldn't do this. Not to Baba. I'm dreaming.

But she walks to me, gripping a rumpled sheet to her chest, and when her hand falls on my shoulder, doubt vanishes and reality pulls me into its whirlwind. "Don't touch me!" I fling her hand away.

"Azere, please. Please let me explain."

"Explain what? No explanation in the world can make this okay! You're in bed with Baba's brother."

"Azere." My uncle approaches me with sheets wrapped around his waist. "Give us a chance to explain." His dark eyes, guilt-stricken, are pleading. "*Omwinwen.*"

"No," I say sternly. "Don't call me that. Don't ever call me that again." I turn away and hurry down the hall.

"Zere, wait!" My mother races after me. "Please!"

"How could you?" I stop at the front door and spin to face her. "How could you do this?"

"I can explain. Let me explain."

"How long has this been going on?"

She's quiet.

"How long?" I demand.

"Over a year."

I stagger until my back hits the closed door. "A year! How in the world did this even happen? Why did it happen? How could you let it happen? How could he? Do Efe and Jacob know?" The last question seems more important than the others. "Do they know?" This will destroy my sister as it's destroying me. And Jacob? How will he take this?

"Azere, no one knows."

With one question answered, I focus on others. "How could you do this? What were you thinking?"

"It just happened."

"It just happened? Seriously? Is that your excuse?"

She shakes her head.

"Then explain this to me, Mom. Explain it because I don't understand!"

"Azere, please don't get upset. You're pregnant. Just stay calm."

"Are you going to give me an explanation or not?"

"Okay. Okay." As she gathers her words, her eyes wander. "Your uncle is a good man. For years, he took care of us selflessly. He never asked for anything in return. As the years progressed, I started having feelings for him. I tried my best to hide it.

"One day, he came to the house. We were alone. We talked. One thing led to another. He told me he had feelings for me. I admitted my feelings. And then we started to . . ."

"Have an affair."

"Affair?" She squints, considering the word. "Azere, he is not married, and neither am I. We are not having an affair. We are in a relationship."

"A relationship!" My jaw drops. "With your husband's brother!"

"Late husband," she says. "Azere, your father has been dead for thirteen years. I mourned him. I respected his memory and took care of his children." Tears fill her red eyes. "Until your uncle, I refrained from having a relationship with any man. Zere,

I have done everything I can, but he is dead. Your father is dead, and I am alive. I cannot live my life for him."

"But you've made me live mine for him."

And this is it—the life-altering moment of realization.

For years, I clung to something that didn't exist—a phantom made of blood, flesh, and bones. My father, dead, was very much alive in my head. The strong, resourceful farmer who cultivated lands and used its harvest to provide for his family. The proud Edo man who passed on stories of his ancestors and hundreds of years' worth of tradition to his children. The patriarch who, on his deathbed, bound his eldest daughter to a promise that gave him ease but imprisoned her. For years, that man lived in my head. I struggled to obey him, to please him—to please a man who was long gone, a man unable to speak, a man not entitled to opinion. I lived for him. And now, the realization dawns.

"Baba is dead, and I am alive." I nod at this simple logic that has somehow evaded me for thirteen years. "He was a good father with good intentions, but he is dead. And for thirteen years, I've been obeying a dead man, striving to keep a promise I ignorantly made. And you have been holding that promise over my head."

"Azere, you—"

"No! Don't speak!" My voice booms around the house, causing my mother to flinch in surprise. "Listen to me! For the first time in my life, listen to me! Hear me!"

She purses her lips and nods.

"When we were growing up, Efe was stubborn. She never obeyed instructions. I was determined to be better, to be an example for her, to make you and Baba proud by any means.

"So I was obedient—a good daughter. But you took advantage of my willing compliance. You governed parts of my life you had no right over. And I foolishly allowed you because I didn't know how to be anything else but the obedient daughter."

"Azere," she says. "You are a good daughter."

"Of course. But only when I do what you want. Right? I'm a good daughter only when you can control me."

"That is not true."

"Of course it is. You told me to be with Elijah. You pressured me into it. When I obeyed, you permitted me back into the family and accepted me as your daughter again." I wait for her to deny these events. She doesn't. "Mom, I know I hurt you, but you didn't love me enough to just forgive me. Your forgiveness had conditions."

"Azere." Her mouth falls open, her chin trembling slightly. "How can you say such a thing? Of course I love you."

"No, you don't." It's agonizing to admit this—to say it out loud, to breathe life into the terrible words I've been mulling over for days. "Mommy, you don't love me enough. Your love, like your forgiveness, has conditions."

"Azere, stop saying that. It is not true."

"Then where were you during my pregnancy? I needed you, and you weren't there for me. Meanwhile, I gave up the one person who was always there."

I broke up with Rafael because of my mother, because of her words that were constantly in my head, because of the guilt and obligation she laid on my shoulders, because of the promise she never let me forget, because I was so damn terrified of not pleasing her.

"I gave up Rafael because of you, Mom. I love him." And there goes the muzzle that's been confining those words. I couldn't say them to Rafael, but by some miracle, I can say them now. And it's incredible, exhilarating, emancipating in every sense. "Mommy, I love him." I hold her gaze, ensuring she sees the sincerity in my eyes. "I love Rafael so much."

"Azere, listen." She takes a small, cautious step toward me. "Ending your relationship with him was for the best. You cannot be with him. I cannot allow it. Don't you see that being with a man who isn't Nigerian threatens our culture—puts it at risk of being diluted? Azere, don't you see that?"

"You know, if you wanted me to marry a Nigerian, you should have left me in Nigeria. I mean, the odds of marrying a Nigerian in Nigeria are incredibly high. And if this country is such a threat to our culture, you shouldn't have brought me here. But you did.

"You brought me to a country that has a culture of its own, a country that's also home to people from all around the world, and you've expected me to ignore these facts for years." I groan and ruffle my hair. "Do you have any idea how crazy that is?"

She opens her mouth, but words don't come out. She closes it and looks at me. We look at each other. A single tear rolls down her cheek, and she rubs it away.

"Azere, your father—"

"Don't." I squeeze my hand and pound my small fist in the air. "Don't talk about him. Don't talk about what he wanted or feared. Because you're right. He's dead. And you've obviously moved on without him. Let me do the same."

Wait. I'm not asking for her permission. Not anymore.

"I'm going to do the same. Whether you like it or not is of no interest to me." I look over her body that's cocooned in layers of white sheets. There's so much more I could say, but I choose to say only one thing. "Over the past few months, you've done so much, said so much. Just so you know, I will never treat my child the way you've treated me. My child will never have to question my love. Never." I turn around and twist the doorknob.

"Azere, wait." She grabs my arm before I can step out. "I . . . I . . ."

"You know, I never told you how Rafael and I met." I yank my arm backward, separating it from her hold. "It was this strange coincidence. I used to think fate played some sick trick on us for its own amusement. Now, I know better.

"Rafael was meant to enter my life. He was meant to interrupt it—to disrupt the plans I had made because if he hadn't, I would still be under your thumb. And I would have remained there my whole life."

In my car, as I reverse out of the driveway, I notice something. It's quiet—too quiet. I continue to drive, and as I pull farther away from the quaint bungalow, the truth becomes apparent.

For the first time in ages, I don't hear my mother's voice.

chapter
41

It's late at night. A few hours ago, after returning from my mom's, I called Elijah. I apologized and explained I couldn't be with him because I was in love with Rafael. Despite the hurt and disappointment in his tone, he accepted my decision. He didn't fight it. After a long moment of silence, he wished me all the best, and I did the same. Now, I'm in bed, burrowed under a heap of covers. My iPod is connected to a speaker, and I'm on the second hour of a Whitney Houston binge.

Minutes ago, "It's Not Right but It's Okay" was playing. The lyrics gave me a boost. I sang along—loud, proud, and determined. In the moment, I felt somewhat empowered and optimistic but those feelings passed. The next song—"I Have Nothing"—came on, and it quickly revived my sadness.

Now, another ballad is playing, and I sing along while sniffing and whimpering. "And I will always love you-ooh."

When the instrumental solo begins, I quiet down and notice an offbeat banging. *Well, that's new.* I pause the song, isolating the sound coming from my front door. *What the hell?* I get out of bed to investigate.

"Who is it?" The real question is: Who the hell is banging on my door, disrupting my Whitney Houston binge at eleven thirty at night?

"Azere."

"Rafael?"

"Yeah. Hey." Even with the door separating us, his voice is clear, and it's gentler than it was earlier.

"What are you doing here?"

"Azere, I dropped by before, but you weren't home. I've been calling you for hours. You didn't answer your phone. I was worried. Are you okay?"

"No." I don't have the energy to lie or to disguise my pain as something else. "I'm not okay, Rafael."

"I know. Why don't you open the door, so we can talk?"

"No. I don't wanna talk." I just want to hide under my covers and listen to the next song on my Whitney playlist—"Heartbreak Hotel."

"Open the door, Zere. Please, *cariño*."

Even after everything, he calls me that. *Cariño.* Does he think the word will generate memories of who we once were? Does he think it will make me open the door? If these are his thoughts, he's absolutely right. I turn the lock and pull the door open.

He stares at me. I'm a mess—red, puffy eyes, untidy hair, and a wrinkled T-shirt with blotches of tears and snot. As I walked to answer the door, I caught my reflection in a mirror, and I was a little horrified. I wonder if he is too.

"Zere." He draws me into him. "I'm so sorry."

The hug is tight and long. I cling to him. My sharp fingernails dig through the knitting of his sweater, and a hint of his smooth skin touches my fingertips. I never want to let him go.

"I'm so sorry about today," he says. "The . . . the way I treated you." Regret makes his voice shaky, uncertain. "I was just hurt."

"I know, Rafael. It's okay." Even without him asking, I know what he needs from me. I stand on my toes, and my puckered lips reach for his. For the first time in so long, we share a kiss. In an instant, everything is better.

"Come in." I step aside, and he enters the apartment.

"I'm sorry too," I say, rubbing my arms, trying to flatten the goose bumps that sprouted due to the sudden chill in the room. "Sorry for breaking up with you. And I'm so sorry about Elijah. Can you ever forgive me?"

"Of course." He takes my hand and holds it to his lips, kissing each pointy knuckle. "I forgive you, Azere. Now, come." He leads me to the living room. "We need to talk. Please sit." I do, and he grabs the fur blanket on the couch and places it over my shoulders. The beige fleece covers my upper body and falls to my bare knees. After ensuring my warmth and comfort, he sits beside me. His expression is grave.

"Rafael, what is it? What do you want to talk about?"

"Sofia," he says. "Azere, it's time I tell you the truth."

"Okay." I'm nervous about the information he's about to offer, but I don't show it. I take his shaky hands, giving the support he clearly needs. "I'm listening."

"Sofia and I met when I lived in New York." His stare drops to the floor. "I loved her. Very much. We got married after dating for two years." This isn't the easiest news to hear. "Our families were ecstatic—my parents and hers. Her parents being the couple at Pottery Barn."

Of course. It makes sense.

"We were so happy." A smile touches his lips briefly. "During a Fourth of July weekend, we stayed at her parents' place in New Haven. We were supposed to drive back to the city on Sunday evening, but she wanted us to stay another night and drive back early in the morning. A storm was coming. She didn't want us to get caught in it, but I convinced her we would be fine. So we left."

For a long while, he says nothing. His jaw contracts, his brows furrow, and his hands turn clammy.

"The storm started, and it was bad, but we were managing. We were halfway home. Then it all happened so fast. Screeching tires," he says. "I heard screeching tires and a crash. Then everything went dark. When I came to, she was unconscious. Her blood . . . it was everywhere. A car had lost control and T-boned ours—crashed right into her side of the car. She didn't survive the impact. She died. They both did."

"Both?"

"Yeah." Tears gather at the rims of his eyelids and drop. "She was nine months pregnant. Due to have the baby within days."

Immediately, my hand drops on my stomach. Though I try to stay strong for him, a sob rumbles out of my mouth. He lost a child, experienced an incredible loss. What was it like for him to see me pregnant? Did the sight of me trigger his past? Was the preparation for our child bittersweet? It must have been on some level, and he dealt with that alone. As I watch him, it all becomes clear. This is the pain that's been haunting him, the pain that created an eerie void in his striking blue eyes.

"In New York, I visited her grave—their graves. That's why I didn't want you to come along. That's why I was distant when I came home."

That's everything—all my questions answered, all my suspicions put to rest. There are no more secrets between us.

"Rafael, why didn't you tell me sooner?"

"Because I was afraid you wouldn't want to be with me."

"Why wouldn't I?"

"Because it was my fault—Sofia, our child. That was my fault. I should've listened to her. She didn't want to go. I convinced her to. I promised her we would be okay, and she trusted me." He shakes his head, remorseful and distraught. "It was all my fault. They died because of me, and I carry that guilt every single day. Azere, I'm messed up. And who wants to deal with that? Who wants all that baggage?"

"Rafael." I take his face in my hands. "Listen to me." My thumbs move over his wet cheeks. "It wasn't your fault." I say the words again and again, ignore the tears pouring out of my eyes and speak with tenacity, attempting to convince him of what is true. "It wasn't your fault." When he nods as if understanding and accepting the words, I wrap my arms around him and hold him tight for seconds, then minutes, until he pulls away.

"Azere, I've mourned Sofia and our child for three years. I decided to leave New York because it was time to move on. But even so, I came to Toronto in the same state I had been in for years—miserable and hopeless.

"But the instant I saw you in that lounge, drinking and staring off into space, something happened. I'm not sure what it was, but for the first time in three years, I didn't feel absolutely miserable." He smiles. "Even without talking to you, there was this instant connection that drew me to you."

I felt it too—that pull. In fact, I feel it now. It's as if the ends of one string are lassoed around our hearts—mine to one end and his to the other—and we can't part from each other. Rather, we are pulled to each other.

On the night we met, that pull led me to his hotel room. And in the early morning, as I quietly slipped away, it took every ounce of resolve to resist that pull. And that same resolve has been exercised many times since, and sometimes, on many occasions, it has failed.

"Azere, when I woke up in my hotel room and you were gone without a trace—without a number or any way to reach you—I was devastated. But you were there—at Xander. It was like . . . like—"

"Fate."

"Exactly." He nods, his smile expanding. "Azere, you were the best thing that happened to me in a very long time. The past few months with you were incredible, the happiest I've been in years. But then you broke it off. You chose Elijah and . . ." He stands and walks to the other end of the room, his back to me. "It hurt. Zere, losing you hurt so damn much."

"Rafael." I toss the blanket that's been draping my body and stand as well. "You haven't lost me, and you never will. I'm right here, and I want to be with you. Look at me."

He turns around, but his eyes don't focus on mine. Instead, they are fixated on my legs.

"Rafael?" Color drains from his face. Something's wrong, and I'm finally aware of what it is—warm, sticky wetness sliding down my thighs and soaking my T-shirt. I look at the spot where I sat. The teal sofa is drenched with blood. "No . . . no." My knees wobble like they're about to give out. I sit on the couch again as blood continues to pour out of me.

"My God," Rafael says, kneeling at my feet. This scene is so parallel to one he experienced before. I'm not certain how he's going to react. "I did this." He assumes blame. "This is all my fault. I upset you today—stressed you out."

"Rafael, look at me." His eyes are set on the blood between my legs. He isn't responsive to anything I say. It seems like trauma has unhinged him slightly. *God, how do I help him out of this? What do I do?* "Rafael, look at me!"

The zeal in my voice forces his head to snap up.

"This is not your fault. You didn't do this. Do you understand me? This isn't your fault."

He nods like he did minutes ago, when I repeated the same words.

"Rafael, I need you to be strong right now. Can you do that?"

His head bobs keenly this time. "Yeah."

"Good. Call the paramedics. Call them right now."

"Okay." He reaches into his pocket and pulls out his phone. After dialing 911, he talks to the operator, giving my address and explaining my condition. "They're on their way." He ends the call.

"You see? Everything will be just . . . fine," I say this even though I'm lightheaded. "Everything will be fine," I say this even as Rafael's face blurs. *Stay with him, Zere. You can't leave him—not like this.* I coach myself inwardly. When I blink firmly, things are clear again. "We're going to be fine, Rafael."

Despite the confidence that straightens my voice, I can't put faith in my words because my bloody legs are a heavy dose of reality that underline the inevitability of tragedy.

chapter
42

In most romantic movies featuring a pregnant protagonist, there is a dramatic yet equally comical scene where the water breaks and the expecting parents race to the hospital. In the movie *Bridget Jones's Baby*, Mark comes over to Bridget's apartment to reconcile their differences. As he's about to attempt an emotional declaration, Bridget's water breaks, and they begin their journey to the hospital. With a feminist protest obstructing their route, the couple faces a few hilarious hurdles before reaching their destination. When Bridget finally gets into a hospital bed, she's screaming and cursing as she suffers contractions. Mark stays at her side, holding her hand, stroking her hair, encouraging her with loving words.

Inspired by this scripted scene and a few others of the same nature, I have envisioned various delivery scenarios. In one, my water breaks while strolling in the park, and Rafael, desperate to get me help, steals a tandem bike and peddles me to the hospital. In another fabricated scenario, we have access to a car. Unfortunately, we're stuck in heavy traffic. I scream—you know, like every woman who's in labor and hasn't been drugged—and a miracle occurs. Dr. Jackson Avery from the TV show *Grey's Anatomy* appears. In my fantasy, he isn't an actor but a certified doctor, and he delivers my baby right in the middle of rush hour traffic on the Gardiner Expressway with "Circle of Life" playing in the background.

My fantasies, no matter how bizarre, have one thing in common—the birth of my child. Now, in a hospital room filled with scurrying nurses and a slightly frenzied Farah, that no longer seems like a possibility.

When we arrived at the hospital, Farah was waiting for us. After a quick examination, she explained my placenta had partially separated from my uterus; this caused the excessive bleeding. Because the placenta wasn't obstructing my cervix, a Caesarean section wasn't required. She broke my water, inducing labor.

Now, it's happening. Based on what I've seen in movies, I expected my delivery to be painful. It's not. It's excruciating. I'm ready to call it quits, but that isn't an option. The baby is crowning. I dig my fingernails into Rafael's arm and screech.

"I can't," I say, breathless. "I can't anymore."

"Zere, yes you can." He strokes my hair. "You can do this. You're strong. I know you are."

"I'm . . . tired, Rafael. I can't." I'm motionless on the bed, weak and defeated. I'm mortified by my reluctance to persevere. If not for myself, I must persist for my child and for Rafael. He can't suffer another loss. I can't allow it.

With that understanding, I gain a newfound resolve. I grip the layers of sheets beneath me and grit my teeth, pushing past the pain, the frustration, and my desire to give up. The piercing muscle contractions in my lower back threaten my determination, but I don't quit. Holding on to my legs for support,

I sit up and push harder than before. Tears and sweat cover my face, my heart thumps, and my body quivers under the strain of severe pressure. Certain I can no longer push, I fall on my back. Between my throaty inhales and exhales, there's a cry—sharp and vibrant. Rafael's head spins to Farah. I want to do the same. I want to see what . . . who has him overjoyed. Instead, I shiver. There's a repetitive beep coming from the heart monitor machine.

"Blood pressure dropping," a nurse says. "She's going into shock."

Rafael's focus is on me again. He says something, but I can't make out the words. He reaches out to me, but nurses enclose my convulsing body. I want to talk to him—tell him to take care of our child, tell him I love him, tell him to be happy no matter what. Unfortunately, my shuddering lips can't form words.

Now, my eyelids are too heavy and can't stay open. Rest, whether permanent or temporary, beckons me and its call is so enticing. As my lids close, Rafael's distraught face appears between the spaces in my lashes. Soon, the world around me fades. There are no colors, no shapes. Merely darkness.

chapter
43

My father died at thirty-nine. He was young—too young. There were so many years he didn't get to live. But those years weren't wasted. They were inherited.

Often, my mother would say to my sister and me: *Your father died young. You will not. The years he did not have will be added to your lives as inheritance. Untimely death is not your portion.*

Considering this, I never thought much about death. I assumed I had been guaranteed a long life. I forgot that death is a greedy force that's always prowling, always taking, impartial to youth or beauty or innocents. I was foolish.

Now, the strings leashing me to life sever, and I'm held by nothing. I'm falling into a vast, dark void that has no beginning or end, screaming and crying and clawing at blank spaces, pleading to nothing and no one in particular.

The fall is endless until something hooks me. I dangle, suspended by a single string. *A single string.* It lassos around my heart and tugs, pulling me out of oblivion and toward a speck of light. There's something . . . someone else at the end of this string—another heart tethered securely to mine, calling me out of death by the sheer force of love.

As I move upward, the speck of light transforms, altering from a dot to a circle and increasing in size until it comes at me in a fierce, blinding radiance.

chapter
44

Light seeps through the seams of my closed eyelids. After opening my eyes, I blink until Rafael appears clearly. He's standing over me, cradling a white blanket in his arms. My heart skips with excitement, and I prop myself up on my hands and shuffle to a sitting position.

"Take it easy, Azere," he says. "Please."

I peer at the infant sleeping in his arms. "Is that our . . ."

"Our baby girl."

"Really? A girl?"

"Yeah. A beautiful girl." He extends our child to me and places her in my arms. "And healthy."

She's gorgeous—fair skin with copper undertones, a head covered with dark, curly locks, and pink lips that pucker like the early spurt of a rose.

"She's perfect, Rafael."

"Yeah. She really is." He sits on the edge of the bed. "How do you feel?"

"Great. I'm great." Mostly because of the gem in my arms. I can't take my eyes off her.

"Azere, you scared the hell out of me. I thought I was going to lose you. Both of you."

"Well, she's here now."

"But you weren't." He cups my cheek, and I'm forced to look at him. Tears sparkle in his blue eyes. The trauma of almost losing us still haunts him. "Azere, when I saw you lying there, I thought I lost you."

"I know. But by some miracle, I'm here with you and her." I smile. "I love you."

He watches me blankly. It's the first time I've said it. Maybe he thinks he's misheard me.

"I love you, Rafael. So much."

Now, his lips turn up in a huge smile. "And I love you, Azere. Very, very much." His adoring gaze drops to our sleeping daughter. "She needs a name. I've been waiting for you to wake up, so we can pick one."

"How long was I out?"

"A few hours. She was born at four fifteen a.m. You became unconscious immediately after. It's a little past ten now. And she still doesn't have a name."

"Then give her one. You're her father, Rafael. Give her a first name. Every other name will follow." He deserves this honor. "What do you want to call her?"

He takes our daughter's tiny hand, and it coils into a fist around his finger. "Hope," he says, gently stroking her knuckles. "I want to call her Hope."

I smile and nod in full agreement. "I love it. Hope Castellano." Because of her, the branches on my family tree will extend far beyond the borders of my village. "It's perfect." We watch our child. Minutes pass before I look at Rafael. "I heard you went to my mom's like a hundred times."

"You heard wrong. It was about fifty times—tops." We laugh.

"I thought I could convince her to get over her anger. It didn't go well."

"But you kept going back."

"Yeah. Well, that wasn't the only reason I went there." He clears his throat. "I wanted to ask for your hand in marriage."

"Oh." Didn't see that coming. I draw the blanket over Hope's neck, keeping her small body snug. "You know," I say after a few seconds, "you don't need my mom's approval or permission. If you want to marry me"—I meet his stare—"ask me."

As he opens his mouth, perhaps to ask a question that will change my life, the door creaks open. My mother's face appears.

"Rafael, what is she doing here?"

"We had a baby. I thought it was appropriate to inform our families."

"Azere." She comes into the room, moving toward me cautiously as if treading on thin ice. I suppose she is.

"Mom, why are you here? I don't want you here."

"Azere." The stern disapproval in Rafael's voice restrains me from lashing out further. "I'll give you two a minute," he says.

"No, Rafael. Stay."

His feet, which were already moving, still. He retakes his place. At my side.

"This is the family you almost cost me, Mom."

"Azere, I thought I knew what was best for you."

"You can't know what's best for me when you don't even know me. You know the daughter who obeys your every command, who bites her tongue, and bends to fit your will. You don't know the daughter who's in front of you."

Maybe it's time you show this part of yourself to your mother. Maybe it's time she sees the daughter who has been hiding from her. Rafael's words come to mind.

"The daughter in front of you loved that Antonio Banderas

poster you tore from her bedroom wall. She hated almost every guy you set her up with. She fell in love with a man you don't approve of, and she doesn't care because she's done living her life for anyone but herself.

"The daughter in front of you is proudly Nigerian and proudly Canadian. She isn't choosing one over the other. She's both. And it's okay."

My mother cocks her head. Confusion makes her brows bend and her eyes dart across my face. She looks at me as if searching for recognition, for the daughter who didn't speak up, who was so easy to tame. She won't find her here. That girl is long gone. And my mother nods as if she sees that and accepts it.

"Azere, everything I did—making you keep that promise, setting you up with those men, asking you to end your relationship with Rafael—I did because I was scared." Tears shine in her eyes. "We came to this country and everything is so different. There are so many people, so many cultures. I didn't want you to get lost in it all. I didn't want you to forget where you come from."

"And I never will." My village, the people, the traditions, the ancestral stories my father told are woven into every part of me, as deeply rooted as bone marrow. "Mommy, I still remember home. I can never forget because it's who I am, and no matter where I go and who I love, I will always, always know who I am. That will never change."

It's silent for a while. Rafael and I watch our slumbering child, and my mother dries her teary eyes.

"I'm sorry," she says. "Azere, Rafael. I am so, so sorry—for everything." Her remorseful eyes wander around the room. "I am so ashamed of myself."

"Mom." I wait for her to look at me. "I forgive you."

"Really?"

"Yeah. I forgive you."

"We both do," Rafael adds.

"Thank you." She smiles at him and then turns to me. "Azere, these past few months, I have acted stubborn. Remember your father always called me stubborn?"

"Yeah." I giggle at the memory. He also called her a trouble-maker because she had her ways.

"The truth is, I missed you. So much. I worried about you and my grandchild. I prayed for you both all the time because I love you, Azere. Even when I am too stubborn and proud to say it, know that I love you. You and Efe are my whole world. Don't ever doubt that."

My mother has never been this candid about her emotions. Growing up, she expressed her love with the things she did—how she took care of Efe and me, especially after our father passed. Love was in her actions. But these past months, her actions and even her words were spiteful, and I believed she didn't love me. But I was wrong, and it's such a relief to know this.

"I love you too, Mommy."

"Azere, I just want you to be happy."

"And I am happy. More than I can express." I take Rafael's hand and place it over my beating heart. "And it's because of him. He's my everything. He's my lifeline." The single string that pulled me out of oblivion and back to life. "Mom, I want to spend the rest of my life with him." I should turn to Rafael and see his reaction to this news. Instead, I watch my mother. She's nodding and smiling and crying all at the same time. "If you can't accept that, if you can't accept my choice, then you can't be in my life. You can't be in my daughter's life."

"Okay." The tears stop falling, but the smile remains. "Okay, Azere. I accept your choice. As long as you're happy, I accept."

"Good. Now, do you want to hold Hope?" I ask. "Do you want to hold your granddaughter?"

"Yes. Please." She leans into me and scoops Hope out of my arms and into hers. "She's beautiful." She rocks her gently. "When is she going to wake up? I want to see her beautiful eyes."

"They are beautiful," Rafael says. "Big and brown. Like her mother's."

"Really?" I ask, ecstatic.

"Yeah. Really. Just like yours."

The room fills up soon. Jacob, Efe, and my uncle enter with balloons and stuffed animals. Christina twirls in after, declaring herself godmother before I can do the honors. When Rafael's family arrives, everyone takes turns holding the baby. I watch them laugh and bond with one another. Selena and Efe are flipping through a celebrity magazine and critiquing every Hollywood starlet who pops up on the page. Jacob and Max are talking sports. I can tell by the imaginary basketball they're dunking. Rafael's parents and my mom and uncle are discussing the joys and aches of parenthood. Christina is taking selfies with the baby, probably flooding her social media with pictures of my kid. And Rafael. Well, he's smiling—really smiling. I've never seen him so happy. His blue eyes, once hollow, seem occupied now; emotions pour into them like the sand that fills an hourglass. Joy, serenity, love, and hope fill the void that once existed in him. For the first time since I've known him, I see a man who is whole.

In this moment, I reflect on how far my life has come—how it twisted and turned, diverting from my original plan yet bringing me to a place I was always meant to be, to a man I was always meant to love.

How did I get so lucky? Fate.

That's the answer that comes to mind, and I'm right—partially.

Fate had a hand in this love story, but so did Rafael and so did I.

I believe in destiny, but I strongly believe destiny isn't all-powerful; it gives a portion of its influence to us. We have the choice to accept or reject its plans.

For so long, the ability to choose, to voice my opinion, was taken from me. In weakness and then in strength, I retrieved it. Now, I remember months ago when Christina said, *Let go of the life you've planned and accept the life that's waiting for you.*

That's exactly what I did. I let go. And this—Rafael, our daughter—was the life waiting for me. It was predetermined— intricately designed by forces unseen and unfathomable.

I simply sealed this fate by making a choice.

I WAKE UP AND THE ROOM IS EMPTY. I'M ALONE UNTIL THE door breaks open. The face that appears makes my heart flutter. "There you are," I say, beaming at Rafael. "Where's Hope?"

"The nursery."

"And everyone else?"

"I asked them to go home. They'll be back later." He kisses my forehead. "I'm proud of you."

"For what?" I ask.

"Standing up to your mom. You did good, *cariño.*" My reward, a kiss on the lips—brief but appreciated. "Have I told you how much I love you?"

"Well, only like ten times today." I watch him bashfully through flapping lashes. "I could use an eleventh."

"I love you, Azere. I love you so much." He pecks my lips.

"You're my heart." Another peck.

"You're the light of my world." Another peck.

"Everything else is a shadow where you are."

Another peck, and my lips quickly hook his. I kiss him fiercely as if I can taste those sweet words on his velvety lips.

"Marry me," he says, breaking away. He digs into his pocket and pulls out a little black box. "Azere Izoduwa, the mother of my child, I am absolutely, irrevocably in love with you." He opens the box and presents a champagne-colored princess-cut ring.

My trembling hands come over my mouth, and he starts reciting words I've heard before. My mind instantly makes the connection. He's quoting lines from romantic movies we watched.

"'You make me want to be a better man.'" *As Good as It Gets.*

"'When you realize you want to spend the rest of your life with somebody, you want the rest of your life to start as soon as possible.'" *When Harry Met Sally.*

"'Love is too weak a word for what I feel—I luuurve you, you know, I loave you, I luff you.'" *Annie Hall.*

I laugh at that one, and he does too, but he doesn't stop.

"'You're a beautiful woman. You deserve a beautiful life.'" *Water for Elephants.*

"'I have never needed anyone in my life the way that I need you.'" *The Wedding Party.*

"'I've come here with no expectations, only to profess, now that I am at liberty to do so, that my heart is and always will be yours.'" *Sense and Sensibility.*

"'You have bewitched me body and soul, and I love, I love, I love you. I never wish to be parted from you from this day on.'" *Pride and Prejudice.*

"Azere, I want to devote my life to you. It would be my greatest honor." Those are his words—simple and sincere. "Marry me."

"Yes. Absolutely."

Before the ring comes to my finger, his lips come to mine. With us having restrictions—the hospital room, my body that's still recovering from labor—the kiss ends with both of us half-satisfied. He slips the ring on my finger, and I raise my hand and admire the delicate undertones of pink and copper that complement my brown skin.

"I'm guessing you didn't pick this up at the hospital gift shop."

He laughs. "I've had it for a while. Do you like it?"

"I love it. It's perfect." And it really is. It's stunning and big enough to make a statement without being obnoxious. "So? What now?"

"You become my wife, and I become your husband."

"And . . ."

"I buy us a house with a huge yard where Hope can eventually run around."

My eyes urge him to continue.

"And maybe down the line, when we're comfortable with the idea, we can have another baby."

I nod in agreement. "Definitely."

"And a vacation house in Muskoka."

Confused, I frown.

"Christina suggested it." Of course. My brilliant best friend. "And a chicken coop. With four chickens."

I mentioned this to him a while back.

"Gatsby and Daisy and Shrek and Fiona."

I bob my head in full support.

"Am I missing anything?"

"Nope. Now, there's only one thing left for us to do."

"And what's that?" he asks.

"Live happily ever after, of course."

epilogue

"Story, story . . . ," I chant.

"Story," my five-year-old daughter responds.

"Once upon a time . . ."

"Time, time."

"There was a beautiful village girl called Osasu. Unfortunately, Osasu didn't have a voice."

"She couldn't speak?" Hope says, twirling the tight curls that fall over her shoulder.

"Nope. Not a word. When Osasu was born, a wicked witch knew she would have the prettiest voice in the village. So, the witch put a spell on her."

Already, Hope is intrigued. She looks up at me, dark eyes eager to acquire information.

She has her father's features—the slopes that shape his face, the gentle fullness of his flushed lips. But she has my eyes and my spirit—the same spirit that seeks romance and a happily ever after in every story. Tonight, like most nights, I'm telling her one of the many stories my father used to tell me. There were stars in the sky whenever he told these stories and insects buzzing around a lit kerosene lantern. Usually, his orotund voice would break through the stillness of night, and my sister and I—seated on the ground—would look up at him in awe as he skillfully combined action, drama, a struggle between good and evil, and of course, romance.

When I tell these stories to my daughter, it's in her princess-themed bedroom—pink curtains concealing the view of the moon and the stars, a nightlight illuminating the space, her body tucked under a blanket, me sitting on the edge of the twin bed, and Milo curled at her feet. The setting is different, but the sentiment of the storyteller and the listener remain the same.

"Then what happened, Mommy? What happened when the prince kissed Osasu?"

"Well, while they were sharing a kiss, Osasu felt something move in her throat."

"What was it?"

"Her voice, coming back. True love's kiss broke the witch's spell."

Hope claps, thrilled by the triumph prompted by love.

"Osasu started talking and singing for the first time in her whole life, and her voice was absolutely beautiful."

"Did the prince ask Osasu to marry him?" She always likes to skip to the good stuff.

"Yes, he asked. But she said no."

My daughter's mouth falls wide open. "She said no?"

"Yes. Osasu had just gotten her voice and she wanted to use it. She wanted to travel the world, learn different languages, become a famous singer, and do other incredible things."

This wasn't part of the original story. I made some reasonable, timely adjustments.

"And after making all her dreams come true, Osasu said yes to the prince."

"Then they got married?"

"Yes, honey. Then they got married."

"And they lived happily ever after." Rafael steps into the room at the last minute and wraps up the story.

"Daddy!" Hope stretches out her arms, reaching out to her father.

"Hey, baby." He leans down, lifting her off the bed and into his arms.

"Mommy told me the best story."

"She always does." He looks at me and a beautiful smile, one I am never weary of seeing, spreads across his face. "I suspect she might be the best storyteller in the world."

"I think so too. I wanna hear another one. Mommy, tell another. Please."

"Not tonight, Hope," Rafael says, tucking her under the covers. "It's bedtime now." He kisses her forehead. "Good night."

"Wait." She holds my hand. "Am I still going to the aquarium with Grandma and Grandpa tomorrow?"

She's referring to my mother and my uncle. They're married now, so calling him grandpa is only appropriate. "Yes," I say. "They'll pick you up after breakfast."

"Yay! Good night, Daddy. Good night, Mommy." She leans forward and presses her lips to my round stomach. "Good night, baby brother." She's quite certain about the gender even though it hasn't been revealed to us.

"Good night, baby," I say. "Good night, Milo."

Rafael and I walk to the door, his arm around my waist and my head resting on his shoulder. We're about to exit the room, but Hope calls for me.

"Are you and Daddy living happily ever after?"

I look at my husband, and he looks at me.

After four years of marriage, after building a life together that far surpasses anything I could have ever envisioned, after every minor and major argument that led to reconciliation and us falling deeper in love with each other, the answer is clear.

"Yes, honey. We are. We are living happily ever after."

And those are the words that put our daughter to rest.

As Rafael and I walk to our bedroom, down the hall from Hope's, I'm reminded that I hate when romantic movies end without giving the viewer the slightest glimpse into the happily ever after the couple is promised. Personally, I want a few more heartwarming details. What happens after the stern businessman faces his fear of heights and climbs up the fire escape to prove his love to the spirited prostitute? What happens after the eccentric socialite and the straight-shooting writer kiss in the pouring rain with a cat called Cat nestled between them? What happens after the iconic chase to the airport or after the public declaration of love? What happens after the final kiss?

Notting Hill doesn't end after Will subtly implies his love for Anna during a press conference. After that scene, others follow—their summer wedding and their red-carpet debut as husband and wife. In the last scene, the couple is on a park bench. Will is reading a book. Anna has her head on his lap and a hand over her baby bump. Needless to say, this is the perfect glimpse into the happily ever after the couple is promised.

In my culture-clash love story, the glimpse into ever after is this moment—my daughter sleeping peacefully in her room and me in bed with my husband, his hand on my stomach, securing my body to his, the thread that stitched our hearts together years ago still very much intact.

ACKNOWLEDGMENTS

I unconsciously wrote my family into this book and didn't realize it until I was editing. Azere's village is the picture my mother painted whenever she told me stories about her village. Christina is my hilarious sister, Precious. Jacob is my kind brother, Divine. Chapter forty-three—the shortest chapter and dearest to my heart—is dedicated to my father, Fred. He died before I knew him, yet he found a place in this book somehow.

I am so thankful to these people who unintentionally inspired this story and these characters. I am especially grateful to my mother, Joyce, who is such an extraordinary person. She knew she had given birth to a writer—she just didn't know which of her three children it was. Growing up, she would say, "One of my children will become a writer, and they will tell my story." I was certain it was one of my siblings—not me. It couldn't be me. Even at ten, I struggled with reading and writing. But it's me, Mom. I'm going to tell your story one day, and it will be the greatest story I ever tell. Thank you for supporting this dream, even when it seemed irrational and impossible to achieve.

Kristin Wright, my wonderful Pitch Wars mentor, thank you for loving this story just as I did, for dedicating your time, your knowledge, and your support. Brenda Drake, thank you for creating Pitch Wars; it continues to give writers so many opportunities. Kevan Lyon, you are seriously an incredible agent. Thank you for your support, for replying to emails so quickly, for calming my nerves. You have prevented many meltdowns you aren't even aware of. With you, I am confident and at ease. You're a dream agent. Kate Seaver, thank you for not seeing what my book was but what it could be. You knew exactly what this book needed. I am still amazed at how far it has come. I am so grateful for your brilliant insight, and I seriously couldn't ask for a better editor. To the entire Berkley team—Fareeda Bullert, Danielle Keir, Dache Rogers, Megha Jain, and Mary Geren—thank you for helping me share this book with the world. A huge thank-you to Fatima Baig and Emily Osborne who captured the essence of my book with a stunning cover. You guys gave me the cover of my dreams.

To my friends, family, and critique partners who have offered endless support over the years—there are so many of you—thank you so much for dreaming with me, for believing with me.

More than anything, I am grateful to God. He placed this dream in my heart, but it wasn't easy to accomplish it. Getting a book published is the hardest thing I have ever done. There were so many years of rejections. At one point, my dream felt like a burden, and even then, I didn't know how to give up. God wouldn't let me. Proverbs 18:16 became my mantra. My faith in those words and God allowed me to achieve this dream. But it's more than a dream come true now. It's a testimony.

ties that tether

JANE IGHARO

Discussion Questions

1. Azere describes her Canadian citizenship as a title that is both empowering and demanding because it requires her to give up part of her Nigerian culture so she can fit into her Canadian setting. Do you think many immigrants believe their citizenship is both empowering and demanding? Why or why not?

2. What do you think of the promise Azere made to her father? How do you think the promise constructed her perception of what a Nigerian woman should be?

3. When Azere is around her family, she doesn't feel the pressure of being wedged between two worlds. According to her, she isn't Nigerian Canadian, but just Nigerian. Do you think some immigrants often have two sides to them—one they present to the world and one they reserve for the comfort of family? Why do you think that is?

4. Both Azere and Rafael experienced the death of loved ones. How do you think their losses impacted the development of their relationship and how they interacted with each other?

5. Azere's mother was often harsh. Knowing her actions were provoked by fear—fear that her children would lose their culture—do you think they were justified? Why do you think this?

6. What role do you think Azere's family and friends played in her growth? Who do you think was the most influential character in her development and why?

7. Azere constantly compares her experiences to romantic movies. What was your favorite movie reference and why?

8. In the novel, Azere's mother asks: *How much more of yourself, of your culture will you lose to accommodate him in your life?* Do you think people who marry outside of their ethnicity have to give up part of their culture in order to make their relationship work? Why or why not?

9. Azere's mom and Rafael's parents are immigrants. How do they approach preserving their cultures with their children? How do their methods differ?

Photo © Borada Photography

JANE ABIEYUWA IGHARO was born in Nigeria and immigrated to Canada at the age of twelve. She has a journalism degree from the University of Toronto and works as a communications specialist in Ontario, Canada. When she isn't writing, she's watching *Homecoming* for the hundredth time, and trying to match Beyoncé's vocals to no avail.

CONNECT ONLINE

JaneIgharo.com

📘 AuthorJane.Igharo

🐦 VictoriousJane

📷 Jane_Igharo

Ready to find
your next great read?

Let us help.

Visit prh.com/nextread

Penguin
Random
House